Tweakerville

ased Arsonist Admitted Using Crystal

Father Pleads Guilty to Meth Tr

3 lbs. of Meth Seized in Bust

Teacher Charged with Meth Trafficking

Death Toll Will Keep R

Meth Linked to Abnorma

School Neighbors Spur Ice Bu

Man sought trea

$1.

Security Chief, Liquor Inspector Adm

Guilty Plea in Meth, Rifle Case

Dru
Diap

Federal officials agree
lower percentage of imm
because Ha

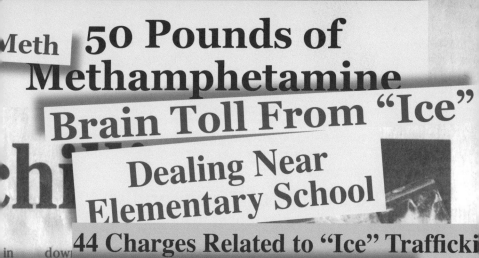

Meth | **50 Pounds of Methamphetamine**

Brain Toll From "Ice"

Dealing Near Elementary School

44 Charges Related to "Ice" Trafficki

sing as Long as "Ice" Rules Isles

ities in Fetuses

Oahu, Vegas Ice Raids

and minors have different addiction risks.

ment before fatal shootir

Some 52.8 percent of minors en-
tering division-funded treatment

m of Ice a Month

who en-
g treat-
meth

sought treatment for alcohol use addictions increased to 3,536
last fiscal year, up about 19
fiscal year 2008.

ted to Extorting Business

that dropped from 2.5 percent in
fiscal year 2006.

rug bust in
Honolulu is shown above.

Ring Used Women Wearing

s to Ship the Illegal Substance

The People of Tweakerville
as we first meet them

Jesse. Seventeen going on eighteen. Kicked out of his family home, crashing in a drug house. He is having the time of his juvenile life running crack and ice on his moped–until death by OD rears up right in his face.

Robby. A bigtime ice dealer who has kicked his own addiction. The leader, he is teaching Jesse the ways of the world.

Dingo. Robby's sidekick and hanger-on. A drunken clown. Does not carry his weight when it counts.

Mikey. Third-generation chronic drug addict, hustler, thief, sometime pimp. Supersmart, self-educated while in prison, and a deep, deep thinker–but watch out, you never really know what Mikey is scheming.

Dwayne. Jesse's cousin, in and out of rehab, jobless, new father of a child who may be a meth baby.

Charlene. A military brat who wanders off base into the world of ice and into disaster.

Janice. Charlene's mother, wife of a career marine officer away in Iraq. Hawai'i is foreign territory to her, incomprehensible.

Rawlings and De Luca. Marine enlisted men on leave from Afghanistan. They cross paths with locals, and it gets ugly.

Dos. Another ice dealer with brains, in cold-war competition with Robby.

Kody. Dos's muscle. Town bull, a killer.

Amber. Beautiful ice addict, prostitute and single mother, tough enough to rebuke Robby and Mikey. Robby falls for her.

Kapika. Jesse's girlfriend. Private school dropout, working at Longs Drugs. Father an Audi dealer, mother an English teacher. Kapika has her own private sorrows, but she believes in the good and hopes for the best.

Vili. Jesse's friend from way back. Great family guy who has a steady job, happy with his life. Vili is generous, easygoing, accepting–and it costs him everything.

A blind man. Nameless.

Tweakerville

Life and Death in Hawai'i's Ice World

Tweakerville

Life and Death in Hawaiʻi's Ice World

a novel by
AlexeiMelnick

Mutual Publishing

ISBN-10: 1-56647-933-9
ISBN-13: 9778-1-56647-933-2
Library of Congress Cataloging-in-Publication Data

Melnick, Alexei.
   Tweakerville : life and death in Hawaii's ice world : a novel / by Alexei Melnick.
      p. cm.
   ISBN 1-56647-933-9 (pbk. : alk. paper)
   1. Drug dealers--Fiction. 2. African Americans--Fiction. 3. Ice (Drug)--Fiction. 4. Hawaii--Fiction. I. Title.
   PS3613.E4488T84 2010
   813'.6--dc22
                                    2010033155

Design by Jane Gillespie
First Printing, September 2010

Mutual Publishing, LLC
1215 Center Street, Suite 210
Honolulu, Hawaii 96816
Ph: (808) 732-1709
Fax: (808) 734-4094
e-mail: info@mutualpublishing.com
www.mutualpublishing.com

Printed in Korea

In loving memory of the acclaimed novelist,
Ian MacMillan, 1941-2008,
whose five years of close mentorship
and belief in me became the novel,
Tweakerville.

Chapter One

Robby's house jus look like any house in the neighbor hood, bags of cans and bottles, the hose wrapped up around the nozzle. The cinder block walls and high bushes make it hard to see in to the yard. I keep the drive way pretty clean, sweep up the Heineken caps, cigarette butts, sun flower seeds. Some times there would be a Q-tip, a strip of cloth or a paper clip straightened out, nothing the mail lady would prolly notice. But if you knew what to look for you would know.

Over the walls and the bushes you could just see the tarps Mikey put up like camping tents. If you saw through the tarps you'd see all the sealed windows barred up. The black security gate, took three guys to mount it.

The lights were on all the time so it looked like some one was home. In side the air con was always on. No windows open in the living room where Mikey blew the smoke on his pinky to test out the new batch and spit on his shirt and the pipe hissed as it cooled. Then he'd lick his finger and do it again. If it's re freeze, the ice smoke can leave residue.

Under the black light, ash trays over flowing with butts and roaches. Empty bottles in the shower, by the beds, on top of the TV, on top the roof cuz of Dingo. Holes where Robby punched the wall.

Once you knew what you was looking at from out side, you know this is a house where guys making fast money selling hard drugs. No camera over the door. No alarms. No guard dogs. Robby said he never needed um.

Robby put down the lease under his Aunty Jen's name that I still never met. Some guys had legit jobs. But drug money pay for every thing else. The pre paid phones, the Toyota, the Acura, the El Camino, the 50-inch screen, the PlayStation, the propane grill, the steaks, one full ice box only green Heineken bottles, and every thing else. All drug money. Easy come. Easy go. Clean cars. Dirty finger nails.

If the music stopped you could hear the tarps moving around from the air, but the music never stopped at Robby's house. The bass slammed so hard you could feel in your ear rings, your belt buckle, the weed pipe in your pocket. You could feel um in scabs in side your nose from banging lines the night before. The rain gutters would buzz from the sound system.

For guys that grew up in small apartments or cramped houses, was one big thing to have your own land and your own things. But none of them was from big time linked up families, even if Dingo tried to tell every body he was, dropping all kine names. Any rank, any rep they pulled they made for them self.

And before, if I want new clothes for school year, I had to go thief um, put um in the ice box, freeze the ink pack, pry the ink pack off. Now no more school, I jus go up and buy three from the lady at Urban Gear.

And the thing you never would believe is how Robby would talk to his customers.

"I love you, my Uncle. Dis your nephew. Sorry I never call you back. You know how come ah? I jus gon tell you da same ting. I nothing smart for say, you my elder, but I wish you never call me up for dis kine. But if you like . . . yah, can. Jus do me one favor, please, be safe, drive safe, do um one safe place. I know you work your late shiff. Da ting going fass, but I save some goodies for you. Call me when you pauhanas. We die together in da night."

Unreal, he just met that guy five months before. Jus some old lonely weekend tweaker fucka that work security at the capitol building. You would think Robby sold shave ice or ice cream. Not rock and not ice.

I heard when he used to handle the rock him self, he would weigh um out, put um in side one balloon with little bit air, that way can tell if the middle man is stealing. Middle man floaters like Mikey.

Robby always said he never burn no body, never bunk no body, never cut his drugs too much. Straight deals. After, they always come back to us, not Kody-Dos guys and that bent shit they pump. Some smokers chase the cloud, they like to see a big cloud. Real smokers chase the higher purer dope. They come to us.

And Robby would say, "Drugs are for da weak, Jesse. If not us guys, who gon take care dem?"

Trippy, yah?

Back then I even believed him.

Before he was twenty one, Robby already got banned for life from every bar in our town for fighting. So now Fridays, we would party at the house. Stupid. But we did it any way, until that one night before Halloween.

I thought it was the best night of my life. Every body all cut, all gone, good fun.

I was seventeen, by five years the youngest, running dope for the older guys, getting lit, getting burnt, getting blind, the house about to fall down kine parties in the yard.

Had some *men* there that night. Violent men. Little things can become big things. Deadly things. Spilled drinks. Funny looks. Old grudges. He said she said. Guys standing with their back against the wall, looking over shoulders. Was like the whole yard could ignite, jump off and blow up in to action any minute under the drunken moon light.

I shook my head watching more and more cars parking up the road.

Up on the porch Robby was punching the bag. Dingo was scratching his nuts, I swear that guy got herpies.

Pretty soon, all kine girls we never knowed was showing up, dressed like slutty Halloween fairies, cheer leaders, vampires, asking, "Who dose guys up stairs?" And guys was like, "Dat Robby and Dingo guys, you never heard of dem?" Then it was like, "Oh, *dats* Robby."

No body ever heard of Jesse Gomes.

All snob girls that never drank was getting high and loving it, hands in the air, shouting, making drunk girl squeels. And if you could snort it, rock it, rail it, poke it, chong it, smoke it out of glass, you would get it until you drop dead on it. Heaven wouldn't feel as good. You could launch bowls, bang lines, take whacks, cut up Vicodin and rail it. Every body buzzing. Every thing spinning. The lights start getting more bright. The night getting more dark. Guys getting more loud. The neighbor's windows getting more closed. Mikey coming out from the shadow down stairs where he was sitting with his best friend in his jacket pocket. Black circles around his eyes.

Then the rain came hard and started pounding on the tarps, and every body in their bare feet squeezing in together in the mud, spilling their drinks on each other and no body give a fuck. Dingo flew his bottle over the gate and you could hear the thing smash. Robby put his arm on my shoulder, pointing with his beer at people under the tents. Scrubs, he called them. Worms, midgets, no bodies. Robby never have time for soft feelings.

He was about five ten, one eighty five, but he was quick. Guys used to say he look like that MMA fighter Wanderle Silva, but never to his face.

He usually wore a black beanie over the top of his ears to his eye brows.

He poked one ring of small bad boy faces around his wrist and the mafia stars on his shoulders and under his wrists. On his neck had the two masks and the words Laugh Now Cry Later. Real big on his fore arm had the double bar cross, the chain dangling from his neck.

On his back you could see the beatings his dad gave him. The scars was all mis shape too. You would think, what did that? One cigar? One car antenna?

He was pointing over the rail at the girl with his Heineken. "Dass da kine you like, Jesse?"

She looked up when she seen us and smiled.

"Nah," I said.

His throat moving as he drank the beer.

"She tink you handsome, you ugly fucka. She said she need one daddy for her baby. I told her my friend like try, he like see your in sides. Go handle your candle, Jesse."

"No," I said. He always did this.

"So deadly. Same age as you, her. Good girl too, dats da kine dat would go church and pray for you."

She was looking back at us again, wearing her jacket, trying to stay out of the rain.

But Robby was the one she wanted.

"Nah," I said.

He spit off the balcony over the truck. His phone was going off, the new song from Three Six Mafia, but he just let it go.

"Jesse, you no scared for slang dope. You no scared for scrap guys. But you scared for talk to girls?" He shake his head to me. "Weak, Jesse."

He put his beer down on the rail and picked up his phone. Business.

Some of our regular chronics was trying for grab rock from us, cocaine cooked up with baking soda so you can smoke it.

Robby was trying to get the guy to up the order, cuz we was heavy right now. He said, "I not trying for tell you how for live your life, but I was you I would grab da whole gram while you can."

Then I could hear the guy crying, whining, Mikey prolly rip um off last time.

"I no tink Mikey would do dat," Robby said in to the phone, shaking his head to me. "Whateva. Your ting, bra. Ova wit me. Between you and Mikey."

Then the rain stopped and Robby told me go down stairs, get the rock, make um, weigh um, take um to the guy. I was the runner. They used me cuz I was still under eighteen and if the cops caught me trafficking they treat me like one juvenile.

I started breaking off the crack rock in to the digital scale. Back when I wen school I stole a scale from my science class for the guys. Before my dad kicked me out last year. I get one way meaner scale now, my pocket scale, only like six square inches.

Rock, you can just break the thing down with your fingers until it weigh out right. You jus fold um up in to one baggie or receipt, or one small gum wrapper size paper. Not like coke or clear, you gotta scoop um from one half straw.

Our way goes by points. One twenty point of ice, meth, clear, batu is one tenth of one gram, 0.1 grams. Think how small that is. Could fit on your finger nail. Nuts, ah?

I left the party on my moped about eleven thirty, gassed it toward the beach, the wind coming up through the neck of my shirt.

The guys was waiting for me on the side of the road some place. When I start getting close they started the car and I followed them around the block. I just pulled up to the window at the stop sign, hand um right through the window real fast, grab the money and shoot out. If HPDs watching, hard for them follow the whole thing.

No matter what you tell some of those fuckas, they just keep buying twenties and forties the whole night instead of grabbing more one time.

And every time Robby or Dingo's phone ring I gotta go back out. Some times the same fucken guys already putting in the next order by the time I just got back.

Chronics.

When I was by the house again, Robby was calling to me–

"Eh, no get mad, kay, Jess? Dis kid show up, telling us he your long lost cousin or some thing, caught bus for come down here. Rat tail, hoop ear ring. He said you was gon front him two points. Shady looking fucka. No BVDs. Said his name, James or Wayne or some shit. Mikey–what he said his name was?"

"Dwayne," I said.

Robby coughed and spit. "Yah yah, Dwayne. I told dat fucka he come to da wrong house. Private party. I never did one wrong ting, Jess?"

"Nah," I said. "Tell dat fucka go home, bra. Dat fucka's losing it."

"So now what, Jesse?" said Robby. "You can make one real fast beer run? Nab some Heinies for Dingo?"

"Afta twelve already," I said.

"Take da Toyota, take one of da young boys. Lass time, I promise."

"You said lass time was da lass time."

"No. Dis time. Hard luck, boy. Hard luck."

"Fuck," I said.

At twelve thirty I parked in the parking lot across from the Safeway. I told the kid Kaika you never park um in front. If can, park um one whole other parking lot. I re versed in, left um in drive with the hand brake on, the two girls sitting on the truck bed whispering. They said they wanted Kaika grab um some Smirnoff Raspberry.

The kid Kaika was big time in front the girls, telling them he gon grab dem Smirnoffs. Kaika was one menace to society in front the girls. But when we was walking in side the Safeway, the poor fucka was all shittin.

Telling me, "I cannot get busted, Jess. I no do dis kine stuffs, Jess."

I told him, "Shh. You gon be all right. Watch and learn. Watch and learn."

I get um wired already over here. You just gotta walk in like you know what you doing there. We went around the table with the Halloween candies. We got the beer, three twelve packs plus the Smirnoffs from the back of the stacks, that's the coldest.

There was just the one aisle open and the check out girl was busy any way, some old haole lady snapping at her over some thing. She never see us go out.

I keep telling the kid, "No need run, jus cruise, jus cruise."

But then the doors open behind us and we heard some one shouting, "Eh!"

"Kay," I said. "Run."

The kid Kaika dropped one of his twelves and flew in to the truck bed, he almost took out the two girls. I scooped up the twelve, jumped in, let go the hand brake, peeled out. I hopped the curb, busted one full on U turn over the median. I buried the needle in the RPM meter. Flying it up the road. The wind ripping through the cab. The JL W-6s buzzing the seat. The girls going nuts laughing.

"Grab me one, Kaika," I shouted through the cab window, and felt back for the beer to come in to my hand. I opened the bottle with my seat belt.

Away from the house about a mile I seen Dwayne walking down the road. I ducked behind the steering wheel. I couldn't tell if he seen me. Look like he had hurt feelings, jus walking down the road alone by him self. Fucka caught bus for come see me. I felt all sick. Me and him was tight before, cousins. We grew up same house for a while, my family house. He got kick out by my dad two years before me.

Back at Robby's had all kine cop cars in front saying on the loud speaker, "If you guys want to get arrested, keep making noise."

We jus walked right past under age with the stolen beer.

And all these dumb fuckas partying that didn't even live with us, they start shouting all one time. Then the cops jus drove away, like was one Halloween miracle.

Robby was still up stairs on the porch by the front door. Right after the cops left I gave him the money from the last delivery, and he never count um this time, he jus fold um, put um in his pocket. He was all red about some thing.

"Eh Jesse," he said. Pointing with his nose at this one big guy. "Eh, dat fucka in the brown Ecko shirt, da kine Raising Hell shirt, dats the toughest fucka hea? He going around telling everybody he jus did two years, he like do five more. He telling everybody, boring in O Trips, next time I like go Halawa. He must be one real gangsta. Hoo fuck, I *scared* of him." Robby made this fake scared face. "Who is dis fucka? Smash dis fucka, Jesse. Dis fucka get hiccup, Jesse, now he gotta get burped."

"I dunno," I said. "Dat guy was cool to me."

That made Robby more nuts.

"Kay...kay...nah, nah," he said. "Dass your friend. I thought I was your friend, but I guess dat guy he your good friend?"

I took off my slippers and went in side to my room to get my shoes. When I opened the door there was this girl sitting on her knees on my bed, loading the end of a crack pipe. Her skin was all shiny, drug sweat. Dingo at the other wall, his arm around his girl friend, a bottle floating in my fish tank. No body ever respect my room.

The girl on my bed placed the rocks in the pipe. She looked at me. "I never do dis."

"Sure," I said. "You never told me da same thing last week?"

Dingo clapped his hands. "Dis young kid is wise," he told the girl, then point his beer at me. "I cry for da future. Come, Jess. Take one wit us, launch one wit us, blass one wit us."

"Robby would palm me," I said. I never do crack rock.

"Fuck Robby," said Dingo. "He not your dad."

I tied my shoes, jumped to my feet, punched my palm with my hand. The girl put the flame to the end of the pipe and took a hard draw, burning the rock, the crack, sucking air, making that loud crackle sound. The smoke has this sweet chalky smell, nothing like clear smoke, ice smoke smells bitter, like melting chemicals.

Crack rock not really one friend ship drug. The high last fifteen minutes. After that you jus chasing. One blast of clear? You could stay up for sixty two hours.

The girl started scraping the pipe like she knew what she was doing jus fine.

In the same store that sells the glass pens you make a crack piece. You could grab the glass air freshener bottle you never see in any one's car. You wash um out good with hot water, get one blow torch, make you one ice pipe with that. Next to that they sell gram size baggies with one candy in side for one cent.

I got my shoes from in the closet. "Robby says I gotta go whack some body."

"What? Again?" said Dingo. "Let me guess, da guy with da brown–"

"Yah, him."

Dingo laughed and bobbed his head. "You like fight dat fucka? Good luck, Jesse. I know you get one strong arm too, but shit, I dunno, bra." He raised his beer. "I guess I gotta get up den."

Any time Robby like fight some body now he like me fight him, cuz that way other guys might say, "Ho, Jesse, dat young boy, he off, bra. Seventeen only him–watch, he gon be one hammer one day." But nobody ever does say that. If it look like I gon lose the fight, Mikey would jump in and burp da poor fucka. We no fight fair.

I came out the front door jumping and stretching. Mikey turn up the music so the neighbors couldn't hear the fight.

"Sup, gangsta," I told the guy in his Raising Hell shirt.

The fucka look over my shoulder at Mikey and Robby. I ran up, caught him one clean one right on his chin. I could feel the jolt in my fore arm.

He went back wards, blocking. "What I did to you guys, Robby?"

"Nothing," I said. "I wen whack you for no reason. You ax him, dat give me one reason."

I heard Dingo. "Burp dat fucka, Jesse!"

The guy kept blocking, he hardly even try to fight. Then he started running to his car. I followed him down the road, yelling at him.

"Dis your cah? Ho—nice your cah." I kneed the side door, dented it. He jumped in and start gassing um up the road.

I walked back to the house, put my hand in Killas's cooler with the melted ice. My thumb went right in to the guy's tooth.

I almost felt bad for him after. But he know what he did.

The rest of the night Dingo was all joking with me, he was like, "Ho, sorry, I no like trouble. I no like cruise with dis kid Jesse. Ho, dis fucka one loose cannon."

And Robby would watch, drinking his beer.

Every day Robby fought me. Yelling at me, stay on the balls of my feet, move my head. He tell me remember, throw more under hand. I would pound the bag. Then he go pound the bag, shake the whole house, scare the neighbors.

Chapter Two

By four o'clock all the light weights was gone already, it was jus the die hards camped out on the porch coming down from the high, some of them scraping pipes, but no body was launching bowls. Robby closed shop.

Mikey was trying to get guys to throw in scrips with him. He said he like go grab from some where else but he had to go alone. Anybody that ever gave Mikey money before was calling it a night already, pounding Nyquil or popping Valium, Codeine, Percocet, Xanax, just trying to come down from the high.

The guys that only did soft drugs was dropping dead in our living room, sleeping on the wood floor under the black light in one big pile of bodies. I was one body, passed out with my bottle.

About five, around then, Robby was kicking me. "Wake up you slut. We go."

He dropped this one pair boots down by my head and threw one trash bag on top dat.

"No wayz," I said. I couldn't open my eyes and my mouth tasted all sick from drinking hards. I put the sleeping bag over my head.

He started again with the kicking. I was all, "All right, all right, nuff nuff."

He handed me one beer. "Nothing wake you up like one red and white fire cracker. Dingo killed all your Heinekens."

I rubbed my eyes. My neck hurt so bad from sleeping funny. "What is dis, Robby? What is all dis . . . boots?"

"How else you gon climb around in cow shit? Now go throw up, I no like stop on the way."

In the bath room I ran the water in the tub so no body hear nothing. I knowed I was gon get up set stomach later, so I put my finger down my throat and wen throw up for little while until I fell asleep again in there.

Robby came in and kicked me again, in my stomach.

And then we was walking out the house when I seen Mikey on the porch. He was sitting next to this old tweaker girl, in the dark, like how he did all the time with the hood on his huge black jacket up over his eyes. Hard core tweakers no sleep after they party, they like vampires, jus slide up some where stone cold and tweak. Coming down. Mikey had raccoon eyes but his face was all intense, like he was looking at the sun all day or he saw God. The girl was chewing on her gums. Tweakers.

"Where you guys was going?" said Mikey.

"I gon take Jesse out for pick mushroom," said Robby. "You don wanna be dere, bra, gon be all sloppy. Why, you wanted for shoot with us, Mikey?"

Mikey jus sat there all quiet.

"I need one more point, Robby," he said.

"You no need one point, Mikey, you need Jesus."

"Eh Mikey," I said, "no go in my room this time. Please."

The way he looked at me I knew he going in there as soon as I turned the key and the El Camino left the drive way.

Sucken Mikey. Every time with him.

Mikey didn't get a room at the house, he was one full blown chronic tweaker.

He was too chronic to sell the dope. Robby never let him near the stuff. He might disappear for two weeks, smoke four thousand dollars of clear before you see him again. Every body love Mikey. He was way smarter than all us, he read the whole paper every day, not just the buy and sell, looking for where to press off scrap metal and auto re cycle parts, copper wire without the U.S. seal.

It prolly hurt him real bad too that he couldn't stay at Robby's house. But you know, when you get one tweaker living your house you gon have five more coming by every day, yelling, whistling, trying to get in the house, throwing up tweaker hand signs.

Tweakers bring heat. Every night for them get action. They gotta do it but. Even if you get money, staying high is hard work. But to one chronic tweaker, it's clear or it's every thing else.

Me and Robby was drinking through the hang over in the car on the way to the ranch. Robby was telling me how he know this guy from the main land that pay choke for Island shrooms, cuz shrooms up there all hydro grown.

I said, "Better I thought, hydro grown?"

"Nah," said Robby. "Cow shit more organic."

When it jus rains little bit, but there's not that much clouds so the sun can hit the cow shit first thing, that's the prime time for pick. But you gotta get there before all the hippie fuckas come over in their hippie vans, snag um all.

One other thing, when you pick shrooms you no can just really pick the fuckas. What dat really mean, picking, is ripping up big bricks of cow shit with your hands, trying for not hurt the shroom.

We had to hop the fence and we were bagging the shrooms, but soon enough the guard dogs started for chase us up in to the trees, going nuts barking. Robby was yelling at the dogs, "Dog! Shhh!" Hanging there in the tree, yelling at me, "You fucka, no drop da bag." And shrooms falling out through the rip, spinning in the air, landing all around the dogs.

I was laughing, sucking breaths, jus happy to be alive. Robby going nuts chirping at me, I never even cared.

Chapter Three

When we pulled up at the house was almost seven already. We came in with the two bags, bra, we was all brown, all kine thorns in our shirts. Sloshing around, the boots all water logged.

Dingo was trying for evict all the non residents. "All right, every body. Get home safe." Then he seen us taking the shrooms to the bath tub for wash them.

"You guys smell like shit."

"Not," said Robby, all wise. He was still salty cuz I wen drop my bag when we jumped out over the fence.

But after I seen my bed, bra, I yelled out, "Mikey! What da fuck, Mikey! Odda room I said, cuz, odda room!"

But I never like argue, I could feel my ears starting to pop jus from not sleeping. I went out my room to the living room couch where dis one haole girl was taking up all the real estate, out of it, still in her vampire costume. She had white make up on her white skin but black around the eyes. Her fake vampire teeth had fallen on the floor. By her black wig. She had one of dose spike neck lace leashes around her neck with a chain hanging down, like goth chicks wear even when it isn't Halloween.

Time for dis chick re locate. I dragged her all the way down to the other side the couch. People that live here get first dibs. I did one belly flop onto the pillows and that was it, lights out, I fell asleep on my arms. I could still feel the girl's curly red hair on my feet but I never care.

After little while I heard all kine commotions around me. Dingo yelling out, "Mikey!"

I heard Mikey's heavy feet on the wood floor and Robby turning off the faucet in the tub, telling every body, "Shh . . . quiet."

I never open my eyes but I heard couple words here or there.

Load. OD. Drool.

Dingo whining about some thing and every body telling him for shut his ass.

The blackness took over again. I was so tired it hurt.

Dingo was shaking me all around. "Jesse, wake up."

I sat up and then I seen her face, the haole girl.

"She's still alive, Jesse!" said Dingo. "Tell um, bra, tell um she's still alive. See, look–you seen that, Jess, she was moving!"

"Mikey know what he talking about, Dingo," said Killas.

The girl's eyes wasn't moving and her make up was all smeared, her eye liners like dat. She had drool all over her face too. But yah, I seen her arm move. It was more like one jolt but, one spasm.

I was so tired I never gave a fuck if the girl was dead. I'm sorry for tell you dat, but I never knew her, none of us did. She just popped up outa no where. If she had any friends, they left her there.

"Dis your friend, Jesse?" said Mikey.

"No lie, Mikey," said Robby, wiping off his arms with the towel. "If any body hiding any thing, is you."

Mikey shook his head like he never know nothing. Then he went in to her bag and took out all her stuff until he saw the sun glass case. "Right here–look."

He opened the case and took out the burnt blacked out clear pipe and handed it to Robby. About five inches long with the round part at the end. Crusted glass burnt almost half way up the mouth.

"Poor chick," said Robby. "Look how bad she burn um. No body even show her, look all dis fucken dope she wasted."

All up the mouth of the pipe the clear was spilled, dried. Like one rookie smoker wasting all their money.

Mikey took the empty baggie she had with the Superman S print on the outside. He peeled it open and took out this crumb, holding it between his fingers up to the black light on the ceiling, trying to see through it.

"Oil base dis one," he said. "Plus, you seen dis green color? Dats Kody's new batch right dere."

"See, Dingo, wasn't even ours," said Robby.

"Dis Kody's dope right here," said Mikey. "Kody-Dos rip her off on dis shit, guarantee. Dats da kine bag dey get too, with the Superman S. "

I laid back down again, trying for get back to sleep. But I could hear Mikey's voice with all that deep bass. "Dingo, some time the body never like die for a while, even when every thing else dead. Dis girl wen die hours ago already." His voice going even more lower now. "Only one thing for do, is drop her ass off in the dumpster behind da old theaters. Boarded up, no cameras dere."

Robby was saying we had to get her out of the house now in case any body come looking for her. We had to chance um with the body in day light, other wise we could have waited for to night. She had to go now.

Dingo no like hear any of this but.

I was half sleep still but I heard Mikey asking Robby if he wen tag the girl dat night. Robby said no. But Mikey took off all her clothes any way, for burn um, jus in case she had any kine fibers or whatever from the house. He cleaned out her finger nails, and even—well, I no like say, but Mikey made sure the girl was all clean before he rolled her up in the carpet. Okay, I jus tell you I guess, he wen fill her up with da kine Clorox.

"She's alive," said Dingo, still yet.

"She no more pulse," said Mikey.

"Fuck dat, I felt her breathing," said Dingo.

"Fuck dat," said Mikey. "We go."

Killas backed the truck right up to the stairs. When we knew the neighbors wasn't watching, Mikey and Robby took her body in the carpet out the back door, around the side of the house with high bushes, and put her in the truck bed.

Mikey and Killas rode in the back with me and her. Dingo was in the front and Robby driving. The wind was keeping me awake, sitting on the girl for keep her from rolling around in the carpet. She was squirmy as fuck for one dead girl, and like half way there she wen shit all over the carpet. All day already I was smelling shit.

Mikey was picking his teeth, his back to the cab, the hood from his black jacket blowing down over his face, riding in back too, for make sure every thing, keeping one eye on her and us too.

Mikey, he was one for life tweaker, he seen it all before already. That's why he took charge with dis, not Robby.

Him and Robby was two different breeds. From far away, guys would think Mikey was the bull. Robby would pound a guy out, talk shit after. Mikey would pound the guy out, pad his pockets, take the wallet, take his quarters. Mikey had the I no give a fuck long time already kine tweaker face. He had real green eyes too, like voodoo charms. One hard look from him, guys was jus planted.

When we was behind the old closed down theaters Mikey got out for check every thing real fast. Seem like no body was around, but you never know.

Was strange, but the girl got the most nuts when we backed up behind the theater and Mikey open the lid of the dumpster and about to put her in. I thought I heard noises. One last time Mikey reached in to the carpet and felt for the pulse, looking at Dingo, shaking his head. With those voodoo charm eyes.

We was all relieved driving home, to have it done with. We parked by Safeway, waited in the truck for Killas to go grab beer and hamburger. It was the same store I took the beer from the night before. Mikey was gon make hamburger steaks when we got back, with all the left over gravy. I could feel the bed already. We was gon watch the game later, go beach in the afternoon. No body was gon talk about no drugged out dead haole girl trying to make like she was alive.

And then her phone rang. Ring tone No Woman No Cry, Bob Marley.

For some reason I still cannot understand, I went in side her bag and opened the phone and was holding it up.

"No, Jesse!" said Mikey.

Every body was just staring at me, bra, mouth open.

And I said, "Hello." I still cannot understand why.

"Hi?" said this shaky voice from one older haole lady. "This is Charlene's mom, Janice."

"Oh," I said.

"Can I talk to her please, darlin'?"

"I–I dunno."

"Can you put her on the phone? She's not in trouble, sweetie. I just wanna talk to her, okay?" The mom sounded all sick. She had this accent.

"I dunno–"

Mikey grabbed the phone and put the receiver to his chest.

"Who dis?" he said to me real quiet.

I told him, "Da mom."

Mikey started to make the sound with his lips he always make when he thinking.

Mikey had one voice he only saved for girls. It had some special power too. It was all slow and soft, but you could feel all the horse power. It made girls feel safe.

"Dis Charlene's mom?" said Mikey in his voice. "Janice? Kay, Janice, dis Charlene's new boy friend. Me and your daughter, we going up to da main land for start one new life up dere. You can come up visit us when we ready, but you no can talk to her." I could hear the mom going off at him, losing it. "I sorry but I still cannot let you talk to her. You gon tell her come home and I cannot have dat. I gon take good care her, no worry, kay." Mikey closed the phone and slap me in my head with it.

Robby grabbed the phone, smashed it, took out the SIM card and threw all her shit down the gutter by the side of the road.

Then Mikey said, "We gotta go back get the girl now. One haole girl like dat, the cops all come out serving old warrants, raid houses till they find us. Plus, before dat even, somebody dat knew her was dere last night, gon talk to some body."

"No," said Dingo. "Fuck dat, we never did nothing."

Robby rubbed his eyes. "Not gon matter, Dingo."

"One haole chick li'dat," said Mikey. "They gon try say we gave her da dope."

Robby turned the truck around.

The dumpster was making noises in side. We was waiting dere for little while, jus watching out, making sure no body was around. The noises was awful.

"I told you dat chick was alive," said Dingo.

"Shh," said Mikey. He was leaning on the cab, looking over, waiting for this one old man trying to cross the road, his old man scooter with the orange flag dangling at the end.

I was out of it. I nearly fell asleep on Killas. He pushed me. "Get off me, Jess, you smell like shit, cuz."

Mikey threw open the lid from the dumpster and all these cats jumped out and took off. And the girl was in there naked.

She was still twitching all the way up to the place where we wen bury her. I no can tell you where, sorry. But there was trees every where, pine cones, and no body around for miles.

I was the guy had to dig the hole too, cuz I was the genius who picked up Charlene's phone and talked to Janice, the mom.

Naked haole girl, she was blinding, so white there on the ground, staring up at the grey sky. Every time she wen jolt her arms, or her fingers would lock up or some thing, Dingo would jump too. But she was more relax now, out there by the trees and the cool wind.

Killas and Robby was throwing the foot ball around. Mikey was doing a bowl, smoking his dope in, you could see the fire from the lighter flickering. I started to see all these wavy lines.

After a while of digging Mikey came and told me to dig the hole with square edges, you can't jus dig a hole, you have to shape it. His shadow standing right next to mine.

"You know what," I told him, "go smoke your dope. No tell me how for dig my hole." I threw another pile.

My thumb was still cut from punching the guy and the shovel was digging in to my hands.

The girl Charlene had one little dolphin tattoo on her ankle. I never cared about the little dolphin but. Even though I knew her mom never was gon see her baby again and I was sleeping right by her when she died the night before, I was jus thinking how hard all this digging was, I was all sweating through my shirt, and how that girl was jus lying there with that stupid look on her face, not doing shit.

I got all pissed off thinking that, and then I jus felt so tired, so I made pretend I was digging the hole for me. Even when we dropped her in and I was shoveling the brown dirt all over the pale skin on her breasts, I was thinking dat was me, I was the one with the warm dirt covering me up like one blanket, little by little. I was gon get to sleep finally, with no noise any where, no loud music, no fighting, and no drugs, jus warm. Like how my mom used to put the laundry pile in the living room and I would go dive in and no one could find me. Smell warm and clean.

I could hear Killas and Robby laughing and the foot ball landed in the hole and jus wen miss the girl's foot, the one with the dolphin on the ankle. I was so red I wen pick up the ball and punt the fucka in to the trees.

Robby came up to me all smiling, slapping me around, jus play play kine, trying for get me to smile too.

"Last chance, Jesse," he said. "She not bad for one dead chick. Last chance for finally get some from da party. Hit dat real fast, no body gon watch."

I looked back down at the girl. Half covered in brown dirt, half white poking up through the ground. I took one mean swing at Robby but he blocked it, grab my neck and took me to the ground in one head lock. Every body else turned around.

"Easy tiger, easy killer," said Robby. I stopped fighting and we both just sat on the hard dry dirt.

I told him, "Bra, what if she not fucken dead?"

"Yah?" he said. "She look dead enough to me. What if she was alive? You never tink of dat? What she gon tell da cops after she wake up and her mom start asking who was dat guy on da phone, whose house you guys was at? Mikey get warrants, Jesse, I get one house full of dope, we all lock up for the rest of our life. You no can get any good kine sleep in dere, Jesse, guys crying out, I like die, I like die."

He threw one cigarette that landed right by my knee. The pine trees moving and creaking in the slow wind.

He shook his head again and took one deep breath. "I always forget, Jesse, you grew up one nice house, nice family." He reached out his arm and pulled me up.

And I finished shoveling and packed the dirt down and we covered it all over, pine needles and cones.

I sat down again. Robby sat down beside me. "Da girl had her own pipe," he said. "She know, Jesse."

"She know what?" I said.

"She know."

Getting back up, Mikey was watching me from under the hood of his jacket.

Riding home in the truck bed, the shovel bounced around every time we hit a bump. Nobody was saying anything. I fell asleep and dreamed about nothing.

Chapter Four

De Luca and Rawlings sat in the Lancer, looking at the cinder block bar across the road. The sign said HOME GROWN in big letters, homemade-looking printing.

De Luca pointed. "See, Rawlings? That's one of the places in the video."

On the base, Recreation and Welfare had this video they showed to all the marines rotating back to Hawai'i between tours. Places to stay away from. The message of the briefing was, be advised, there is a history here, the locals are not necessarily friendly to the military.

Most of the guys listened, but Rawlings was not all that good of a listener. He was famous in his unit for going in harm's way not just in war but in time of peace, which was what the next thirty days was supposed to be, before they rotated out again. Rawlings could be crude, crazy definitely–he said odd biblical things. When he drank it was even worse. De Luca knew Rawlings's thinking from experience: I am here, and if I want to go there, that's where I will go, God is on my side and I am a god-fearing man and I don't fear anything else or anybody. The gospel according to Rawlings.

Rawlings's father had been in Vietnam, and Rawlings liked to recite the version of the psalm that the old man brought back. "Yea," he said out the window of the Lancer in his biblical voice, blowing Marlboro smoke, "Yea, though I walk through the valley of the shadow of death, I will fear no evil, for I am the meanest mother in the valley." He knuckled De Luca in the shoulder, hard. "And thou art with me, aren't thou?"

De Luca jabbed him back, not seriously, he didn't want to end up wrestling with him again. Rawlings had six inches and fifty pounds on him.

On a weedy patch by the bar, in the yellow light of tiki torches that smelled of kerosene, a pickup was parked, with a cooler hanging out the end of the bed, and four guys, some in board shorts, drinking from cans, laughing.

The truck had a bumper sticker. I LOVED THIS TOWN, THEN YOU SHOWED UP. De Luca read it off. "You sure they're not talking about us?"

Rawlings got out of the car. "Come on, De Luca, you pussy. We got our aloha shirts on, don't we?" His had yellow pineapples. "XXL-size aloha, that's me." He unbuttoned the big shirt, flapped it loose, and puffed out his chest in his undershirt.

"Alright then," said De Luca. His shirt had comic-strip palm trees. "Just don't be doing any of your IED behaviors tonight."

Rawlings bowed his head. "I sin, I know I do. But I repent. God knows I repent." He flipped his cigarette butt to the ground.

"Yeah," said De Luca. "I've seen you repent more times than you give up smoking."

The HOME GROWN bouncer was sitting on a high stool by the door, and the closer they came the bigger he got.

"Man," said Rawlings, "he's gotta go, what, three fifty easy."

The girl standing beside him was small and slim, in shorts with a green blouse, holding her arm out straight, tapping ash from her cigarette.

"Hey, beautiful," said Rawlings. "What's your name?"

She took a slow draw, blew smoke in his face and walked inside.

Rawlings shook his head and turned to the bouncer. "What's her problem?"

"I dunno. Wat you tink?" said the bouncer, hoisting himself to his feet. "ID, guys."

He took what seemed an ungrateful amount of time with the purple flashlight.

"Rawlings, Arkansas. De Luca, West Virginia. You two a long way from home, ah?"

"Iraq," said De Luca. "Now Afghanistan. You know, defending our country."

The bouncer looked down, nodding. "Right on. No offense. You guys saw action over dere?"

"You could say that," said De Luca.

"You want to see his war wounds?" said Rawlings.

The bouncer waved his big hand in a fist, with the IDs between his fingers. "Nah, nah. Jus, I can tell you guys like party tonight, enjoy yourself. Dats fine. Good. Good for you. You earned it. But jus like how it was back home, you prolly never like guys, you know, out of town guys, showing up making all kine noise. For your own good, may be you like da sports bar down da road, better for you guys, for your kine."

"Our kind?" said Rawlings. "Our kind? What is this, ethnic profiling?"

He planted himself in the doorway, fronting the metal detector, legs apart in his tight jeans. "Profile this, boss."

De Luca shut his eyes. No, Rawlings. Not again.

Kody was leaning on the bar, looking at the big haole making ass at the door, measuring the distance with his eyes, ten paces.

Dos put out a hand to him. "I know you how long. I know your mind. I tol you already . . . If get mil-i-tary tonight, jus leave um, please."

"Me?" said Kody, sounding offended.

"Yah you," said Dos. "Every time you come over here da ambulance come, den da cops. Den we gotta go court afta."

"Nah," said Kody.

"All dat hate inside gon be you down fall," said Dos. "You go beach you launching haoles. You go movies you launching haoles. Leave da haoles, let um haole around for one night."

"Me?" Kody drained his beer and set the bottle down on the bar, gently. He stretched his neck and it made a loud pop. His yellow diamond earrings sparkling. "I love haole people. I was gonna go shake his hand. But you wanna go home so bad, we go den."

De Luca watched the two of them coming, slippers on bare concrete. The smaller one not really all that small. The big one with the limp, shouldering ahead, tattoos, bleached hair and a white scar. He would weigh in a lot heavier than Rawlings. And Rawlings standing there in their way, not budging.

"Listen," the bouncer said to Rawlings. "You gotta move, bra. For your own good. Or I can move you."

Rawlings shook his head. "You think? I don't think so."

The bouncer said, "You not worth my time. If you was bigger may be."

Rawlings gave a snort. "If you was a little bigger, boss, you could be my dick."

Kody stepped out through the door, smiling ear to ear, clapping.

The bouncer shrugged. "I was tryin to help you stupid fuckas. Now too late."

Two paces, and Kody was head to head with Rawlings, the torches flickering behind them.

"Come on, man," said De Luca. "We're just back from Afghanistan."

"I know," said Kody. "You my hero."

Rawlings reached back, but before he could unload Kody had him wrapped in a headlock and he could hardly breathe. Kody pushed him against the wall, held him there, then let him go and stepped back, arms out, palms up, smiling.

"Eh," he said. "I jus fuckin wit you." His voice was warm. "Come, lemme shake you han."

He took hold of Rawlings's right hand and pulled him in close, breathing in his face.

"You tink you one tough guy. I tink I one tough guy. I dunno . . . but I guess one of us always gotta be wrong ah?"

Chapter Five

Back when I was still seventeen, that's when I starting slanging on my own.

Robby told me, "You been pumping um for us long time. You know plenty guys by now. Pump um for yourself, Jesse. Make your own money."

Next day my phone was blowing up all day, guys telling me, "Yah, eh, Robby said for call dis number if any thing, for da kine . . . grab."

Dingo told me, "Learn from Mikey. Dat guy was born and raise. He know da drug game better den any body."

Mikey was one hard guy to crack. He hardly let any body in. Jus Robby. But after a while, day by day I would learn from him. I even found out a little about him.

The first thing you would notice, da guy Mikey jus look like one murderer jus escape from the circus. He was one big wide round fucka with huge shoulders, NFL middle line backer build. Funny thing but, he was quieter than mouse shit. Even the way he would move stuff around and sit down on the cooler, you never heard nothing from him he never meant you to hear.

Guys that never knew Mikey good never like drink around him. You could drink with that fucka all night, he might not say one thing at all, like he only knew how for say three

words any way. Like you ask him what kine beer he like, he
go, "Whateva kine beer." Whatever kine music. Which way
you going, Mikey? "My way."

When he does speak he choose all his words careful too,
he always say, "I never seen but I heard" or "supposably."

He was kinda pale with short bushy hair, hairy stomach,
his face had all kind creases and stubble. Mikey was the only
guy too that hardly poked nothing, jus the zip code on his fore
arm (not your zip code, whoever you are). He always sport the
same huge black jacket that never was in style, but he could
fit his pipe kit, the cloth, the scraper and some times even
rubbing alcohol on the in side. And he always some random
weapon not too far away, machete, sawed down bat.

Every where we went guys was bowing down to Mikey.
We would drink til six and shut down every party. You heard
every body whispering, "Not dis fucken guy again, fuck,
every time."

Mikey was one infamous tax man on this side the island.
Small time dealers was one snack for him. You would see
him with the hood up on his black jacket, creeping around
corners, jus gliding, no sound, all the moms telling the kids,
come in side.

When Mikey stop you on the street, tell you, "I like borrow
money," you already feel your hand moving to your pocket,
cuz the next thing he gon tell you, "Like lose teet?" He had
the most raspiest, deepest voice.

He would tax the same guys over and over again and
there wasn't nothing they could do about it.

But there was one other side to Mikey that prolly he never
even really know. The guy was the most ticklish fucka you
ever met. Dingo's girl would sneak up to Mikey all tickle tickle,
and Mikey would jus go nuts giggling like a baby, but right
after that you never seen him so mad in your whole life.

His foot too, bra, he had one weird thing with his foot, that if some thing touch him that he never was expecting he would jump back six feet and start throwing combos.

And they say God watches over children and drug addicts and maybe that's true. Cuz Mikey always got away with every thing. He jus had this look like he was too smart and too fucken evil to ever get busted. You was jus glad he was on your side.

The legend is that Mikey grew up in one car, hiding, running from CPS so he never got taken away from his chronic mom in to foster care. Mikey never talk about um. That's jus his way.

This is what I know. Mikey and Robby both grew up from small kid time in one of those low rises where half of every body there taking whacks, smoking clear every night. Robby told me when Mikey was still young, his mom made him drink choke water and then she would take him to get her drug test, have him piss in the Ziploc bag for her to take in side for her test still warm.

But Robby said there was so much clear smoke in the house between her and Mikey's aunty, even Mikey's piss no pass some times.

When Mikey was twelve his aunty would send him out to pick up the drugs for his aunty and the mom and the grandma.

They was all tweakers.

Mikey was third generation tweaker.

Mikey got smart, he started for tax the other young boys in his building and grab extra from the dealer for him self.

Mikey would always tax this one skinny kid from up stairs named Robby. Robby would always fight back but Mikey was more big than him.

One day Mikey taxed Robby's older brother and pounded him out pretty good. Robby's brother was real weak too, his organs in side was all katsu, he had one scar down his chest from the surgery. Robby came back the next day and stabbed Mikey all over his chest and neck with the box cutter.

After that they was best friends. Mikey put him on to the clear and they would go out taxing and smoking all night together, losing it on the pipe for whole weeks.

Pretty soon every body know about them.

But Robby never was as sick as Mikey. One time Mikey had this real young girl Alisa have sex with these military guys for dope. She was supposed to set them up so Mikey could tax them, but she felt sorry for one of the guys and told him the whole story, so they got away. She wasn't even in to the guy, she said he was just a nice guy and she couldn't do it.

Mikey slapped her around until Robby showed up. He ask Mikey, "What? Your heart no more soul?"

One time Mikey called up Robby for bail and Robby told him, "Good, you fucka. You belong in dere."

Robby gave the pipe up three years ago when he starting selling full blast.

One word guys say a lot is "gone." Gone is when you no more one light crush on the drug any more, it's one life partner ship. You get tired of getting up, making speeches about your changed life, jus to fuck up that same night. One day you jus quit quitting and say fuck it.

Guys used to say about Mikey, dat fucka's losing it. Not any more. That fucka's gone.

And when you seen how bus all his fists. All cartilage.

How much scars he get from ripping guys for money. Taxing guys. From jumping fences, from throwing cracks with other tweakers.

Two through his chest from one forty four in one deal gone bad.

He thirty one years old by now and he already know what he gon be doing for the next thirty one.

Being chronic was his life's work. One thousand dollars a week habit he gotta raise. Meth addiction no take vacations. You gotta keep feeding um. With drawals come like swarms. First come the hard fast panic, you like pull out your hair, scratch through your skin. But the slow Sunday afternoon pain that grind you down is the reason you never see the other side of the pipe.

In side but, Robby was crying out for the pipe too. That's why he smoked weed like a chronic, he was waxing off. And he knew Mikey was where the pipe was at. He cannot have Mikey in the house, tweaking around him all the time. And even though every body would try for act like Mikey in the house, even Robby, even though every body try for talk in Mikey's deep raspy coal miner voice, no way he could stay with us full time. He bring too much action.

Mikey wouldn't make one big deal about it either. He would jus shoot out for couple months, sleep other houses, sleep his old apartment with his mom and his aunty.

I still no can understand tweakers. One night tweakers is scheming on how for rip each other, break in the house li'dat even. The next night they melt the clear in the same pipe saying, pass dat shit and you my cuz. They get one kinda bond us guys never would understand, you and me guys.

Tweakers get one whole secret community with all kine rituals, trade agreements li'dat, they own official sign language, all pulled together by one single purpose, get high or die or die trying. And it's all right next door, you jus never seen it. That's where Mikey lives every day. Even when he's with us his mind is there.

My friend Ola had one pretty off way for say um. One tweaker is one zombie, stumbling around mind less in the night eating brains. But when you get one tweaker in the group, you gotta cut him off fast before it spread and then every body out there with him. And you gon do him one favor too cutting him off. The sooner he hit bottom, the better chance he get re join the living. Better than being one undead thing that never sleep or eat, just one mouth that keep swimming or die.

Mikey was king of the tweakers but. He knew exactly how for stay high every night even without money. This is one tweaker move, you put some body on to clear that don't know any body, they no more line to the dope. That guy, or even worse, girl, cannot get to the clear without Mikey, cuz he was the guy that put um on. Mikey scores li'dat. That's one floater move. You get in between the users and the dealers, middle man li'dat. Whenever they getting high, Mikey getting his too, getting high. By the time they could find some body that would sell to them, Mikey would just move on looking for fresh blood. And you could say that's pretty sick, but to one tweaker the only sick thing is them not tweaking.

Mikey grew up more worse then any body, but his whole life you never heard him complain. He felt like he was lucky and any thing happen to him he knew he had it coming. And even though pretty much every body wanted Mikey dead, they wasn't gon do shit, cuz other than Kody-Dos guys, Robby pretty much ran shit, and Mikey and Robby was gon die together.

I tell you one story.

Mikey was sitting on the couch eating hand fulls of Captain Crunch without making any sound. It was the third game of my three team parley and all the Niners had to do was do nothing and I would be up plus five hundred for the day.

They couldn't even do that. The nose tackle stripped the quarter back and Ray Maualuga took it back for a touch down.

I put down my beer hard. "Forty Niners. Dey couldn't even lose by ten and half."

Mikey changed the channel to the financial channel. That fucka watches some weird shit. I told you his mind, all the books he read when he was lock up.

Then I was telling Mikey how I crashed my moped in to one mail box, asking if he know any body selling one.

"Yah," he said.

"What kine moped?" I ask.

"What eva kine moped," he said, all slick. "I get what eva kine you like, Jesse."

We nothing else for do any way, he told me come hop in the do whateva truck he borrow from some body, come with him shoot up Manoa side by the college.

I had to make one delivery on the way. The guy never brought the money, he like me front him, but no. So after I still had three points in this match box in my pocket plus the scale.

I was gonna leave um in the truck, but you never take out dope in front of Mikey. That guy was Houdini when it come to the clear—now you see it, now it's gone and he don't know nothing. And then for the grand finale he disappear.

"Gotta be fass," he told me as we was rolling up Dole Street past all the students walking to they cars. He just hopped the curb nice and slow, right on the campus, driving over the grass, pulling up to the library, the engine still running, the truck facing back at the inter section.

By the time I got out the passenger side Mikey was already going down the bike rack with the bolt cutter, tink tink tink.

He popped the locks like it was nothing. We was just launching mopeds in to the truck bed, letting um get dinged up.

These two old teacher looking guys walked by. But they couldn't think of what to do so they just looked the other way and went about their business.

I thought Mikey was throwing the tarp over the bed, but jus when I was closing the passenger door I heard him shout from far away, "Run, Jesse."

When I looked around he was gone.

I was hopping out the truck when I felt some thing grab me from behind and take me down.

That cop was the worst under cover of all time. He was wearing this base ball jersey, tuck in even, plus he had the cop hair cut. Mikey had seen him coming a mile away.

I wen ask the cop, "What? You gotta slap da cuffs? I jus one kid, Uncle."

He looked down and he told me, "Gotta, boy. Sorry." I could tell he felt shame. He knew I was too young to plan one whole thing li'dis.

Soon had all kine cops over there. Plus security. All the students looking at me like I was one show for them. I held my head up, looking at the tree tops so they wouldn't feel sorry for me. I felt stupid asking the cop to let me go. Shame is the most worse thing. Better to let some body think you're a prick than have them feeling sorry for you.

At the police station they give you this jelly to get the ink off your fingers. I decided I wasn't going to be scared any more.

I watched the lady cop putting all my things in the clear plastic evidence bag. The scale was in one little pouch. Good thing I had the dope in one match box. Most times I keep all the rock and ice in a prescription pill container.

The detective with black gel hair smiling at me. I nodded at him and he nodded back, drinking his Pepsi. He jus stood there smiling, watching my eyes watching the scale pouch.

After they took my picture I got the inter view. No, wait, was the other way around, first I got the picture, then I got printed, then the inter view.

The lady was saying if I never ratted on Mikey I was gon have to eat all the felony charges. I was almost eighteen too. She said they might try me as one adult. So one last time she asked me about Mikey. I jus looked down.

"All right," she said. She took her folders and left.

I thought they would jus put me back in to holding, but five minutes later this detective with gel hair showed up in the room smiling, and I knew I was gonna be there for a while.

But he seem like he was in a really good mood or some thing and you could fuck around with him. He told me, "You want a drink, Jesse? Pepsi, root beer?"

"I take one Bud Lite if you guys got . . . Nah," I said.

"They love that attitude in court," he said and smiled.

He didn't really look like one cop. Early thirties, prolly think he dress sharp, his hair slick back, you could tell he partied too when he was younger, maybe he still party.

"Yah," I said. "Look, bro. I tell you what I told da odda guys. Just one mistake identity charge– "

He laughed. "I'm not here about the mopeds. That's not what I do, Jesse."

"What den? Yout couselling or some thing?"

"Do you want me to be?" He put on this look. "Why'd you steal the mopeds, Jesse? Was it the white man's fault?"

I cracked up laughing. "No you–I am da white man. So what den?"

"I just thought you could use a friend."

This fucka.

I looked him in the eye. "You seem like one cool guy. But I usually cruise with guys more close to my own age."

He laughed a little and walked around me. Jus eye balling me until he got back to the front.

"You not gay?" I said. "You like girls, right? Your life, bu, I no judge you. But I not like that."

He took the plastic evidence bag out of his pocket and put it in front of me. I stopped laughing.

"You know what's in that bag, Jesse?" he said.

Now I get it.

"I'd say you've got about ten to fifteen years in that bag, if I had to open it. Take it to evidence, weigh it. If I felt like doing all that paperwork."

"I know you guys gotta eat too," I said.

His face came all serious. Like I insulted him. "Oh, I don't want your money, Jesse."

"What you want from me, bra? I don't know any names."

He put one card down on the table like he used to be a dealer at a casino. DETECTIVE RANDY VALSKI.

Valski? What kinda fucked up name is that any way?

Then he put down the flyers, color xerox. I started flipping through the pictures until I saw hers. My mouth opened, but I came off smooth like I was yawning. It look jus like Charlene, except, you know, alive.

She had her red hair in these weird braids, not really smiling, like some body was making her be in the picture.

"So what?" I said. "Your job is to figure out whose fault it is?"

"No," he said. "I let other people try and figure out whose fault it is. I just try and get the kids back to their parents."

His whole face changed, he was looking at the pictures too. He spun his wedding ring around his finger with his thumb and tapped it on the table. "I'm not very good at my job, Jesse."

I looked up.

"You know who would be good at my job?"

I shook my head.

"You."

"Me?" I said.

"Yeah," he said. "You, Jesse. I worked in Phoenix. Sex crimes in Vegas. But over here with missing kids, most of the time it just comes back to this." He shook the evidence bag. "You follow the drugs, you'll find the kids."

"So what you want from me any ways, man?" I said.

"I just want you to take this with you." He pushed his card across the table. He opened up his file and took out more xerox copies and photos and descriptions. All kids, missing persons. "Look at those pictures. Ask around. There's rewards if that helps. If you can bring one of the kids back for me, give me a call. Maybe I can do you another favor later on down the line. That's what friends do."

He shook my hand and then he picked up the evidence bag and shook it. "I'm going to go flush it."

I guess it's only three points.

I was more worried about the scale. I love that scale.

But in the end I know I was lucky, even if it's jus cuz they don't got room in the court to charge every body for every thing. Or maybe they jus like keep the stats down. I dunno. I really don't. Maybe the guy Randy jus wanted one friend.

At least I had my own holding cell. Was pretty clean. The two benches and the toilet bowl and the sink was all stain less steel. I put my feet up on the bench and did sets of incline push ups until I couldn't even do ten. But I slept good on the hard surface for some reason, even though I was craving beer and weed. I never sleep sober for how many years already.

In the morning they came and took me out of the cell. That's when I heard the voice, my dad.

Peeking around the corner I saw my dad in his under shirt tank top, talking to the cops at the processing desk.

They kept trying to joke with him, get him to relax. My dad just kept apologizing. He even told um, "His mudda was soff with him."

Then they told him, "Your son's record will expunge the arrest automatically when he turns eighteen."

In the parking lot the morning sun light was coming through the monkey pod trees.

My dad wouldn't even look at me. First thing he said, "Your mudda smoke cigarette now cuz of you, Jesse."

He had his work pants on and he was putting on his work shirt over the tank top.

I asked him, "When can I come home, Dad?"

He jus hand me the court paper work and got in his old Ford and drove away until he stopped too early at the yellow light like he always did. I put the paper work with all the pictures of missing children that Valski the detective gave me.

I still had red line marks around my wrists from the cuffs.

Mikey got away clean.

He slipped in to some shadow or some ditch with his black hood up. He could do that. You turn your back on him and when you turn around again the fucka is gone.

Chapter Six

One word some guys say is "game."

Game can mean pretty much any thing. Could be like talent, like dat guy got game. Or you say one girl is game, that could mean she one slut, not like in one bad way, in one good way.

But you say one guy is game, that mean he one fear less fucka, down for tax any body, down for scrap every time he go drink.

Another kine, you ask your friend about some body and he tell you all serious, dat fucka game, that mean he one stand up guy, like he stand for some thing. That's the most, the best thing some body can say about you.

No body I knew was picking up the phone to give me one ride. May be they was afraid I wen rat um out. Or may be they just wasn't awake yet. I had to mission it in my slippers looking for one 57 bus back home. I took plenty wrong turns too. I don't know town for shit.

I wish my dad had picked me up after they feed me, my stomach was growling. Even more than that I was craving beer. You never realize you one alcoholic until you stop drinking, drinking and burning first thing when you wake up.

I was walking down this crowded street between little restaurants and tables in the middle, home less guys every where. I took all the pictures and threw um in the trash except for Charlene. Then I remember the court paper work and fish it out, with little bit ketchup on it that I wipe off. When I looked back I saw this one old guy with long nails going through the trash, looking at the pictures.

I found one uncle sleeping on the curb by the McDonalds to grab us one twelve pack bottles from the liquor store. But he came back with one cold pack cans.

"Ho," I said.

"I go return um?" he said.

"Nah, if cans can. Gotta watch for HPD but. I just got my first arrest last night."

"Oh, den we gotta drink," he said and handed me one.

We started crankin um in this alley by the white church. I was jus pounding beers super fast, putting the cans back in the box I was hiding under my legs. Then I grabbed us couple ninety nine cent double cheese burgers. Was like eleven o'clock when I started to catch buzz, laughing, cracking jokes, jus killing beers in the alley together, watching all these older kids walk by with their back packs.

Uncle said we was by HPU campus. "No way," I said.

He was telling me, look all the chicks, I should sign up, get one ed-u-mu-cation li'dat. I told him I not book smart.

"Why you say dat?" said the uncle.

"I dunno," I said. "I took one test in elementary."

"One main land test? Pff," said the uncle. "How you tink dem guys would do on one test from down hea?"

"Shitty, I guess," I said.

I chug my beer. I always put one dent under the mouth my can to make the beer pour out more smooth and mark my can from the other beers. Some guys tip the tab to the side.

Soon enough this chubby girl with pig tails and thick frame glasses came around the corner with one clip board asking for signatures.

"Are you eighteen?" she ask me.

"I twenty one, you," I said. "Twenty two even."

The uncle started laughing. We was all cut already.

She made this weird smile. "Do you want to sign our petition to save the manatees off the Florida coast?"

"Da who?" I said.

She showed us the picture, some kine weird marine creature. "They need our help. The motor boats just drive over them and the blades cut them." I saw the little guy had one scar on his back.

"Dats one ugly ass fish," I said, burping. "Poor little fucka. They should kill him, put him out his misery before he see him self."

The uncle was all rolling, laughing more hard. Then he calm down. "How's da meat taste? Mean, da fish meat?"

The girl shook her pig tails. "Please. If you could just sign it. I'm trying to get the most signatures."

"Awright!" I said. "Gimme da pepa. I go sign um. You gon win um."

Jus for fuck around, I signed Dingo's real name and gave his phone number. I even checked the box that said if you wanted to volunteer.

Uncle smile at her. "Take one break from saving da world. Sit down, grab one beer with Uncle. Tell us all about saving da fishes in Flor-i-da."

"Thanks," she said, and left.

About twelve I finally found the right bus stop and the bus hissed and lowered to the ground. In side was almost empty, was clean and the air felt good. I went all the way to the back.

I slumped down in my seat and watched as the bus left the city, the glass buildings mirroring each other, up the highway past the pagoda tower in the grave yard towards the mountain that split the island in half.

I was tired from drinking in the sun, starting to sober up. I started thinking about what the cop was saying, detective what's his name Valski.

I leaned in the corner with my hat over my eyes, like I was going to get to sleep.

I guess for most guys they can't remember the one day their life took one left turn.

Since small kid time I wanted to work Pearl Harbor like my dad. The first time I was ten, I think, when he took me out to work with him and Uncle Bill, tug boat, night shift.

When we came in to the harbor, the stadium lights came over the black water. The old timers fishing off Sand Island nodded to us as we went by the pier. The heavy bass from the engine vibrated the riggers as we passed Aloha Tower Market Place on the right. When we got closer you could hear the sounds of the water lapping in to the row of tires and the music from the bars.

Everything was so new, new smells, new sounds.

We chugged past the gift shops, the restaurants, all the people partying, shouting and laughing. I watched it all pass by and the neon lights behind the man shape of my dad.

My mom told me how my shoulders would come big like him one day.

He let me steer um too for little while, holding the wheel from behind, telling me, "Hard work, boy. Dats da meaning of life. Dats what men do."

Uncle Bill said, "If never was for us guys and dis boat, bring all da ships in, no body would have any kine food for grine tomorrow, Jesse."

The radio hissed when the helicopter flew over head. I was just one small kid thinking how I was gon tell all the boys at school, "Ho my dad is Superman cuz. Me too."

My dad took off his gloves and picked me up in the air by my arm pit to pull the fog horn. Was like sand paper, my dad's hands. And that horn just blasting, echoing all down the ship yard down to dry dock 4A where the stevedores rigged cables.

After we finish, all the uncles was standing around laughing at me, saying, "Look. Watch um. In da blood. You gon be da next Gomes over here work harbor. Your dad dem gon get you in, boy, guarantee."

I ask my dad how come the boat got the name Atlas. He said Atlas was this guy, he carry the world on his shoulder.

My dad's neck would fold up in creases over his shirt when he gave orders.

Leaning over the edge above the water I seen all the oil spots, garbage, bottles floating by. Then I seen this school of twenty hammer heads shooting under the boat like bullets. My dad yelled over the engine, jus playing around kine, "Ch-out, fore you fall in dere, Jesse."

That water was so black like it jus swallowed up light. I was thinking how any thing that could live down there would have to be pretty nuts.

When we got the last ship in was after mid night already and my mom and my sistas Shelly and Gummybear was waiting for us in the truck, watching us with the riggers and the surface hook.

My mom came out the Ford with her camera telling us sit down. My dad, he never like having his picture taken, but my mom made all the fuss too.

My dad did his double eye brow raise. Then he sat down for the picture and he talk soft, just to me, no body else, "Shweatin? Feel good?" The stadium lights around him.

"You gon be all right, Jesse," he said with the flash going off. "Jus be careful in da night. No make da same mistakes as me."

After my mom took the picture I wen ask my dad, "Eh, I did pretty good tonight, Dad?"

He looked away. "You did okay."

Later on my sista Shelly called it the picture of dad smiling. My dad wasn't there when Shelly was born. He was lock up.

Through the radio static now we heard some body calling for my dad. There was one last ship, the Monticello, that had stalled out far from the harbor. It wasn't on the schedule and the uncles was grumbling.

"Fuck um," said Uncle Bill. "Let da next shift get um."

"Every body waiting for us," I told my dad.

But my dad told um, "Da guys workin on da Monticello probly want for go home too. Plus over time." And to me, "Jesse, your mudda rather us get da over time pay. She could take her day off dis week, take your sistas up for see grandma."

My dad cranked the latch and the engine started up again. The water shooting out behind us, my dad working the wheel.

From far away the Monticello ship looked all white but up close it was other colors too. There was this band playing and strange laughing. There was people on top the boat, men wearing dress jackets and long pants and ladies with robes and wine glasses. This one lady even had a long scarf dangling over the rail.

You need take all kine care hooking up to tow. Dad giving the orders. Then all of sudden Atlas's engine sputtered out and died. We was jus drifting there, getting closer to them. People started yelling at us from on top the Monticello to get going already again, and my dad was hustling around with the flash light to figure out what was wrong with Atlas, covered in engine dust and grease.

The lights from Monticello shined on our deck like we was on stage for them. Looking through the haze the faces all looked the same.

Then I saw a kid holding a bag of M&Ms, grinning at me like the whole thing was funny.

My dad was one man to humble all men with one hard honest look and one strong hand shake. And the kid smirking at us, like it was good fun on Friday night to watch my dad pour sweat.

I heard my dad. "Boy. Come. Hold da light."

I turned around.

I felt some thing hit my neck.

When I looked down on the deck I saw the M&Ms, hitting my dad.

I yelled up. "You like fuck with my dad, you fucken punk?" But there was nothing I could do.

The kid jus smiled with that stupid smirk.

My dad snapped at me. "Eh, Jesse. Get over here. Hold da light."

I couldn't look at him. My dad jus letting them do it.

And there we was in the middle of the ocean. All of us stuck together. The two ships locked in with bolts, steel cables. Getting no where.

Pretty much all my family work tug boat jobs. Or they work for the city and county, work in the sun laying slabs. They work hard.

I wasn't going to be the first guy or the last guy to take a look at the other ship, tour ship, and figure it never was meant for me. Not if you gotta act that way, bull shit every body and call it people skills. I gon talk like my gramps.

So I wasn't gon carry luggage for tourists. I wasn't gon park cars or mow lawns for chump change. And they can jack up the price to live here all they like, I not leaving, so they jus gon have to deal with me at the other end of it. May be one day I gon live rent free off them in jail.

I wasn't gon work tug boat either. If the guys partying on the Monticello was cool, I would have been proud for do da job, help out, do my part. But sorry, I jus being honest, they wasn't cool, most of them was dicks, all stuck up about the wrong things. But no more pride.

Six years later my dad kicked me out the house, me, my scale I stole from school, and the dope. Now one more empty chair at the family parties.

We all living some where in that harbor. I guess I'm in dirty water with the hammer heads.

Chapter Seven

When I got back to Robby's, two hours from town on the bus, he was sitting on the porch throwing out hamburger bun, watching the birds. He always pull for the under dog birds to get the food. Robby.

I know every body was thinking I was gon rat. But when they seen me walking through the black security gate, they knew I took ass for them.

I went in side the house and I hid Charlene's missing picture behind my fish tank. I left jus the edge hanging out a little.

But Robby was punchy the whole afternoon, pounding the bag, kicking the bag, kicking me.

He start strutting up and down the porch waving his Heineken, giving speeches, yelling, sun flower seeds shooting out his mouth. "No scared Jesse when you go court. No shame." Behind him Dingo was shaking his head to me.

Soon as Robby slammed the door to the house and we heard water from the shower, Dingo told me forget every thing Robby said. "Just go in court dere, act like one total bitch. Cry if can."

Dingo opened my bottle with his and handed me the Heineken. "You gon be all right, Jesse. Even if you get lock up, they gon send you O Trips. Half my family stay in side dere, Jess. Da good half."

I looked up.

"Da other half stay Halawa."

I laughed.

"Jesse, you in. In for life. You wen prove um to us cuz you ate da charges for Mikey. You know what dat means? Plenty guys love Robby cuz they fear Robby, or dey use Robby, use his name. Had plenty guys come through dis house before you, Jesse. You know in da end Robby not gon draw blood for them. But you in." He smiled. "What's your middle name, Jesse?"

"I no more one."

"Mine's Eugene."

"Eugene," I said, nodding my head.

Dingo told me how Mikey got banish from the house again and he was up Chinatown hiding out with guys up there.

"Cuz why?"

"Cuz you," said Dingo. His chin lifting up as he smiled. "Not a very good mind, Jesse? You flooding da town with rock and clear, and you get lock up over one fuck-en mo-ped." He shook his head. "Dey never catch you for doing one smart ting. But dey catch you every time for doing one dumb ting. How you feel? Stupid?"

Worse, I almost miss court. Dingo told me how for get there but he sent me to the grown up court building. I seen all these guys I used to drink with, all in line waiting to get arraignment. They never smile either, they jus nod. All of them hardly talking, looking back and forth, trying to think of what to say when their time came to get judged. All these cool guys, good guys, guys honest with me, standing in line to go jail. The state seal of Hawai'i on the wall behind them.

I found out juvenile court, in the old building, was way down Punchbowl and I had to book it. By the time I got there

I look all chronic. All stink, sweat pouring. And my dad there. He no speak to me, jus watch.

In side the court had all the micro phones, the bright flags, dark varnished wood, lawyers and court people all dressed up, talking lawyer talk. It made you feel like you must have did some thing.

I had one whole speech worked out too, about how sorry I was supposed to be. But when the judge lady ask me if I wanted to say any thing, even with my dad watching, the words wouldn't come out.

I didn't even know if I was sorry.

All I know is if I had to choose whose side I was on, then I was with my friends them up the road and I would be for ever.

It pretty much goes li'dis, good as I can tell. To those guys that seen the system working for the guys they know growing up, they believe in the system and they think the law is messed up because all the crooks getting away with it. For other guys growing up, they seen family, they seen some the coolest guys they knew getting taken away by the law, and they never had to be told whose side the system was for.

And of the guys I know, it's the ones going back jail that get more respect for the cops than the rich guys the cops is protecting. Cuz only one broke fucka gon under stand that the cop gotta do the job for his family to get chance living over here. Only one broke fucka gon under stand how much cops gotta put up with for shit money and respect. Messed up, yeah?

The judge lady told me take one no contest plea to the felony charge thiefing the mopeds and she would defer the sentencing for twelve months and if I stay outa trouble the whole thing go away.

But I had to go Olomana School for punks. Saint Olomana's they call it, like one joke I guess.

But I never had to go to the boys home part, jus come from the house for school.

You gotta get up early, catch bus down the Highway and walk it up the long road between the cow pastures and the base ball field. In the afternoon you can hear the aluminum bats, the kids at little league practice, their coach yelling at them.

Behind the wire fences the cows would moo all together some times, munching on the grass.

Some guys in my class was pushing dope on they own, small time, jus trying to get started. Word traveled fast and pretty soon all the young kids my age was asking me for work, cuz I had the better lines. Not even jus the punks that got kicked out, the good kids that graduate even. Trying to find legit work, there was shit jobs for shit money with no medical. And you prolly gon need two or three of those fucka jobs. So, my kine work.

I fronted some of them work. I figure I help out, let them sell the dope, pay me after. But most of them was too nice, too soft. The chronics ate um alive and I lost out.

I went around with my bat with the top part sawed off trying to get my money back from the chronics jus to make myself feel better. I knew all of them.

They never had any money to take, that's why they chronic.

I never used the bat.

I had to pay Robby out of pocket.

Chapter Eight

I almost thought Mikey forgot about me. He should have at least shook my hand.

But then, on my eighteenth birth day, Mikey came scooting up the road super slow on this moped. He could barely ride the thing, his fat ass weighing um down, dragging, his jacket hood bulging with air behind him. Mikey would have been super fat ass status but he was on the batu diet plan.

He threw me the key trying to make like it was no big deals, like he just showed up by accident on my birth day, like he never thief the moped just for me. "I cannot ride dis fucka, I too fat. If you like um, take um, Jesse."

The next half hour I was all proud zipping around the block, showing um off, gunning the motor super loud. I seen all the neighbors flying by, cranky old man yelling out over the motor, "I guess you got your moped back, huh?"

"Yups," I said.

The color was off but. Mikey had um painted red white and blue, cuz the fucka was stolen.

When I pulled up the drive way I was trying for tell Mikey we even now, fair and square.

He raised his whole head in side the hood. "Dis nothing. Wait til later." His voice had all kine mischief. "I show you some ting, Jesse."

So one hour later I came in to the living room under the black light, I heard Mikey on the phone. He was using that voice he saved only for girls. "Eh Amber. You like take whacks? Get poked? Come down here. Get some thing for poke over here. Gon have me, my friend Robby and one young kid. Come to pound."

That tweaker Mikey, no shame ever, he just tell um.

The girl ask him how was his supplies and he said, got.

"Amber?" said Robby, munching his chips for lunch. "Who's dis one? I never heard of her."

"She live town," said Mikey. "College girl, used to be."

"One college girl?"

"Too smart for her own good, dis one," said Mikey.

Was about seven when the Jetta pulled up in front the gate, music booming bass. The driver was this surfer looking guy with one long black pony tail.

Robby ran up to the window, leaning over the sink in the kitchen. "Who dat blassing dey sounds in front my house?" His eyes got huge looking out. "Come, Jess."

He put down his Heineken on the micro wave, opening the window panes, spying, his silver chain dangling, pointing. "Jess, look."

I watched her walk through the metal gate. "Ho sista!" said Robby. "Good night! How's dose missile tits, Jesse?"

She came up from under the tarps, up the porch, long legs, short shorts, squeezing between the El Camino and the Toyota, she almost tripped over the tow hitch, talking on her cell phone. Real tall girl with ash color skin, soft hair, her eyes was just a little bit too close together, but other than that, cuz, she was tap tight tick. Slammin. Had a plastic red hibiscus in her hair.

She just threw open the door too without knocking, still on her phone, "Yah, yah, whateva, kay, yah."

She seem kinda stuck up, but she had this cute little nose that made her look young and innocent under all the make up.

She closed her phone and put it in side her bag.

"Kay, I'm here," she said, looking around, running her hand over the furniture, looking at the dust on her palm. "Boy house." She spit her gum out in to her hand and stuck it right on the table.

She took her sun glasses off, her head shaking out her hair, eyeing me. "Do me one favor," she said, in this tough aunty stance with her hand on hip. "Smile. Laugh. Do some thing. I don't do da serious analyzing kine looks."

Robby was watching me watch her. I smiled. "Yes, ma'am."

She put the plastic red hibiscus and her shades in her bag with the Play boy Bunny logo and took out her lotion.

Right when I was gon ask if she like one beer. But she was already in the kitchen opening the doors, raiding our liquor cabinets.

She looked back at me over her shoulder. "If you gon keep staring, at least say some thing."

"Some thing," I said, looking at her legs as she reached up and took down the bottle of Patrón, her top lifting up over her pants, you could see the top of the g-string.

She had tats, the name Bronson on the bottom part of her neck just above her shoulder blade. Then the girl's name, Lisa. She had the islands under that. I never seen too much girls with the islands huge like how she had.

She talked without looking back, moving all the bottles around, fidgety. "I know you got some Grey Goose in here? No? 151? Nothing?"

"Nothing," I said. "Jus da Patrón and da Smirnoffs."

When she turned around again she rolled her eyes to me. "My name's Amber, by da way," she said. "You might want to know, jus in case."

She downed whatever was left of the Patrón, straight out the bottle in two cranks. Then she jus held the bottle up over her mouth, fidgety, waiting for the last drops. Robby not saying nothing.

She put her bag down nicely on the couch, jus one small bag for put all her girl stuffs, like my sista's ones. Walking back and forth, her heels clacking around on the hard wood, looking at herself in the TV screen putting up her hair. She couldn't sit down or hold still. She rolled her eyes at me again for looking at her, so I looked down.

"I'm a bitch, yah?" she said, scratching at her wrist. "Don't worry. I'll feel better soon. Where da hell is Mikey? Mikey!"

"Right here," said Mikey coming from the bath room, getting his kit together. He nearly trip over him self running.

Amber went back to her tough aunty stance. "What you was doing back there? You think you slick, but you not slick, Mikey. Trying to sneak one in? You better get left what you said on da phone."

If you never seen any body smoke a bowl, the whole thing kinda look like one magic show, when you melt all um up one time. Mikey was sitting on the floor in front of Amber on the couch facing the TV, scooping the last of his .5 grams baggie with the half straw. Placing it down the mouth of the pipe gently. Clear is so small, so potent, you cannot afford to waste. Mikey would treat the whole thing like surgery, trying to conserve to the very last. It can take years for perfect your smoking skill.

Mikey swirl the flame under the pipe, melting um down from hard crystal in to one puddle, like glowing wax, almost like mercury, and he was jus rocking the puddle back and forth.

Mikey can melt um down without hardly letting the pipe burn black at all.

He cooled it off with the towel and it left a black smudge.

But Amber, she never even give Mikey chance, never giving him the pipe, holding it in her lungs. Sitting on the couch where Charlene was.

"Easy, easy," said Mikey. "No suck um dat hard. You like collapse your lung?"

"Ho, sorry mom," she said, sarcastic. Then, "Bra, I suck um as hard as I like, kay?"

"Nuff," said Mikey.

I never figure out till later, she only had barely enough for her, couple for him. But Amber, the girl was more hard core than even Mikey. You could tell. Her habit was ridiculous. She didn't smoke to have good time. She smoke to get to go one other world. She made Mikey look healthy.

She was the worst kine chronic, the kine gets loaded up as fast as they can, end up stumbling around. Too high to cruise, too messed up to talk, sitting alone, tripping out, sketching out, all paranoid.

Robby looking at her close up. Three years off the pipe, but still yet you could see him with his mouth open, not for the girl with the strap sliding off her shoulder, for the smoke.

He shook his head at me. "Go out side, Jesse. I no like you around dis kine chronic action. Next thing you gon start reaching for um."

But I couldn't leave, I had to stay for Robby, make sure he never start reaching for um. The smoke drifting up in to the black light.

Mikey watching her, hoping she was too high to take the last hits. "You good for now? Good? Kay."

Jus as Mikey was about to take one for him self, jus enough to make the craving go away for a couple hours, she grab his arm. She could hardly move her mouth. "I take one more."

"Kay, no more," said Mikey. "Dats all we got for tonight."

"Bra, you bull shit," she said, wiping her mouth, chewing on her lips. She could hardly talk, her mouth was dry and her breath was short.

Mikey showed her the empty bag. His face trying to look innocent.

"I seen you switch out da other bag in your hand," she said.

Houdini, I told you.

She got in his face. "Give da pipe or I go walk out of here right now, try and fucken stop me."

"Go," said Mikey, his eyes never leaving the pipe. "Try go."

So she stood up.

"Sit down," said Mikey. "I hold um for you."

This time when I looked at her I had to smile cuz I knew what she was doing. Her eyes was frozen stiff by now. But before, you could tell from the way she look around, she didn't miss much, that girl Amber.

Mikey was out hustled and he knew it. She was jus making the point to him, you not the boss of me, I do any thing I like.

She took two last deep rips off the pipe, coughing hard this time. You could see her strap all the way down her shoulder now, her head wobbling. Her whole face look like she staring at some thing far away, but there was nothing.

"Kay," she said, sounding like the boss again. "Get me water."

Robby went in to the kitchen and I heard him washing out the glass for her. Mikey went to the bath room to clean the pipe, so it was jus me and Amber.

Ten minutes ago she would have got snappy at me for checking her out, give me one wise crack. Now I not sure she even notice me. I tried to smile anyway, cuz that's what she said, she never like the analyzing look.

I could tell she jus shaved her legs, they was all shiny with this super strong lotion that smelled kinda like grape jelly perfume.

Now, under all her blue eye shadow you seen how heavy her eye lids. She prolly been up drinking and chonging for days. And that's why she had all the make up too. The wrinkles was coming fast. Five years of clear age your body like fifteen years hard labor. Tweaker years.

She started leaning for ward, putting her arms on the table. Robby came in with the water, tried to get her to sit up and drink. But she slapped his hand hard. "Touch me when I tell you you can fucken touch me."

Robby put the water down. Watching her head wobble, her eye lids wide open. He snapped at her, "Amber, you jus smoke all my friend's dope. No make like you tweaking out on us, kay? Amber?"

After she drink the water she put the glass down softly on the table. She pulled the strap back up on her shoulder. She glanced at herself in the TV and brushed her hair with her hands.

"No worry," she said, breathing out heavy through her nose. "You gon get what you wanted."

They talked about it like it was one business deal or some thing. She was like this, this and this is okay, not this and that.

Mikey and Robby was like, shoot shoot shoot, they was just happy to get any thing.

I got up and went to the bath room.

I heard her say, "And no matter what, I not staying here tonight, I gotta be some place later."

When I came back in she was gone. Mikey and Robby was sitting on the couch cutting up weed in a film canister.

"What you think dat girl, Jesse?" said Mikey.

"She's dope," I said.

Mikey got up to go to the kitchen, he gave me one soft crack on my arm. He tell me, "Go in da back room." He always called my room da back room. "Do whatevas. First cracks. Amber is game."

Robby was all blazed, high on weed, smiling at me. They was like proud parents. As I walked down the hall I heard Robby saying, "Easiest ten bucks I ever made."

The only light on in my room was my fish tank light.

At first Amber never notice I was there, seem like, lying on her stomach under the sheet. There was two empty air plane size bottles of rum on the floor. You know how powerful clear is when you gotta drink liquor to get more sober.

I could see the tan line on her back. She had hung all her clothes and her under wear on the chair. She was fumbling with the radio but then she gave up and was looking at the fish tank.

She ask, "What's your fishes' names?"

"Dis one Shelly," I said, pointing. "Over here Gummybear."

"How can you tell them apart, they look the same?"

"Gummybear da nice one," I told her. "I gave dem–"

She cut me off. "Kay, I never ask for your life story."

I asked her what she went school for li'dat, but she never heard me. I couldn't read her face. Was stuck in that frozen tweaker stare.

When her phone start buzzing she told me find it and tell her who is calling.

I found it in her clothes and looked. "Bronson," I said.

"Shit, give it to me. Don't say a fucken thing."

She cleared her throat trying to hold the phone up to her ear.

"What's wrong?" she said. She was trying to sound normal but her voice was all fuck up. "I cannot come tonight. I coming to get you on Friday, we'll go beach okay?"

I could hear a voice just barely, a kid.

"I know. I would, you know I would. But I gotta see you on Friday. Okay, go sleep, go back sleep, Bronson. Good boy. Mommy loves you, kay?"

She closed the phone and dropped it and laid back down on her face.

"How old is your kids?" I asked.

"Don't," she said. "Just don't."

When I sat down on the edge of the bed, her head barely lifted up to look at me. She was in one better world now, on the in side. She could just see me and the real world from far far away. That's how she wanted it.

I hadn't been with too many girls before and never one as deadly as Amber.

Sometimes guys talk about chicks, I dunno, the way they make it sound you would think one fine girl is one pair bangers with one mouth that never shut up. If you could jus lose the mouth, keep the bangers.

And now I jus wish she would say any thing, instead of staring at the roof. Amber and her naked body under the sheet.

"Come here birt-day-boy." Her eyes still looking the roof.

Her breath was so fuming with alcohol it made me shiver and my eyes tear. Jus her heart pounding away from all the dope.

She started feeling around for me under the sheet until she found my hand and put it on her breast. I could feel how fast the blood was pumping.

She had that sticky lotion all over her, pulling my hand lower and lower. Then she start taking off my belt.

Her ice cold lips that didn't move. And what came in my mind was Charlene.

After a while she ask me, "What's wrong, boy?"

On the way out the door I told her, "My name's Jesse."

I went back out in the living room. Mikey and Robby looking at me, Mikey more hard.

"Mikey–I no can, Mikey," I said.

Robby bust out laughing, just falling down off the couch laughing.

Bra, Mikey was pissed. He say, "You no like drink couple beers first? Think about um."

"I not gon do um," I said, rubbing my hands on my shirt, trying to get the lotion off. "Fuck um. You go do um."

Robby laugh even more hard. "Keep da ten bucks, Mikey, I know it's your last. I tol you, Jesse saving him self for when dey pass da law you can marry other guys."

The way Mikey's green eyes was looking at me, almost look like he had hurt feelings, he jus wanted me to have a good birth day.

Cuz one guy like Mikey, he not gon tell you, you my little man, Jesse, I so proud how you ate all the charges for me. Every day I crack up in side jus hearing you, bra. I owe you my life too cuz all the warrants I get.

Mikey never would say one thing li'dat. What Mikey did but, was trade all his clear for me. And to one tweaker fiending, clear is more than life.

Mikey took one more good hit off the blunt and let um out when he spoke, putting those green eyes on me. "You feel shame for dat girl, Jess?" He waved with the back of his beer to my room. "Ffff. Lucky ass girl, all dem. At least dey only gotta have sex for get dey dope."

Robby got up and took off his shirt, threw it behind him, went down the hall to my room.

When he came out he was carrying Amber. Her wrapped in my sheet with her head rolling all around. The phone in her hand in case her son call her. And Robby heads for his room carrying her.

Mikey got up to leave. On the way out the door he put his last ten dollars on the counter under the rice cooker by the over flowed ash tray, where Robby would see it. The sweat on his fore head. The clock ticking in side, his mouth making that clicking sound. His mind figuring out where the money was gon come from tonight.

Down the hall I could jus hear Robby in his room yelling over the CD, and the mattress springs. And Amber dead quiet, not making a sound.

Mikey not even gonna wait for his chance with her. He was headed right out the door to find more dope.

I couldn't sleep. My bed smelling like the lotion, but I didn't have any clean sheets. I went in the living room, smoked a joint and drank couple beers watching ESPN news. Then I was geeking out on the history channel I used to watch with my dad. It always remind me of him, he could be watching the same thing as me. Falling asleep on the couch. My mom would put the blanket over.

They had this show about this guy chained to one rock for trying to steal fire from the gods.

It was two a.m. when I heard this car pull up in front our house. I knew it would be the Jetta.

Amber came out of the bath room. She looked jus how she did when she showed up. I kept my eyes on the TV so we could ignore each other. She went through our liquor cabinet until she found the Smirnoff bottle.

"See you around, Jesse," she said.

"Kay den," I said. But she jus stood there.

"Music," she said.

"What?" I said.

"You asked. I studied music." She put her frilly hair behind her shoulders. "What was your fish names again?"

"Shelly and Gummybear. No tell dem guys. I catch enough shit over da fish already."

She came over to get her shoes and she kissed me on my cheek and smiled so pure and proud it would have shamed any one.

And when she saw me smile she said, "Dere, you see? Now you can look at me. Make that face, Jesse."

"Kay, Amber," I said.

She touched my face. "You know, my name's not really Amber."

She touched my dimples. She touched her own face and made her own dimples, smiling.

I could hear her shoes on the wood as she went down the stairs.

I would never say I knew her or understood her. But her smile was the most genuine and pure thing I ever saw. The kind of smile that didn't jus come from the shape of her face, it came from in side. The kind of girl it hurt too much to think about. She wasn't yours, but jus to know her. Or maybe you were jus like all the men that came to have her but couldn't really, couldn't even know what it was they didn't get to have, the things that were only hers and she gave for free. And may be her now, getting older, keeping herself drunk and high enough so she didn't have to watch it or feel what they did.

I went to the window to watch her leave.

I saw the car door open.

She looked back and waved. The islands between her shoulder blades.

The next day Robby got me up early to train. He was trying to laugh and fuck around, but some times he would get that far away look, even in the middle of laughing his face would change and I would know, in side he was crying out for the pipe.

He would train, bang plates, hit bag, lift weights until he crash out, or burn weed to wax out the feeling.

I asked him if it ever goes away.

"What?" he said.

"Cravings."

"No," he said, spraying down the bench and wiping it down with the towel. "Da cravings never go away. You gotta believe in some thing bigger than you gon get you through it. Dats da only way. Dats when I got dis." He raised his fore arm that had the cross tattoo.

"No matta what happen, Jesse, be a man, handle you pain. All those same problems you hiding from still waiting for you when the drug go away."

Chapter Nine

Mikey called, told me pick him up from his aunty's apartment. He said he needed my help. He told me Robby thought he stole one half gram and he was gon kill him.

At the aunty's messed up apartment there was busted hinges where Robby knocked down their door looking for Mikey. He wen pound the wall all over the place. Then the bath room door he kicked down.

I couldn't believe Mikey would jus rip us off li'dat.

We bought a case and drove all around the island, all night. Every place he would tell me stop, wait for him, I knew he was still smoking shit in the bath room.

There was no telling what Robby would do if he found Mikey. When Robby loses it, it takes couple days before he calms. He might take out his piece and put it right up to Mikey's ear.

We needed one place to hide where Robby wouldn't find, and so we drove up to my dad's house.

It was like eight in the morning and I figured they was all gone. When I opened up the car door all the beer cans fell out on to the ground.

Right before we got in side I saw that my mom was in there. I could smell cigarette smoke coming through the window. My dad was right, she never smoked cigarette before.

Mikey stopped on the porch. "Fuck dat. I not going in side. I not gon meet your mom dem."

He looked in side through the window, then wiped his face with the bottom of his shirt, you could see his hairy stomach. He was out for the last four days so he was covered in sweat and dirt and beer.

"Mikey," I said, "my mom is all g. If any thing she gon get you one shirt and tell us come grine."

I never know that for sure. I never seen my mom for the last year. But my mom would love the dog in the street that bit her. I just wasn't sure if I bit her too hard to ever see her again.

I started pushing Mikey for ward to the door. For some reason I wanted him to see how nice the house was. Not like we was rich, but it was one nice family's house.

Mikey just panicking. "No tell your mom dem how you know me, Jesse, tell her I go schoo wit you or whateva."

My mom opened the door. "Jesse!"

She hugged me. She wouldn't let me go either. She said she was so happy I figured out to come now to see her, when my father wasn't home and she could talk to me.

"Howz school?" she said, with one little sniffle.

That freaked me out too. She knew I wasn't going school.

But right away Mikey pipe up. "Jesse doing good, Missus Gomes. He always dat guy, help me wit my home work. We getting ready for go school right now, we was up late studying."

Never mind Mikey was past thirty, some school kid him. My mom look so dreamy, she seemed like she was just dopey. But nice though.

"You boys cannot go school on empty stomach, come in side, come in, boy."

You think Mikey would win one truth telling contest, how he was telling my mom about school, how hard the classes was. My mom couldn't stop smiling cooking up the fried rice. It wasn't bull shit fried rice either, my mom make um with the grinded up ginger and onions, fish cake, every thing.

I never like even interrupt Mikey and her. Them two was doing some sick kinda thing making pretend with each other about my life. They both knew they was full of shit.

"Jesse was always da artist in da family," said my mom. She still had all my clay pieces from when I was in kinder garten. She had them up all over the living room like they was great works of art.

She picked up this one sculpture and put it down by Mikey. It was this thing I made in first grade, one monster with black hair and yellow teeth.

"It's so cute," Mom said. Putting more green onions in the fried rice.

Mikey slap me in my arm. "See dat, Jesse, dats what you teacher always telling you." Mikey was all in to it. I never could say nothing.

My sista Gummybear lived with her room mates now, but all her test scores was still up on the refrigerator. And Shelly, my older sista, gone main land already, her Punahou diploma, my mom put my black monster with yellow teeth right back by it. My mom cannot help but, I was her only boy. Then she tell me, "Shelly getting married, you know." I never know, how would I know. I just say I happy for her.

Mom brought out the steamy fried rice and the passion orange juice. I tried to tell her never make um from the beginning, cuz no way Mikey was gonna eat, cuz the dope. But Mikey made all the fuss too.

"Oh wow," he said. "You guys eat good over here." Then he started mashing, just stuffing him self that guy. I knew it was making him sick too, shoving all that food down. Clear tells your body not to eat. Your throat won't even work right when you swallow. He whacked the whole thing but, scrape the plate even.

I couldn't believe, I thought I was seeing shit that wasn't there. Mikey, grim reaper, shadiest fucka in town doing the dishes with my mom, laughing, busting out jokes.

They was keeping on lying to each other about me and they was loving it. She talked to him more than me even, cuz I dunno, Mikey was doing pretty good with his stories and she was afraid I might tell her some thing else.

My mom was late for work and she never even told us. The bank called her, told her come down so she said she had to go already. She felt all shame when she said to me be sure I was gone before my dad came home. She kissed me couple times and then took off real fast for the bus stop. She was working part time bank teller and part time at Macy's.

After she left Mikey went back to being quiet. We was sitting in the living room watching the NFL top twenty plays of all time count down, totally quiet.

I told him, "Eh Mikey, what if you tell Robby you was with Killas or some thing all this time? I could go back to da house, you could say you was in Chinatown even, if any thing. What you tinking?"

Mikey was wiggling his toes on the carpet. I tell you that guy get one thing with his feet. The rest of his body look all piss off but his feet was just happy as fuck on that clean fluffy rug.

"You tink dat would work or what, Mikey?" I said.

He looked me up and down, like measuring. "What you doing wit us guys, Jesse? You not like us."

Chapter Ten

It was the worstest day at work ever. So here I am at my checkout stand, aisle 4, in my green checkout girl uniform, with my name pinned on, KAPIKA, and I've got a cold, and I need to pee so bad, but it's the afternoon rush and my line is backed up into Cosmetics.

There was the noise of coins and shopping cart wheels and bagging groceries and the bleep bleep bleep from the scanners and under that the register opening and closing. My scanner mostly wasn't catching so I had to punch everything manually. Everything needed price check and I had to hear my voice on the speaker. I hate my voice. Everybody had a coupon or a question and the whole time I'm squeezing my knees together, saying shoot shoot shoot in my head, trying not to think about peeing.

And the girl working register 2 with the mustache and the rat face had told Aunty Ruth, the manager, that I was late. I told Aunty Ruth how my car stalled out. That was true. Aunty Ruth just smiled. I'm her favorite. I looked over my shoulder at Rat Girl. I gave her my meanest stink look. You look like a rat! Your boyfriend looks like a rat! You're going to have little rat babies!

Even Kimo my dog was against me that morning. He chewed up my only clean work pants and I didn't have time to do my hair so I was putting my hair up in a scrunchy as I ran across the parking lot late.

The light for the N wasn't working, so the sign said LO GS Drug Store. And when I punched in on the time clock I dropped my phone.

And I forgot my flower. When I don't wear the flower gross old guys hit on me.

It slowed down and I put my ones and fives and twenties in order and tried not to look at the clock. I wanted to go home and wrap up in a blanket and mom would make saimin.

And then the lady with the baby hanging on to her neck came into my line and I looked down, not at them, as I passed their groceries over the scanner with that beeping sound. The lady probably thought I was rude. I would just look down at their Huggies and their Johnson & Johnson powder, and their little glass bottles of baby food. But the boy made that "g . . . g . . . g . . . g . . ." sound and started crying and the mom patted it, spoke to it, and he cooed, and I hate them so much. I wanted to cry too, and after they left I almost did, and Aunty Ruth asked what was wrong.

"Why you always get sad around kids?"

I just shook my head, let my hair fall around my face so I was hiding.

"Jus go home, baby," she said. "I cover you. Go home. Go nei nei."

I was remembering the boy. His little blanket. His little hands on his mom. I told Aunty Ruth I'd stay until Bernadette came in. I blew my nose.

"You always work so hard," said Aunty Ruth. "I have to make you shift manager."

I looked back at Rat Girl to see if she heard.

The sliding doors opened, but it wasn't Bernadette. He came through with his huge shirt hanging from his shoulders, yelling into his phone, "Fuck him, he no body," then he sipped his beer, not even trying to hide it.

He had diamond earrings, his pants were so baggy you couldn't tell if they were supposed to be shorts or jeans. His shirt bulged and clung to his chest and shoulders and trailed behind him like a black cape. He swallowed the last of his beer and put the bottle on a pile of rubber slippers by aisle 4.

I knew his name, because all the girls check out Robby. They can have him. Even if he has high cheek bones and tiny line eyebrows more perfect than mine. Even if his mouth smiled up and down so you could see both rows of teeth like Ricky Martin.

And following just behind Robby was the younger, quiet one, trying to strut like Robby with his own triple-X shirt and his face under a black hat with a flat bill.

I looked down. I couldn't see him and Robby checking me out, I just knew, like how you can tell when guys are.

They went straight to the back of the store to do their guy shopping. I knew they would come back with no cart, lugging five twelve-packs of Heineken and a bag of sunflower seeds. I knew they would come to my line.

And the quiet one put down his cases of beer and stood right over me. My head was chest high to him. I looked at the stain on his shirt. They both smelled like weed and Heineken and way too much designer cologne. The quiet one's veiny arm reached deep in his pants pocket and scooped out a thick wad of twenty-dollar bills in a rubber band and I thought he must sell drugs too.

I sneezed.

And I could feel Robby giggling inside. I knew he was about to try and set me up with the quiet one. I found that even more insulting. I just kept looking straight at the reddish purple stain on the boy's shirt.

"You guys got ID?" I said. Trying to look tired.

And when I looked up at the quiet one, I saw his face was mostly hiding under his hat but his hauna breath smelled like weed, Oreo cookies, and beer. He had a four-hundred-dollar chain that he didn't clean.

"No, I no more one," he said. "What? Gotta have?"

"Gotta have ID, guys," I said.

Robby put his hands on the counter and leaned in like he was telling me a secret.

"What, sista?" He made a little move with his chin pointing to the door. "You no can jus slide um through for him? He not gon tell on you. Look at him. Look at dat face. Dats da kine face you can trust."

I raised my eyebrows. I looked at the quiet one. I looked back at Robby. "He looks fine. I still gotta see ID."

"You heard dat, Jess?" Robby said. "She said you look fine."

"No ID, no Heinekens," I said. I crossed my arms and leaned back. I made my most bored and irritated face.

"Kay," said Robby. "I tought you was one cool local chick, but I guess I was wrong."

He took a hundred-dollar bill, crumpled it and slammed it on the counter with his ID that had a circle poked in it. Even their money smelled like weed. Then his voice was loud. "I gon show you my ID. And you know what? Memba my name cuz next time you ID me I gon mafia dis whole fucken store."

And the old guy standing behind him in line took his bag of dog food over to line 3.

I gave Robby his change. I put my hand on my hip.

"You know what?" I said, in my other voice. "I no give a shat, kay? No ID, no Heinekens. Not now. Not ever." I looked past them, and then in my Longs voice, "I can help the next in line." An old lady with can soups.

But the quiet one just stood there, his head cocked sideways in his sideways hat, staring at my chest, mouthing words. I was about to tell him off too.

"Kapika," he said. This time when I looked up at his sideways face under his cap, he looked different. His big droopy dog eyelids and long eyelashes. "Easy, girl, easy. I just wanted for tell you your name tag's upside down. "

He had dimples. I could see his collarbone through his shirt. His big lumpy Adam's apple. He put his palms up to me like he was saying sorry.

His voice was soft and slow. "I jus thought you would wanna know, dats all." He kinda laughed. "I no like trouble."

As he watched me turn my name tag right side up, it seemed like he wasn't hiding under the hat anymore. I could see that his face was saying, this isn't really my face, can't you see that?

Suddenly I felt all funny. I couldn't figure it out. I thought, he's not even my type. I had chicken skin. I think he saw it too, because out of nowhere he said, "Kapika, I can call up you some time?"

I didn't know what to say. I just said, "I gotta work."

I started running the old lady's can soups over the scanner.

I didn't understand yet. It happened too fast.

"Next time den?" he said.

"Maybe," I said. But I smiled.

And as I was bagging the old lady's soups, I kept looking over my shoulder, watching him going to the door with the boxes of Heineken.

Somehow I thought that if he turned around and came back . . . Somehow I just knew. I know how dumb that sounds.

But all I could think was, come back, at least look back. Come back. The door closed. Frick.

Bernadette came in so I started closing my drawer. I was counting my pennies and losing my count every time I sneezed and starting over and over, when I began to have that feeling that I was being watched.

I looked up but there was just the small bags of chips and the candies over the magazines. I put my chin down and dumped the pennies out of my hand and started all over again. I heard someone crawl under the wire.

"Sorry, I'm closed," I said, without looking up.

Just above the counter, I saw two veiny hands holding a pack of gum and some quarters. When I looked up, he had his hat off and I saw his short buzz cut hair with the silver patches. I saw again that he had dimples. I smiled. I looked down at my pennies.

"So?" I said.

"So . . . you said next time?" he said.

"And what?" I said.

He shook his head and shrugged like he was saying, duh. "Dis da next time."

I tried to look down at my pennies and start counting again, and he said, "Tir-teen."

"What?"

"You got tir-teen pennies."

I looked up. I looked down.

"You seem nice," I said. "But I don't date drug dealers or wannabe gangsters or . . ." I looked at his hands. "Or . . . even real ones."

He kept trying to look in my eyes. I looked down.

I said, "This is the part where you try and tell me what a good guy you are."

He waited for me to look in his eyes, and when I looked up his shirt past the stain his smile was sad. He started to shake his head slowly. We just looked for the longest time.

I put one hand on the back of my hip and two fingers on the counter pointing towards him. "Do all the girls fall for your honesty approach?"

"I dunno," he said. "I hope so."

"Why?"

"Cuz you're my ride."

And this time I couldn't hold my mouth. And when I looked up, I did that thing with my eyes that I do. And he liked it. And he has dimples.

I told him to wait outside and I went to pee. Then out in the parking lot I told him about my car stalling out.

Under the shower tree, I was holding his shirt, scratching at the stain and watching him kneeling down, the hood of my car propped up and his hands on either side leaning over the engine. I could see his ribcage from the side and the line of his boxer shorts lifting above his board shorts. His eyes moving over all the parts. The eyes so intense. His mind full of gear thingys and carburetor thingys, concentrating so hard on guy knowledge.

I saw our reflection together in the silver-tinted window of the Honda parked next to us and it looked like we were touching. People passing by would think we were a couple.

"Oh no," he said, kind of chuckling, holding that rod thing. "Dry. When was the last time you wen put oil?"

"I don't know. Too long, I guess. That's how come?"

"Nah," he said. "It's da wire part going to da battery."

He shook the Diet Pepsi bottle and poured it over the cables. And as it fizzed, the greenish white scum melted away. It was like magic. He unhooked the cables and hooked them again. He stepped back and put his hands behind his head thinking more guy stuff, and I watched the line down the center of his spine until he caught me and I smiled and quickly looked down at the shirt. It smelled like too much cologne and Heineken and weed, but under that there was the faint sweet animal smell of a boy.

"Try start um up if you like," he said.

I got in and the motor started almost right away and it made that gr . . . gr . . . vroom when I pumped the gas. I laughed. And he grinned.

"First try," I said, getting out. I even did a little jump.

"Can I have my shirt back?" he said. He reached out for it.

I held it back and showed him the stain. "I can get this out for you."

"Dat's blood," he said.

I scratched at the stain again. "I'll get it out. I can get anything out."

He put his hand on mine over the stain. "Hey, can ask you some thing? I never saw any body talk to my friend Robby li'dat. You grew up over here? You know who he is?"

I smiled. "I no care who he think he is." Talking like him. "Who are you? Mystery mechanic. You're not wearing a name tag."

"Jesse Gomes," he said. And I had heard of him.

He still had his hand on mine. "You get one boy friend right now?"

I made my shy face. "I no more boy friend."

"How old are you?"

"Eighteen."

"But how old on your driver license?"

I looked down and took a step closer. "Seventeen and three quarters."

He smiled. "Eh . . . by da way," and he looked into my eyes like he was going to say something important. But it was a trick. "Can get my shirt back or what?"

Chapter Eleven

I was watching the wash when I heard the ice cubes in my mom's glass of ice tea. She was swirling a straw.

"So what's his name?"

"Who?" I said.

"The boy whose shirt's in our washing machine. The one you've been staying up all night talking to in your pidgin voice."

Mom teaches English. Mom doesn't like pidgin.

"Nobody, Mom," I said.

She put down her glass, opened the washer and held up the shirt by its collar up over her head.

"Oh my gosh," she said. "He's huge. He must be at least six ten. Is he a basketball player?" She slapped my shoulder and sucked in a quick breath. "Are you dating a black guy?"

I took the shirt back.

"That's just the style now, mom. Boys wear big shirts and big pants."

"All right," she said, laughing. "Don't get upset. You can date a black guy. I don't care. I dated black guys. But your dad and I want to meet him."

"No," I said. I put the shirt back in the washer and slammed the door shut.

"What's his name? Jamal?"

"No."

"Darnell?"

"No."

"Keshawn?"

"Leave me alone, mom," I said.

As she was walking out, she said, "By the way, you'll never get that stain out."

Yes I will.

I told Jesse that my family is not like his family, probably. He just said, "No worry, no worry. I know for shoot shit with da old timers. I used to get all my uncles dem rolling. I know just what I gon do. I got da big plan. Watch."

He showed up with his sideways hat, zipping all the way up to the front door revving his ridiculous red, white and blue moped that was obviously stolen. I could tell he was already drunk off his ass by the way he couldn't get the kickstand down right. He had a slight blue shade on one of his eyelids.

He handed my dad a twelve-pack and my dad just looked at it. I think the idea was that they were going to drink them together and have their male bonding. That was da big plan.

Dad asked him how he got the alcohol, being underage. Jesse didn't know what to say, he just kept looking at me. Then dad said he was just joking, but I knew he wasn't.

Dad opened one of the beers and started drinking, which he never does, and after it seemed like everything was going well for a while, he said to Jesse, "Hey, you know what would go great with this? Do you know where I could score some ganja?"

"Ganja?" said Jesse. "What is dat, ganja?" With that stupid drunk smile. "I think may be I heard of it. But no, no, no, I no can say about dat kine stuffs." Then, tilting his head back, "But why? You needed?"

Mom said it was great meeting Jesse, and that he should walk home.

They waited until Dad got home the next day when I got the long scolding from him. "He just looks like a drug dealer."

Mom and Dad sat on the couch opposite, taking turns. Kimo my dog was running back and forth in between us, barking. He wanted to make sure he got his say too.

"I know what you're thinking," said Mom. "You're thinking you're going to change him. Well, you know what, Pika? People don't change."

"People change every day," I said.

"You're right. People get worse. I know he's cute. There's plenty of cute guys out there. I had a boyfriend like that and I ended up feeling so stupid and embarrassed. Honey, you know your father and I don't care who you date, but I definitely don't want you around drugs."

"You don't know Jesse," I said.

"Neither do you," said Mom. She laughed her fake laugh and leaned back against the couch. "You know what. I'm not even worried. You'll see. You'll learn the hard way."

"You're wrong. You're wrong."

Kimo jumped on my lap, licking my face.

That same night I was on the phone, lying on my bed in my little separate studio in back of the house, telling Jesse how much my folks like him, and they were out. He said that means it's about time, then. I said to be patient. I said I was worth it. He said, just barely, but he laughed, and I can just see his dimples.

Then he tells me my MySpace page is lame. He said my screen name was the dumbest thing he ever saw, Pikabu, Pikabu, and if I was a guy I would get beat up just for being a scrub. He said I was lucky anyone would want to have sex with me at all, he was doing me a favor. I used my sexy voice, I told him keep going, he just got bumped back another week. I crossed my legs, jerking my top foot up and down.

Then I heard a noise. And it came again.

"Crap, Jesse," I whispered. "Somebody's outside."

Now a scratching on the sliding glass door. "Jesse, he's inside!"

"Oh no. Oh no."

Then through the glass I saw the hat and the earrings, the light of his phone against his ear, with that stupid smile he makes when he thinks he tricks me.

I tried to stop turning red.

I turned off the bedside lamp and hid under the covers.

"It's unlocked," I said.

Chapter Twelve

Janice sat on her piano bench by the window and watched the cars go by, all at the same speed, slow, past the barbed wire spirals and the check points and through the officer base housing. After the afternoon drizzle, the neighbors' mailbox flags dripped. The little roof windmill across the street stopped spinning, and then the sprinklers all came on, chuck chuck chuck. The sun went behind the mountains, and it got dark. A girl's footsteps came clapping up the sidewalk, but it was someone else's daughter.

The hours were long, the days and nights all the same, Charlene gone and John in Iraq. She talked with him every chance he had to call, but there was not much to say, silence across thousands of miles. He and Charlene hadn't been getting along, he couldn't discipline her. Janice said him being a major wasn't the point. The last thing he said when he shipped out with his unit was, "Okay, Janice, you're the one who gets to deal with her moods."

The base chaplain had prayed with her. He gave her a sleep CD. In her nightgown, in the dark, Janice listened to the sound of the waves, but her mind did not come to rest.

She got out of bed and went down the hall to Charlene's room with the ridiculous poster on the door, red, green and yellow. Whoever Bob Marley was, a black man with stupid hair.

Charlene always wanted the door closed. Janice opened it and went in. Under the window there was a shelf. Janice flipped through the magazines, Teen, Teen People, Cosmo, and put them back the way they had been. She was careful to do that with everything. The bed was unmade. Janice left it that way.

She looked at Charlene's yearbooks from the schools on the bases in Tennessee and Mississippi. They had lots of signatures, some with messages in careful cursive. The most recent one, from the high school twelve miles up the mountain, had only four. One was from a boy named Tim, Have a good summer, see you around next year maybe. His picture was scratched out with furious strokes of ballpoint pen, tearing through to the next page.

Janice looked in the trash can again. Old homework assignments and a flyer for some kind of after-school club. At the bottom was a white sock with a burn smudge on the heel.

She went through the dresser drawers the way she did every night, in the same order, not knowing what she was looking for. This time she lay on her stomach with her flashlight, shining it under the dresser, back and forth, but there were only dead termites, and a little glint on a square of foil that looked burned. Janice couldn't think where it came from. She left it.

Charlene's dresses were at the righthand end of the closet. Janice looked at them, sliding them on their hangers, hemlines getting shorter and shorter the newer they were. On the top shelf, tucked in a corner, was the teddy bear Charlene's father had won for her in a ring toss game at a carnival back in Mississippi when she was just small. The bear was almost as big as her then. Growing up along the way from base to base, state to state, she had thrown out all her other stuffed animals.

Janice lay down on the bed with the teddy bear's head tucked between her breast and her arm. She patted the plump bear stomach and felt something solid. She turned on the bedside lamp and held the bear in the light and saw a small seam with a zipper. She pulled it open, reached her hand in, and came out with a little diary. It had a floral print on the cover, lavender, and a darker cloth strip that hung from the spine to mark pages. She opened the diary and looked at the odd purple writing with the violent looping Ls. She did not want to read.

Something else was in the bear's stomach, flat and hard. She reached in for it. A plastic case. It had Sony printed on it. She opened it: a travel-size tube of toothpaste, three Q-tips, and something strange made of glass, like an odd small light bulb, with a hole in one end. A pipe, some kind of pipe. She gasped, and saw Charlene coming in late at night, her face all white, and heard her voice, high and harsh, the outbursts that happened out of nowhere and made no sense.

She fumbled everything back in the plastic case and shoved it in to the bear's stomach and zipped it shut.

And suddenly that man's voice on the phone filled her head, deep and absolutely sure of itself, telling her there was nothing she could do, that her daughter was beyond her command, that he had taken her, and she felt as if she had been sliced open with a knife, that she was just a bleeding empty body cavity.

Chapter Thirteen

Kapika's dad had one fat house from his car dealer ship. Swimming pool. Hot tub.

Quiet neighborhood. Big back yards. No dirt bikes. No body pop fire works. No body mow their own lawn. If some body riding one bike they doing it for fun not cuz they chronic.

Some times so quiet you could hear the ocean. Quiet in Pika's studio room with me in there. Gotta be quiet. This one sensitive situation over here with the family.

With Pika too. She always grumbling about some thing and you no can argue with her.

I used to shut down every party before. Now it's lock down. And not jus no more partying, she like me get one work kine job.

Most girls want your money before you hitting it. After too. May be while you hitting it even. But I try telling Pika you gotta let me make it first.

My phone ring. She know it prolly mean I have to go to work. I miss one block number call, most time the next greedy fucka getting the sale. I going broke cuz her.

She wrestle to get the phone away from me. By the time I could get free of her with one arm twist, I missed the call already. How many time.

I shook my head to her. "Every time cuz uh you lose money," I said.

"'Lose money,'" she said, making fun of my voice, slapping at me, scratching, arms getting all twisted up together. Pinching the fat over my under wears. "You talk moke."

"Cuz," I said, "you talk worse than me."

"No call me cuz, kay?" she tells me. "I not your frickin cuz. And you the very reason why. I was honor student before."

"Bull shit," I said.

Then she start pinching again. I start pinching back until the thing blew up in to one pinch war, with her giggling. But Pika, she pinch more hard and I always give up. She smile like she think she all that, rolling over on top of me.

Then she serious again. She think she all hot shit now that they made her shift manager at Longs. She think she got um all figure out now. Every other day now I getting one pep talk.

She even start telling me how we should go up to Vegas or Oregon like her aunty them, where get more jobs and more cheap housing. "And do what?" I say.

She keep on and on about dat, but I tell her, "Fuck dat," and I mean it. "No fucken way. What if you get pregnant? Over my dead body I gon raise one kid over dere."

She make the sad face she has, and I calm down.

She has to have her last word. "So I can tell my dad for sure that you're going to the job interview? He wants you to. It'll make him and mom feel a lot better. And I want you to. For us. Jesse?"

I nod, and she kiss me.

Chapter Fourteen

It was about eleven thirty and I was about to sleep good over there. But then my phone start vibrating and it was block number.

"Yah," I said.

"Who da fuck is dis?" said a deep voice.

"You da one wen call me, bah. Who da fuck is you?"

"Oh yah yah yah," says the voice. "I used to know dis one fag. We used to go out party, drink in to da morning time. Now his chick get him by da nut hairs."

Robby.

I cleared my throat. "I seen you dis morning."

Kapika put the pillow over her head, jus to make her point–if I make big noise the dad gon make big knocks on the door.

"Eh Jesse," said Robby. "Can do me one favor?"

"What?"

"Why you gotta ask what for? If you no like do um just say no."

"But what?"

"I no can say what on the phone. I coming over there."

"Try wait–"

But Robby never like wait. He says, "And go tell her you leaving now cuz I no like hang around for you two guys."

"Robby–"

I heard the click of the phone. I took a deep breath. I know I should never say his name in front of Pika. Most of the time she rages.

"Pika," I said all nice, "I gotta shoot pretty soon."

She started to wiggle back wards until her neck was on top my arm again. For real, I get one permanent stretch mark cuz of that neck. Every day after she drop me off on her way to work I gotta stretch the shoulder out. I had to tell Dingo I get one bus rotator cuff.

"Back rub," she tell me in my ear with all kine sass.

Oh hell no, she think I gon rub her back.

"Or what, bra?" I said.

"I bus you up." Putting on her local voice.

I gotta lose dis chick.

She never even like one back rub rub down, she just like get her way and you no can argue with her.

I don know why, but before I used to listen some times when girls would talk. They all think they so smart, they so slick. Robby tried to tell me, dey all born hustlers. No, girls is more like one can nuts when you all buzzing. You seen the can nuts with the picture the nut in side and you think, right on, those fuckas look prime. But then you open the can, you get that trick yellow spring thing pop out, catch you one good one right in the nose, ka pack.

Now she back to cocking her head, all serious. "What are you thinking about, doofus?"

"I thinking about I gotta dig pretty soon," I said. "Robby gon start honking da horn like last time, memba? Your dad dem gon rage."

"Eh," she said, changing her voice, "where you was going? Sell drugs?"

"No," I said.

I came back by her but I never lie down. I already know what she thinking. She thinking she gon pull her last trick, the most worstest trick.

She roll out of the sheets and start crawling down the bed. "Go den, I gon call the cops," she said, the huge white t-shirt all dangling. Could see the side, all her waist, she in her panty.

Then she stop right there facing me and sit up on her knees, make her legs that shape, arch her back, stick out her butt–ho, that thing cuz. Then she make her hand in to one phone. "911? Yah. Kay. Off-i-ca, get one guy–"

I gave her couple soft slaps on her hand phone just to mess up the reception. "No good your phone," I said, pulling down my shirt.

She turn her phone back to one hand and put um under my chest to keep the shirt off. Then she start kissing.

"You not handsome," she tell me.

"No," I tell her.

"And you getting fat," she say.

"Life is good," I said, slapping my stomach.

"How much other girl friends you get right now?"

"I dunno, forty may be." I make my voice all soft. "But I gotta shoot. Pika. Please please please."

And her, "No no no–"

She make one last kiss, then put her head down and go sit up against the wall like she giving up.

"Jesse."

"What now?"

"Tell me again how you going to the job interview. I heard you before but I couldn't see your eyes."

"I going to the inter view," I said, loud. "You think I wanna be Robby's bitch for the rest of my life?"

She laughed. "After my dad get you one job then you can be my bitch for the rest of our life."

"Fff," I said. I flicked her fore head. "You the one cannot live without me. You da one texting me the play by plays–I went to work I love you I'm at work I love you, muh muh muh."

I went back to the dresser, grabbed my keys, my gum, my cell phone, slid the coins in to my hand.

But she was laying there, all slide up against the wall. Her long shiny pony tail. Nothing fancy, just my over size t-shirt, the one she could never get the stain out but she wouldn't give it back. She always tells me she'll figure out how one of these days.

And then there's the hazel eyes, hands behind her back, little evil smile with her cho cho lips like she could kill if you let her. Like you about to get tapped out.

Choke guys say she deadly, the most deadly if she had big ones. And she got one real thin neck. You never would think the fucka weigh so much.

And she was slide up there with dat look, you know the look. Then kiss. Her hands on my ears.

"Go den," she said.

"Kay," I said, and I turn for the door.

But then I hear all kine commotions from behind and the panties hit the wall right by my head and fell on my feet.

I gotta lose this chick bra.

Now I late for Robby already. I went bathe real fass and hop out the door in to the back yard by the pool. I banish from the living room, the garage, the ice box. House rules. I gotta go out the side gate.

Pika's yard, that's one death trap in the dark. And plus her dog, that little fucka is one cop, one rat too, every time. Pika's father all snoozing, he hear urf urf urf, he know I on the property late. Couples times I thought he like battle, the dog I mean, not the father.

I go, "Dog, shhhh . . ."

"Urf urf urf," he snap back. Little black dog. Pika put all kine braids in the dog hair, look like one My Little Pony doll.

"What! What! All for show, you," I told him. I make my neck all big, just for show him. "Eh, I part Flip you know, I eat dog."

Robby was camped out around the corner, no body can see through the no per cent tint in the El Camino. He open the door still looking at his phone.

"Tanks for showing up," he say, mean sounding. "Every time Jesse, you a day late or a dollar short. You kids no respect your elders."

On my seat was a twenty two ounce Heineken in a paper bag for me. Robby put down his phone and was digging a small pile of cocaine out of a baggie with his key, holding it up to his nose. I could tell he been taking bumps for a while, he was twitchy and sweaty and his pupils was huge. I was pretty sure he jus came from his AA meeting from the DUI.

"I like one bump den, grampa," I said.

He took a snort, cleared his throat, gave one sniff with his nose pointing at me, then he handed me the baggie. I scooped out a small pile with my key too. If coke looks all fine and powdery like how it does in the movies, you're prolly getting ripped off. Coke should have clumps that you have to break down. I felt it as it dripped down my sinus up the back of my throat. That novocaine at the dentist feeling. And then it has that rising feeling, like you're lifting off.

"Dis batch is mean," I said.

Robby laughed. "Dats all you get. I tell Mikey cook um up to night. I bet we get twenty two grams off dis ounce. So deadly."

When you cook crack, the more pure the cocaine is the more weight you come back with after it foams down.

I took a drink of beer and I could feel it mixing with the coke in my mouth.

"I need you for some thing, Jesse," said Robby.

"Kay, what?" I said.

"You still talk to Vili?"

"Once in a while," I said. "I never been up to da house long time."

"Dats what I was gon tell you," said Robby. "Dat fucka Kody. Mikey said Kody flooding every where with dis real green shit. In fack, you memba da shit we found on da girl Charlene? Dat same batch bra. Green shit. Bunk. Cut. Bent. Mikey said Kody giving it away, fronting every body. Mikey think last time had one drought, Kody found one cook up in Vegas. Now he trying to cook the shit up him self but da fucka dunno how."

"I heard dat too," I said. "Why you care? Ours kine is more pure."

Robby shook his head. "I jus like to know what dat fucka doing. And Mikey heard they cooking the shit up at at Vili's house."

Vili's house? Hard for me for believe. "No fucken way. Vili not gon let him do dat."

"Mikey said," said Robby. "Do me one favor. Try call up Vili, ask him what he doing now uh days, you know, howz da family, tell him you get couple cold packs, you like stop by. See what he says."

I still cannot believe. "I no think Vili would get caught up, with all da kids."

"Me too," said Robby. "But Mikey said word is out already. Vili's house is marked. But no make obvious. I no like trouble with Kody, dat fucka. Not for now." He sipped his beer. "I jus like know what he doing, kay? Cuz I no like us end up working for da fucka. I like dat fucka working for me one day, kay?" He grabbed my neck. "I know you and Vili get couple beers in you, the beer gon start talking. So no say nothing about Kody or me."

"Kay, fine," I said. "I go check out Vili. After community service I go shoot him one call. Jus for drink. I let you know if any thing. Can I go now, boss?"

"Ho, you in love?" said Robby. "What's da dad tink of you pluggin his daughter every night?"

"Shit. I set up his new plasma TV for him and every thing and he still give me hard time if he seen me ova dere."

"What you expect, boy? One private school girl, even if she drop out? He threw down all kine scrip keep her away from guys li'you."

I went to my community service. We was supposed to do all this kine shit but we jus sat around watching DVDs all day. The guy even let me go outside for burn couple times. I start thinking to myself I could be one social servant. I tell him, "Eh, you guys ever get job opening over here, pull me in, you get my number."

Driving away from that I checked all my messages. All chronics, talking their chronic talk. Every day the same shit. What? Can? Right now? Where you stay where you stay? When? Soon?

All day my phone blowing up. You with your girl they call you. You making doo doo they call you. You show up they not there, an hour later they call you. They want more on credit, they all say the same thing, "I getting paid tomorrow Jesse. Hook it up Jesse. For da boys Jesse. For da boys."

Then next day you no can find the fucka. You out looking for him, the next ones is calling you. I like one burger. I like one bird. I like one shirt. I like one teen. I like one ball. Hard candy. White boy. Haole girl. What? No more da crip? Da crippage? No more da purps? No more da kills? Jesse I need mara-ju-ana. Jesse hook me up one fatty, I hook you up one blow job afta, was one guy said that.

They can wait. Robby told me I had to go snoop around my friend's house.

Chapter Fifteen

I called Vili. I told him I like check him out. Grab one twelve pack. He tell me, "Yah, shoot, come by, I leave da gate un lock."

Already I was thinking, what gate? Never have one gate before.

I went to da Foodland and bought beers. I wasn't even thinking about Kody, I was just all charged to see my friend Vili. I never seen dat fucka long time. He was my good friend before.

Vili and his wife meet in seventh grade and they never been apart since. He was married to her and the whole family they took him in.

Every body love Vili. You would love the guy too if you ever seen him. That big dummy.

The guy would always make chicken sounds like buck buck buck bu cack! He would challenge the roosters before. He would give rubs to roosters at making one rooster noise. Vili.

And every time the guy go rubbish dump he come back home with more shit than he bring for dump. Would be one off thing too, like urinal cakes. He go showing um off to who ever come over the house.

I tell Vili, "Ho, mean, your urinal cakes? Vili, you no more one urinal. What you gon do with those fuckas?"

He'd be all, "You never know Jesse, you never never know, my brudda." Then he jus go smile real big, lift up his whole huge face with the smile. Sucken Vili. He get one girly ass laugh for one guy three plus almost.

And the guy would jus crash out any where, jus KO in his chair, full Heineken in the one hand, phone in the other hand. All his friends stay calling for talk to Vili, and good luck you try take his phone away too, he hold on for dear life in his sleep.

When the guy would crash in his chair he look like one huge ball and his head would jus float on top his shoulder. He was too thick for his head fall over, plus he no more neck.

You could do any thing to the guy he never wake up, talk shit, "You my bitch, Vili?" Play with his chee chee. Then the wife would come out the screen door, only her could wake him. She grip him, tell him, "Vili, Vili, go sleep in one bed!"

He would jus jump up all shame.

And when the guy Vili would drink, you no can really tell if he talking to you or his self. And all the words come together too like, "Deesfuggadeesfuggandonkay,ehnobusup myfuckenpoomahyoufuggndon-kay . . . k? Ba cack ba cack. What . . . you?" Point his thumb at his chest. "Me . . . Vili!" Then the big fat smile.

Vili never was one hard case or nothing. I mean, the guy would get plenty stupid off jus beer and do one dumb thing. But for one younger guy Vili was from the old ways. Plus he had one good job, he drive truck for Romani.

He jus go on too, on and on and on about his compressor valve and the compass he found at the dump. Like what he gon with the compass any way? In case he gotta off road it one day in the semi? He always try and tell me how to trick the weighing station when you over capacity. I always tell him, "Vili, I no fucken care, I no drive truck bra."

Vili was the kinda guy never needed that much. That's the secret. His wife had the house from the family. She had one good job too, she work one office in town doing da kine office work for them li'dat.

And Vili, of all the younger guys I know he the only guy really seem like he know what he doing. He run his 4 a.m. shifts, go home, crash out in the chair, full Heineken still in his one hand, phone in the other hand. the kids playing in the stream by the house. Other younger guys, they care more about they rank and they truck than they boy and girl.

His wife and him had one true thing too. She love her big dummy. And the gramma would say, Vili, I know you was gon be da firs to give your mudda gran child.

Vili was the peace maker too between his friends. One time it was Vili and his friend Kyle in the front seat Vili's car, me and his other friend Kody in the back seat. (By the way, yah, Kody Scott, the guy Robby talking about, I never met um before then.)

I was all ragging on Vili cuz how in his little ass Sentra his knees would come up on both sides of the steering wheel. I dunno then, I guess Kody wised off to me and before you know it got all nuts.

Kody started for rage, jus like out of no where kine. I never seen it coming. Once his beer spill on his pants he tell Vili, "Pull dis car over Vili, I gon lick dis fucken whore. I gon burp dis fucka." Me.

Kody started to crack the roof, dent the roof, yelling at Vili to pull over. Then he yell back to me again, "Why you all quiet Jesse? What? You know you nothing, you no body. You know when we get out this car you gon drink my piss."

I wasn't gon drink piss. Honestly, I thought I could take him today. So I tell him, "You gon drink mine."

Jus when Kody look like he about to reach up from the back seat and grab the wheel from Vili, this song come on the radio, Cruisin Together, the Cotch version. Vili go turn the volume way up.

So loud all his speakers started to bleed. Then he started to sing, he even did this one little big guy dance. Was classic bra.

What he really was trying for say was, "Girls, for me girls, just cruise." That's what he called his boys. And it worked.

Vili dropped Kody and Kyle off right after. And then Vili yelling at me, "Jesse!" You could see that fat vein in his fore head that come out when he fuming. "What? You shtupid? You know dats Kody Scott?"

I tell him, "Da guy get in my hair, what I gon do? Just sit dere like one door knob, get turned?"

"Next time Jesse, you not gon get lucky. You better squash dat with him. Just go up shake his hand, make like nothing happen."

So later I did. What I gon do? That was Kody Scott.

You prolly heard the horror stories about Kody and Dos. Them two guys was one different breed dope dealers. Fear less, get rich or die, ruth less fucken dealers. Tweakers would be in to them for couple hundred only, and now what, they take the car already, bus fingers, put um to work taxing for them.

The way Robby had um set up, you only sell as much to the guys as you think they can get eventually. Front the guy one forty sack of clear, he gon pay us fifty later and if not then get trouble. But we not gon front one more bag, you know what I mean? We cap they credit, we no bleed. But Kody-Dos guys, those fuckas, they just give tweakers whatever, they feed um the medicine, they push, they pump um, they bleed um.

Then when they customer trying to get clean, they get one six sense. They call them up all nice, "Where you stay bah? I got da goodies. I get da mean one, da deadly one. No worry, cousin, pay me tomorrow."

Then if the guy no pay they snack on him for whatever can get for as long as they like. And they keep feeding um. They no care what the guy owe. He could pay off his first debt three, four times over, he still out robbing for them cuz they keep pumping him. Now the habit is getting more ridiculous, cannot put the brakes any more. What the guy gon do, die? Ruth less, bra.

Dos and Kody guys is how come the other big dogs all got shut down. Got some small time guys floating around, but now mostly it's just Robby and Kody-Dos.

Whatever you think of Robby, remember this. He was trying to make a living off of guys that was already getting high. If one of Robby's customers was trying to quit, that make him happy, he tell every body no sell to them. It never seem like Robby even wanted any thing with money except to lose it on the chicken fights and foot ball.

There was this one house where Dos and Kody would stash all the cars, some times they would chop um for parts, some times they fix um up, detail um, flip the car.

One time this one brave fucka wen thief his own truck back from the house, cuz was his uncle's truck. Sucken guy thought he was smooth, he stashed the truck at his other uncle's house in one whole different town, four towns over.

Two days later, two days only, Kody showed up at the other uncle's house with the red devil gas cans. The uncle come out all smiling, holding the keys. "Oh, I never know dis was your guys truck. Here, take um."

"Nah," Kody tell him all nice, "no worry uncle, relax. I no like da truck. I gon burn da house."

So Kody torched um. The whole house.

A lot of dealers like Kody is closet chronics. He never admit it, but you could tell from the red splotches in his eyes and the tweaker pits in his arms and face, the way his hands was clammy where the drug was coming out through his skin. Dat fucka was one for life smoker.

Kody always seem to make trouble with the last guys you want trouble with.

Robby said there get real gangsters looking for that guy for years and he still walking streets in the day time.

He got shot two different times. Plus he got run over. Dats how he got the limp.

I tell you the story how I heard it. I heard from Mikey, he heard from plenty guys, even Dos.

So one time Kody roughed up this one chick, even after she drop her uncle's name to him. Uncle Errol. This seventy three year old gangster. Not gangsta, old school gangster. Old union. He moved up to Maui for retirement.

So Uncle Errol call Dos family first about Kody, told them all nice, "I no like hurt da boy. I like help him. I no like him get hang up side down . . . you know . . . da tire iron . . . da bag salt, da sand pepa. Too much clean up afta. I jus like hear his side da story."

Dos family respect Uncle Errol and the way he handling um, so they give him Kody's number .

Uncle Errol tells Kody, "Brudda, you wen rape my sista's grand daughter?"

Kody tells him all slick, "Yah . . . why?"

So Kody calls up Robby. They try never talk to each other. Safer for every body. But Kody calls up Robby asking for help. "I need one favor. I do you one favor later. Get some O.G. guys looking for me. Ask around. If you hear any thing. I like find dem first."

"Guarantee," said Robby.

But right away Robby tell Mikey find Uncle Errol's guys, help dem, not Kody. So Mikey did.

When the Uncle Errol's guys came to town Mikey told Dingo find out when Kody was gonna be alone. Kody's boys told Dingo he was gonna be massage parlor in the alley ways behind one strip club. Up on the second floor, between these three alleys.

So the five Uncle Errol's guys show up in the silver tinted van. One guy gets out, gets mama san to buzz the door open. The five guys running up the stairs, walk right through the metal detector down the hall, bus in the door where Kody was catching polish from the girl.

But Kody–the fucka so quick he back up and stood with his back to the corner so they couldn't circle him. Balls naked, dick swinging, throwing combos, head butts, mu tai kicks, making space until he got out the door, bare ass running down the hall in to the room where Dos was pounding this other girl.

Kody flies open the window, second floor, yelling to Dos, "Unlock da cah! Unlock da cah!"

So Dos hits the key less entry for da Lexus in da lot.

Kody jumps, second story, lands on his feet rolling over his shoulder naked in the asphalt.

Mama san guys come busting down the hall with Remington shot guns. Uncle Errol's guys running down the stairs to their van with dealer plates.

Kody already got the gun from the Lexus. He hears the van starting up from the other side the building. He runs around out the corner and jumps in the alley in front the van coming toward him. He gets off one shot through the wind shield until the gun jammed. The story is he could have got out the way but he just stood there squeezing and the van ran him over and gone out the exit.

Kody lying there. Dos came out, took the gun, told mama san he need the surveillance tapes and he gon pay for the damages. Then he starts making calls.

On the news, just said was one road rage incident.

Dos picks up Kody from the hospital, straight to the air port, on to Hawaiian Airlines, Kody still on crutches. Maui. First class. Three days later they come back and Uncle Errol gone missing. No body, no crime. Where he went? One lava tube may be? Swift, silent, no investigation. That's Dos.

The courts too couldn't get Kody. I heard before, he get pull over in the black Expedition for blasting the porn in his ten thousand watt system, plus they gunned the windows for illegal tint, and they got him for DUI, and the chick with him was only fourteen and she open her mouth up about the dope in the car. Girls. But you know Kody, the file went missing some where in the system. Or maybe the cop forget to show up to court and the whole thing got thrown out.

Chapter Sixteen

I no can tell you where Vili's house was, but it was one mission. Off the main road. Back roads, bush roads, way way up away from our town. Miles and miles.

Vili's road was one of the places seem like the city and county forget about. Honolulu could be on another island and you'd never know it over here.

Across the bridge I passed this old man sitting on a cooler by his crab nets.

By now it was almost getting dark. The weather man said it was supposed to pour later and it had that wind chill like jus before the storm. Blue light through the trees, like the valley was haunted.

Some parts of the valley was below sea level and the radio would hiss. Other parts so steep you could see the sky through the tree tops. The first white stars starting to show. High weeds up to your chest.

The shocks was bouncing up and down going through all the pot holes and pig shit every where, and I jus washed the rims on the El Camino.

I seen this guy driving up the road in his Mazda, with a dead pig in the passenger side. The pig had the seat belt on and every thing. Two hoofs sticking straight out and the head to one side like the pig jus came for the ride, shoot to cruise. The guy honked to me and I honked back. I prolly met the guy before but I didn't match him to the car.

About half way up the road past the rusted out truck up on wood blocks with the bullet holes in the side, was this lady sitting on a tree stump in one cow boy hat. Not like Dallas cow boy, like one for real cow boy's hat.

"How you?" I said.

The unlit cigarette hanging out her mouth, sour face. This lady never remember me.

"You not one cop?" she said. The cigarette bouncing up and down, her getting all nuts. "What hospital you was born? Wass your middle name?"

I told her, "I told you last time lady, I not HPD, I'm DEA." She kinda smiled as I drove away toward Vili's house, where the stream was. His wife's dad told me before how when he was a kid the water was so clear you could see to the bottom, see the fish swimming down stream.

I drove past the place where Vili told me some guy and his family rolled the boulder to block the road to their farm. But then the sheriff just got one back hoe.

I usually park up the hill. All the politics about parking. If you block some body in you jus gon have to move the car ten minutes later.

I grabbed the beers and hopped out, pushed the gate open, closed it behind me, hanged the lock back how it was.

You had to walk past all the other houses to get to Vili's. The leaves crunched under my feet down the slope under the tree cover. The ground smelled like wet smushed fruits. Back here had bananas, mountain apples. I followed the clear water of the stream going over the smooth rocks.

Getting more dark now. You felt like a ghost could come from behind a tree and that was all right. Like the ghosts was jus cruisin over here.

I could smell the burning newspaper, Vili's twins fanning the coal fire and their shadows against the closer house. Behind the last house was a small school bus that was converted, like one trailer. Before they would take in any friends and family that came on hard times. Right after my dad kick me out my house I lived in that bus for two weeks.

Some of the benches was sitting in front the house like one porch, and I seen Vili. I had to bust out laughing. Nothing change, Vili sleeping on his chair with his Heineken in one hand, his daughter in the other, her sleeping on his huge chest like a pillow.

The grampa holding the tongs over the grill, his white silver hair. He smiled to me and shook Vili. "Your friend."

"Ho," said Vili, waking up, looking around. "Jesse Gomes. Back from da dead."

"Call security," I said.

"Jesse Gomes, East side mos wanted moped thief."

"Oh no," I said. "You guys heard about dat?"

Villi rubbed his eyes, "Every body hear, Jesse. You famous. Dats what you get for cruising with Mikey. So what, learn your lesson? Staying outa trouble?"

"You know me, I no like trouble," I said. "Trouble always find me some how."

"Pfff," said Vili. "You even talk li'Robby now."

He reach back with his huge shoulder and pull up one chair for me like it weigh nothing. I open one bottle for him.

Before long the gramma brought us fresh banana bread. "Eat! Eat!"

Just like old times, Vili and me drinking, while the grampa piled a mountain of oysters on the grill, laughing at us.

And the coals was hissing with the oyster drippings.

And the kids was lighting up sparklers.

Soon enough the whole family came out to say hi to me, one long lost Portagee they call me.

I told Kapika if I could live any where I would live there again. They had some thing figured out, that family.

The gramma ask me if I get one girl friend and how come I never bring da girl friend with me, bring the whole family?

"I dunno," I said. "I guess her family, I still growing on dem."

She get all quiet. I guess cuz my face look sad.

"Why? What's da matter, boy? Is cuz she from one no good house or is you one no good kid?"

"Da house one all right house, I guess," I said. Looking down.

She put her hand on my back. "One good house can fix. Always can fix."

And funny thing, when you drink with Vili's family they listen. Five guys all talking, some how they never interrupt. They never even own one TV that I know. They jus get each other for entertainment. Watch the kids. Yell at the kids. Hold the kids.

May be they wouldn't know the point spread or even what teams was playing on Monday night. But every one of them know when their niece's test for dental school was. They always talking about every body's health and every body's state of mind and every body they love, and that's pretty much every body.

You could hear the stream behind them, smell the pure water.

And the gramma wearing kids up and down her arms like rich ladies wear jewelry.

Every body laughing.

The things that matter to Vili's family, they don't sparkle, it's in the space between coolers. And by their house you wouldn't even know the rest of the island was there at all, and that was good.

Soon enough they all going down to the neighbors. Next door was having one small party. Not for any reason, just one party, and they going for help cook. They all ask me if I like check um out. Smoke meat, sword fish poke. All age people. Listening to the old timer knowledge and maybe some body would play music. But I told Vili I jus came to talk to him.

After they left I lit up one USA gold. I ask Vili if he ever seen my cousin Dwayne around. I gon ease in to Kody.

"Dwayne," said Vili, sucking his beer. "Yah, I seen. And da kine, what's her name, his chick too, I seen her the other day, like four in morning on my way to work. I try wave to her. I never know they live up around dis side."

"Yah," I said. "How he look, Dwayne? He wen drop plenny weight?"

You know how wide spread the clear is cuz you not supposed to say if some body losing weight, cuz that could mean they losing it on the dope or you accusing them.

"I dunno," said Vili. "You only hear good things come out my mout, Jesse. But yah, I seen his girl friend around some places. Not too healthy, may be." He shrugged. "Her life. But you know, for your baby nephew–"

"What? She had baby? When?"

"Dunno bra, but even for his age da boy looking small, couple pounds small."

"You say she not too healthy. Before she had da baby or after?"

"Afta."

"Good ting," I said. "I cannot handle seeing those meth babies any more. She tink about that or what, Vili? You can be honest, they family to me."

Vili looked down. "Da housing dey live, Tweakerville dey call um. I heard old folks, young kids, every body."

"Ffff," I said. "Getting li'dat every where."

Vili's boy walk up to us all con-temp-lating, his finger so far up his nose, digging, you think the boy would reach his brains already.

Vili go look him all serious. "Boy, what you looking for in dere?"

The boy wen snap back real sharp, "Boogers."

Vili nod. "Okay, go head son. Whateva. If feel good, feel good."

I forget how much I miss Vili. Never had to prove nothing. One family man. Not one hard case. I felt stupid for come up here snooping around on my friend.

Right when I just wen finish rolling up the perfect joint, perfect roll, every thing, I took out my lighter for spark um and the dog's ears stuck straight up in the air and he ran behind the house. Then the daughter open her eyes and grabbed on to Vili's big fat chest.

In this tree all the night birds all at once they all took off like a cloud shifting direction back and forth. And that's when I heard the bass coming up the road getting louder. Boom boom boom.

The black Expedition with black rims and blacked out windows. The music so loud all the animals was going nuts. Dos hopped out to open the gate.

They drove right past the El Camino and parked by the bus behind the second house, out of sight. I could just see this scruffy looking main land haole looking guy carrying all these bags of fertilizer.

Vili shook his head. "Shit. No look over dere, Jesse."

After they was done throwing their shit behind the bus they back up to the gate and stay there. Finally they turned the music down. After a while the passenger door open. Then the door open on the driver side.

Kody. He had tattoos up both his arms, all his neck and his chest. He had the short Mike's buzz cut and he bleach um blond. His skin was real red too, he had all these chicken pock marks on his face and arms. Black Sean John shirt. The white scar through his eye brow. Yellow diamond ear rings worth more than Robby's cars, just blinging.

He took off his shades and his eyes had red splotches, staring at me. The way he strut too, slow, with the limp.

He smacked his chest then point to me. "What he doing hea, Vili?"

"Nah, Kody, jus for drink beer," said Vili. "I never seen Jesse long time, I told him come down, drink couple. You guys never said you was gon swing by."

Dos came up. Short, about five five, but he was thick. And the other guy, scruffy looking haole, jus stood by the Expedition jus eyeing me out.

"Drink beer? Fucken Vili," said Kody.

Then he snapped at me, "Eh, you no can jus come ova here, Jesse. You can stay now cuz we leaving. But next time Vili going ova drink wit you guys at Robby's. Next time you know betta, Jesse Gomes. Next time ax dis fuck." He pointed with the back of his hand to Vili. "No let him put your life in dan-jah."

"You know I never seen nothing," I said.

"You fucken right you never seen nothing."

The daughter was starting to make squeeking noises. Vili he cupped her small head with his huge palm. Her two eyes looking up at her dad, then back at Kody.

I felt sore in side my chest, all sick, thinking Kody prolly give orders li'dis to my friend Vili at his own house in front his kids all the time.

I wanted to fight. I tried to smile, I even tried to laugh. "Wat Kody?" I said. "No body ever tell you you look like one stereo type?"

Kody's eyes jus came huge. He start walking forward slowly. First he look like he in one trance jus full on eyeing me out. Then he start smiling, nodding his head. He blew his nose, all his snots in to his hand. Blew again. Hawked and spit in to his hands. He even smile big now.

I smile back.

He patted my shoulders, like he was being friendly. Giving me one rub now. But he was wiping his snots all over my shirt.

I got red. "Bra," I said. "Robby–"

Now Kody start yelling, "Robby is da only reason you gon live through da fucken night."

He jerked his hand like he was gon pound me and I had to jump back.

But Dos put his arm on him, then turn to Vili. "Kay, Vili?"

Vili looked down. "Kay."

"Vili," said Dos, "we gon drink tonight, come wit us Home Grown."

Vili was still looking at the ground. "Nah. Gotta work 4 a.m."

The gravel shooting out from under the tires. They left the gate open. I knew then. That bus behind the house. That's where the green dope was coming from. The dope that Charlene had. I took off my shirt and threw it in the fire.

I keep thinking in my head, No, Vili. What you did, Vili?

Vili told me later Kody them been coming by for like a year now for cook they shit, like every two weeks if the kids was at school. I wen ask if the wife know and he tell me his wife try for tell Kody. But she had hard time say no to the guy, cuz I guess he lend the family money for back taxes. And Kody was Vili's friend. But Vili was always li'dat. He had hard time to say no if he felt like he owe you some thing. Every time he ever got in trouble was for one friend. But from his eyes, I think he prolly tried before plenty times.

Now he keep telling me, "Nah, Jess, for real, dese guys dey know what dey doing. Between um Kody-Dos dey know plenty pilau HPD. Dey not gon catch dem. Dos one smart guy. No worry so much Jesse, you always worry."

I jus keep watching him. His daughter sleeping on him again.

I told him, "Vili, get one reason why guys no cook um up out here. Dis one small place here. Word get out. Lasers, helicopters."

He looked up at me. Fear on his face. "Word not gon get out?"

I took one hard draw off the joint. Robby would be mad but I gon tell my friend. "Vili, word out already. Mikey said your house is marked. I sorry for tell you dat. I came up hea for tell you dat."

Vili's face came all serious. "Dats why you came over hea den, Jesse? I know you never would jus call me up for drink."

"I come down any time I get one invite."

Vili no say nothing.

After the longest time I finally said some thing. "I know I not the guy to lecture any body. But I always looked up to you, Vili. Da most of every body. You was da one guy dat had um all figure out. You get one good kine job. Da family. Kody dat fucka, he no bleed blood, his heart pump Kool Aid. But I dunno. What, you like dis kine shit around your house?" I looked at his daughter sleeping on his chest. "No be scared for tell one guy leave your family alone. Dats one reason for be one man." I was getting loud. "Shit, Vili, I tell Kody for you, bra."

Vili put his arm around his little girl. "Shh, Jesse, no wake my daughter. I never get her back sleep afta." He looked at her little nose. She still look so peaceful with her hands on Vili's chest. "She's da nuts one dis one. She already sass her brudda."

"I tell dat fucka Kody," I said, loud still. "He not da only guy pull trigger. Robby pull trigger. Mikey pull trigger."

Vili look at the ground. He say all soft, but serious, "What you gon do to Kody, Jesse? More like what Kody gon do to you."

I was standing up, walking back and forth, still yelling. That's when Vili raise his voice to me.

"You never figure um out Jesse? Everything all fuck up already. Da cops know what Kody-Dos doing here. They not trying to stop any body. If any thing dey just want to get on da pay roll."

"Yah, but Vili–"

But he jus keep going. "Jesse, you know when guys would ask me about you, if I seen you? I would always say da same ting, I only know da good side of Jesse. You jus say da same ting, kay?"

"Kay, Vili."

"Ah," he said. "You worry too much Jesse. Drink more beer or smoke weed or get a hug, somethin."

I got up and hug him on my way out. He lift up his whole huge face with the smile. Then held up his little girl up high in the air, she awake now.

"Say good bye Uncle Jesse."

"Bye Un-cle Jes-say."

Walking back to the car, I jus got this weird feeling this was the last time I ever going see my friend Vili. But nah, cannot be.

The El Camino was bouncing up and down the dirt road on the way out until I slowed down. I drove past the lady in the cow boy hat. I figure now she was look out. Kody prolly pay her in dope to call Vili if she see any thing coming up the road.

It started to drizzle, just scattered clouds, down the long road back to Kapika's. I wondered if the old man was still crabbing off the bridge.

I called Robby.

I never really lied to him before, but I promise Vili I wouldn't say any thing. So I said, "No. No way Vili would do dat wit Kody." And anyway, fuck Robby for all this bull shit, making me come up here like this, spy on my friend.

"Good," said Robby. "I don't know Vili as good as you, but I would be all sick too. Eh, you gon make it back for da second half? I slapped five on da over for da pros."

"No, I not gon drink," I said. "I gotta go back see my chick. I get one job inter view tomorrow, memba? Sammy's? Da brake shop?"

"Oh dats right," said Robby, laughing. He kept laughing. And laughing. "Good luck. Look sharp boy."

Chapter Seventeen

At the prayer breakfast, the framed picture of Charlene was on an easel, and when the chaplain stood and bowed his head in closing, everyone held hands.

"Lord, we pray that You are watching over all of our brothers in arms who have gone in harm's way to serve You. Just as You watched over those who have returned safely, and who may yet have to go to serve again, in Your name. We commend Sergeant De Luca and Corporal Rawlings to You, brave men who are new to us. We thank You for helping them to find their way to us in fellowship. But dear Lord, we pray especially today for our sister Janice and for her beloved daughter, Charlene. Janice is alone—yet she is not alone. We are with her, and You are with her. And we know that You are with Charlene, and that You are watching over her, as you watch over all Your children. We know, and Janice knows, that only Your love will bring her child safely home. We pray in Jesus' name. Amen."

Outside, the flags hung still. Janice went to her car, holding Charlene's picture in its frame. De Luca and Rawlings stood off, watching her. It was hot and there was no breeze, but she was walking held in to herself, as if there was a cold wind blowing at her.

De Luca said, "They were giving the girl drugs. Everyone knows that by now, except the mom."

Janice fumbled for her keys and dropped the picture. She stood stock still and closed her eyes.

"Ma'am," De Luca called. "Let me." He stepped and picked the picture up and held it out. "I just want to say–your daughter–I don't have words for it–"

Rawlings said, "This here is just about the most unfortunate thing I ever saw, and I seen some things. I do feel for you."

"Thank you for your kindness," said Janice. "I can use kindness. I don't seem to be finding much of it, not off the base."

"The police?" said De Luca.

Janice shook her head. "The message I am getting–not in so many words, they are careful about that, very polite in their way–but military brats aren't any kind of priority." She looked up and away, to the mountains beyond the base. "I go around with my flyers. I put them up everywhere I can on my own. At the Laundromat. I try to give one to everyone, some will take it, but the others won't. And I put one up on the bulletin board, and next time I come by it's gone, and the ones for the lost dogs are still there. And just try to get someone to let you put one in the store window. Oh, they're very polite, they all smile, and they won't say no, not to your face. They duck their head, they won't look you in the eye. It's like it's foreign here."

She looked at the picture of Charlene smiling with her red hair. "Not to be among your own people. Back home the whole town would come together for something like this, even the coloreds. There wouldn't be anywhere to hide in the whole county."

"I know what you mean, ma'am," said Rawlings. "There's nothing like knowing you can depend on your own."

"Ma'am," said De Luca. "If we can be of assistance–you might find you're not as alone."

"Oh," said Janice, and she put her hand to her heart. "I would surely appreciate it if I could call on you. God bless you for it."

She hugged the picture, and De Luca opened her car door.

Chapter Eighteen

Dad told me when I was a little girl that bad days don't just happen, you let them happen. I decided that no matter what doctor said, and I kinda knew already, today was going to be a good day. The family needed a good day. No matter anything, I still got Mom and Daddy and Kimo. And Jesse. Jesse.

And I prayed. Just in bed when Jesse was sleeping. I never pray! I prayed for Jesse's interview. I even said I was sorry for being mean to Rat Girl. It must be hard for her when she has to work the aisle next to me.

The sun came in through the skylight. I made the bed and the sun made a sun diamond on the mattress that flashed with the fan blades as they whooshed around. I never make the bed! I could hear the water in the shower on Jesse. He would come out soon in a towel smelling like good soap.

I even thought I could hear the bees buzzing in the paperbark trees. The little red hibiscus bushes. The red ti leaves. The plumerias. Even the stinky mango tree.

Jesse wanted to wear a long-sleeve shirt to the interview to cover his tattoos, but I told him he wasn't applying to be CEO and the tattoo of his family name on his forearm was just fine.

But I surprised him! I bought him this long-sleeved collared shirt with the tag still on it. I was buttoning it on him. Then the door was banging.

"Time to get up," Mom said through the door, in her hurry-up voice.

Jesse's supposed to be gone at night by ten, but Mom knows he stays over. Once in a while, that's what I tell her.

Mom said to unlock the door and I did. She stuck her head in and her hair was still a little wet with her bathrobe on.

"We–" Mom did a double take. There was Jesse sitting on the bed, looking up at Mom, his hands in his lap, his shoulders slumped, his legs dangling off the edge, looking like he was ten years old and he got caught stealing cookies.

"Good morning, Mrs. Branch," he said, like she was a second-grade teacher.

But Mom was already shouting at me to get ready to go. I was ready.

Then Kimo wiggled in between Mom's legs and jumped on the bed, put his paws on Jesse's chest and started licking his face. Jesse even started petting.

I wasn't even listening to Mom, I was just watching my two guys.

I heard Dad's voice yelling for Mom, getting louder as he came to the door.

Oh my gosh. It was so–quiet. Good thing I made the bed. There we were, Mom, Dad, Kimo, Jesse, all in my room. I put my hand on Jesse's shoulder and sat down with him.

"Good luck today," said Dad.

"Tanks," said Jesse. "Tanks for da hook up, tanks for every ting."

Dad glanced over at me to be sure I saw him being nice. "Dinner's at seven, Jesse, if you want to come eat with us."

Jesse smiled so big. His eyes and mouth were like three big O's.

I love Daddy.

"Five minutes," Mom said, and they left.

I sat down on Jesse like he was my chair and pulled his arms around me because he is. His voice right behind my ear, "I gotta ask one favor."

"What?"

I couldn't see him, so I twisted around looking side eye when my back popped. He started rubbing my back, down low, and I knew this was a big favor.

Then he's like, "You not gon like da favor. But it's for da inter view."

He unzipped his backpack, took out this little plastic bottle and handed it to me.

I held it, turned it around. It took me a while to figure out what I was supposed to do with it. When I did I almost dropped it.

"Please," he said, with that stupid please-face he thinks I can't say no to.

"You serious?"

"I told you you wouldn't like it," he said.

I didn't. Not at all. But I knew why he needed it. I went in the bathroom and did what he wanted. I brought it out and held it far away from me and didn't look at it until his hand took it away and he put it back in his bag. Yuck!

I looked down, trying not to give him my stink look. He put his finger under my chin. Then his other hand on my cheek with his thumb just under my eyelash. First he kissed my forehead. Then my lips. Then my neck. He doesn't like to, or know how to, but it's so long now and I still get cold.

When I opened my eyes my hands were squeezing handfuls of him and his new shirt that makes him almost look like somebody I would have dated. I smoothed it out and fixed his collar for him even though it was fine. "Now you do me a favor. No get stains on that fricken shirt, kay?"

At Dr. Pisaro's office I signed on the clipboard and gave it back to the guy with the spiky gel hair that made him look like a porcupine. Mom and I didn't talk. It was so cold. I looked at my toes on the grey carpet.

In the hall two fat guys with butt cracks were making banging noises, fixing the water fountain.

I wanted to cuddle up against Mom, but there were other girls and moms there. Even though she was mad-nervous Mom right now, she looked so tired.

When the porcupine guy said, "Branch," we went inside the office.

Dr. Pisaro said his conclusion was that he agreed with the other doctors. I thought he would say more, but he didn't.

Mom walked out into the hall and the door closed.

I watched the seconds on the clock. It said 10:27. I smiled and told Dr. Pisaro how sorry I was for Mom. He said how maturely I handled the whole thing.

"You can still have a family," he said. "I'm sure they told you all this before, about adoption. There's always going to be kids that need good homes."

I nodded.

He had little black spots on his cheeks and a big one on his forehead with the stub of a hair growing out of it.

On his desk was a picture of his daughter in a white dress. Her hair had curls just in front of her ears and she was wearing too much eye shadow. She probably wasn't that cute but she looked cute in the picture.

He took off his glasses. "You're going to live a healthy, long, happy life. You're a very special girl."

"Thank you," I said.

If you just smile, everybody thinks you're nice, even if you think mean thoughts sometimes. If you smile at them and they smile back, that makes everything better and nobody gets hurt feelings. I smiled.

Driving home before the tunnels, Mom was driving too slow, then too fast, then too slow again, and she began to shake, and someone honked and zipped around us. Mom pulled over and drove all the way up to the lookout right before the tunnels. We parked in a stall facing the lookout and the air was fresh and cool.

"Pika," she said. "We'll get a third opinion, okay? There's got to be a doctor in this town that—"

"Okay, mom," I said. I smiled.

"We still can't tell your father. Not yet. He'd just be heartbroken."

Her voice was all crazy, all over the place.

"Jesse will be heartbroken," I said.

"What?" she said. "Do you really think he wants a baby–? He's not just saying it?"

"I just know it," I said.

She put her hand to my cheek. "You can always change your mind, Pika." She looked straight in my eyes. "I mean, you know, sweetie, is he really, really, really, the guy?"

I looked straight back in her eyes. "I just know. I knew it when I first met him."

"It was the same way with your father. But why Jesse?"

"I don't know. Cuz I give him every chance to lie to me and he still doesn't. And it makes everything so hard for him, Mom." I swallowed. "But he does it anyway. He never ever lies, even over stupid things that don't matter." I swallowed.

We watched the birds hopping around.

I shook my head back and forth. "What do I tell him?"

"Nothing," said Mom. "That's the easy part. You just wait for him to screw up so bad he thinks you might leave him.

Then when you tell him, it'll feel like his lucky day. I do that to your dad all the time."

We laughed. The trees moved up and down and smelled like rich trees with new air. Mom held me. We watched out the window and there was this long line of little kids. They were coming back from the trail toward the school bus, making little kid sounds, all holding hands. They had the buddy system. I was worried because there was a shattered bottle on the ground, and one of them was wearing his slippers on his ears. The teacher was counting with her finger to make sure she had all of them.

After a while Mom said, "Then let's do it. Let's get him a job. We'll get you enrolled in classes, and if that's what he really, really wants, more than anything else, you guys be patient—and then you'll have it."

"Do you really think so, Mom?"

"Of course." Mom kissed my head like Daddy does. "This is America."

When I got home, Kimo had undone all of the braids I put in his hair.

"Puppy dog," I said. "Come to mommy."

He jumped on my bed, shaking his whole butt with his tail like he was saying, look at me! here I am! I'm so great! And he is!

"You wanna make pretty-pretty?" I said.

But just when I was getting his comb with the metal bristles, he heard Mom over in the kitchen open the fridge to make a sandwich, and he went running, his little paws scratching on the tile when he tried to stop.

I locked the door.

I turned the fan all the way up and the air was loud. I turned the radio up.

I took out my hoop earrings and curled up under the covers.

I put the pillow over my mouth.

The heat of my breath going in to the pillow and the heat of my breath on my face.

I rolled over on my stomach and got the Kleenex.

After a while I got my phone out of my bag. I opened it and started to text. GOOD LUCK DOOFUS I LOVE YOU PLEASE CALL ;) pikabu. Send. I NEED TO HEAR UR VOICE WHEN U TELL ME U GOT THE JOB. MUH! LOVE U ;) pikabu. Send.

Chapter Nineteen

I was still driving to Sammy's Brake Shop, the wind ripping through my new shirt, when I heard the ring tone on my phone in my pocket.

It was the wrong hour for chronics, a little too late and too early for them to be calling. I knew who it was and what it was really saying, please don't fuck up, my family thinks you're a fuck up already.

I parked the moped by the side of the grey building, put the kick stand down. I could hear the air gun on the other side of the wall. I was sweating some bullets, walking down the side walk to the front. I never smoke all day yet.

One of my ear holes was feeling funny. I never took out my ear rings for long time, pretty much since my sista Gummybear poke the holes for me.

I had this new long sleeve shirt to cover my tattoos but all of the guys there was more inked up than me. Two of them was smoking cigarette by the door. One of the guys had shades, he was rocking the old school dope man Nikes. Rap tunes, Young Jeezy bumping in the back ground.

I nodded to them and they nodded back. From the look on they face I guess they knowed why I was there.

Now I wanted one beer. Just one before the inter view. Just to loosen up. When I sober is the only time I feel alcoholic.

I keep fanning my shirt. It still had that new shirt smell.

In side the girl was answering the phone. When she got off I asked for Sammy. I told the girl Jake Branch got me one inter view with him. She said she didn't know who Jake Branch was. But then she was all nice. I guess I look nervous.

When I filling out the application the girl ask me, "Did your girl friend pick that shirt out for you?"

I thought the shirt was out too, the color. I thought she was messing with me like guys do.

"Why?" I said.

"No, no. It looks good on you."

She might have just been asking if I had one girl friend. Or maybe I just don't look like a guy that would pick that shirt.

Kapika tried to tell me I have good hand writing.

Last grade completed? Tenth.

GPA?

Prior job experience?

Then Sammy came out from the office, over the card board on the floor to the front. "Mr. Gomes, come on back."

Sammy was this big local looking guy with glasses. There was books and magazines all over his desk like he read for fun. You could tell he was trying to act all professional but he still drink prolly. Old timer bars. Sports bars.

"Have a seat," he said.

At first I was quiet. But once I got going with the guy Sammy I felt like I was doing okay.

I told him I never had ASE certification, not for brakes or even jus for any thing. He said no body does now of days. He ask me all these questions and I was surprised I remembered any thing at all till last question.

"When the brakes are applied, the car veers to the left. What are the three causes?"

"What is dat? Um. Brake caliper. Brake hose. Both right side gotta be? Opposite side? And da tird one, f- . . . , uh."

"That's good enough," the guy Sammy said. "So you could learn this job?"

"I not gon say nothing," I said, "but most time I one quick learner."

He was saying I had to work my way up jus to be even a real apprentice. I gotta learn how to work the computer. He said the customers get all nuts sometimes cuz they think they gon get rip off. He told me get plenty snappy guys think they know brakes, you just gotta eat it.

I told him, "If they really know brakes they wouldn't be coming to you guys."

"Exactly," he said. "But we gotta hear em out. They're the customer."

He said that was part of the job, jus eat it if they start lipping. You can't seem threatening. And try and talk professional.

I told him, "I know how for talk good English." I smiled. "Just nerves." I even tried to make one smart guy accent. "I can speak as well as the situation determines."

"Wow," he said. "I'm not playing Scrabble with you."

I knew he was laughing at me, not with me. But he was the boss and I was jus thinking act nice, act nice. Gotta take it from him. I take plenty more shit from Robby.

He put his glasses back on, inter locked his fingers and leaned over the desk.

"So Jake told me you had some run ins."

"I not gon lie. I got one juvenile arrest. Wrong crowd. But I gon work more hard for you cuz of dat."

"What'd you get arrested for?"

I told him what happen with Mikey and I told him there was other stealing stuff too. "I like us be up and up. I was one problem child. But you give me one job, no way I would steal from you. "

"Good," he said. "That's always a plus. Is there anything you want to ask me?"

"No, I guess I just go tell you I need one job bah. Whateva I gotta do. I tink I might be one dad pretty soon. Jus let me know what is da main things for do over hea. I gon be one bus ass worker for you, Sammy."

"The main thing for now is that I need to know you're reliable. You can show me you're serious by coming on time. Showing up to work. And I don't have to tell you to do anything twice."

I nodded.

"All right," he said.

"All right?" I said, all nice.

"Yeah," he said. "Congratulations."

I felt good in side.

He went in to his desk and took out some papers. Then he got a manila file and wrote my name on it. Finally he took out this thick carbon paper with holes punched in the side of it. He clipped all the papers together and handed them to me. It said some thing about diagnostics.

"It's for the drug test," he said. "I'm going to have to ask that you go right now and take it. Is that going to work out for you?" He looked me in the eye like I should be surprised, afraid, full on.

Mikey said, diagnostic labs, the thing makes a ring of colors, one color for each drug. My piss would make a beautiful rain bow.

I smiled, looked the guy Sammy back in the eye. "No problem. So if I pass da test I can work here?"

"Yeah. Starting pay nine dollars an hour."

I stood up and shook his hand. "Thanks for da opportunity. I won't let you down."

He looked surprised I was so cool about it, telling me, "Take that form to the test facility. The address is on the top paper. It's just down the road. I need you to get there in the next hour. Can you do that?"

"Course," I said.

I looked at the time on my cell phone. 11:45.

On the way back to the moped the two guys still there smoking. They seem like all right guys. They was older than me but so is all my friends. I gon like working over here.

I ask them, "Eh brudda, what? When you got hired over here, you had to take drug test one hour after the inter view?"

"No," said the guy in the shades laughing. Seem like that fucka was high right now. "No more drug test ova hea."

So what is it with me?

All this work job kine stress, I had to smoke so bad riding back toward the buildings part of town. I pulled over, put the kick stand down by the side of the road, by this field of bushes. I took off my shirt and hung it on the handle bar but I took the back pack with me. I walked about ten steps in side the bush.

I know I say this every day, but I never wanted one bowl so bad and plus I had the kills.

I pinched it softly and loaded one fat bowl in my pipe, that crip, crystal covered herb with that skunky sweet stink you no can get off your fingers. You come out the shower, you still stinking kine weed.

I was taking man hits.

Holding it in my chest like a champ.

Blowing mean rings.

Cashed it.

Put it in my bag.

I look at my phone, 11:55. I had to get going take one drug test.

So I went to the Seven's by the McDonalds across from the building. I was standing in line with my Big Gulp size plastic cup with hot water by the warmer and I started to smell all the hot dogs, bentos, the huge musubis.

"What's the hot water for?" said the lady at the register.

"Cold world out dere," I said. Then, "Wait, wait." And I grabbed like ten pork hashes for the munchies.

By the pay phone I un zipped my bag and took out the little plastic bottle. I shook it around.

I heard a little girl voice, "Is that shi shi?" I looked and the mom put her hand over the kid's mouth, put her in the van, and drove away.

I walked my moped around the corner by the dumpster, more out of sight.

I put the little bottle in the hot water. For the test the piss has to be a certain temperature.

I sat on my moped smoking my blunt, waiting for the piss to heat back up.

Feeling the nice glaze, watching the small spider weave his web.

I still had thirty minutes and the drug place was the blue window ten story building right across the street. I texted Kapika. EH. THNKS 4 DA PISS. I GOTTA TAKE DA TEST RIGHT NOW. GUESS I GOT DA JOB.

Like one second later my phone tone from her text. YAY! KISS! MUH! MUH! CALL ME WEN YOU PAU! CALL WEN YOU CAN! ;) pikabu

Then the next one. P.S. YOU CAN USE GIRL PEE????????? pikabu

And then mines. DINGO USE DOG P

And then hers. LOL! LOL! I LOVE U ;) pikabu

And then like ten more from her with her girl texts.

Before you only had to be boy friend a couple hours a day. Now with all this texting they got you on the job twenty four seven.

I went behind the dumpster with my back pack. Was so rank. I looked around. I drop my pants. I took the roll of medical tape out of my bag and taped the hot bottle of piss around my in side thigh. The thing might have been too hot for now but it would cool.

At the test place I walked in past the Menehune water jug and I gave the lady behind the counter the papers and I asked if she could time stamp it right away jus so Sammy knew I made his test on time. And her telling me with all kind attitude, "I time stamp it when you take the test." I could see her nose sniffing like I smell like weed.

Sitting on the chair I was feeling good. Nice high. I couldn't get high for a while after I start the job, maybe just drink couple every night.

Kapika's dad, I know what he think of me. Some times I forget just cuz one guy get enough money and he got no reason he gotta lie to you, that don't mean he not going to.

That's why, first time he hustled me in to saying I was one drug dealer cuz I trusted him. This time he set me up for job, then tell his friend be sure you drug test this fucka right after the inter view.

Then he gon try and tell his family he likes you and they gon believe him. Tell you he did you a favor. What kinda guy gon set you up to fail, then he think you stupid cuz you failed. What kinda guy do that? The same kinda guy that's still rocking one George Bush bumper sticker I guess.

He thought he would surprise me. I couldn't stop laughing. Imagine how surprise he gon be when I pass the test with his own daughter's piss.

Just when I thought I got it all figured out, that's when my phone ring.

"Who dis?" I said.

I hear this girl's voice I didn't recognize, crying. "Jesse, I sorry I never call you, Jesse." More crying.

"Who dis?"

"It's me, Jesse. I sorry I never call you."

Now I know it's my sista Gummybear.

"Gummybear? What's wrong? Bobby okay? What?"

"Cutchies is coming here, Jesse."

"Cutchies? What is dat? Vaginas?"

"No, Jesse," she said. "Cutchies—she said she's gonna kill me."

"What, kill you?" I say all shook. "Try hold on, kay, Gummybear. I coming over dere, tell me on da way."

I walked up to the lady at the counter. I hope my sista wasn't on the stuff, the dope. She wasn't making any kine sense.

"Hey," I said to the lady with the string around her glasses frames. "I gotta go. Family emergency. You no can just stamp um I take da test later?"

"Sorry," said the lady.

"I coming back here one hour, I swear on my nephew's life," I said.

"You can come back but it'll say the time you came back."

"Fine," I said. "Fuck you den. Fuck you and your fucken attitude." And I walked out.

On the way out the door I kicked over the blue Menehune water jug and the thing going glub glub glub on the carpet.

I wanted that fucken job but Gummybear my sista.
I got back on the phone. "You still dere?"
"Yah," she said.
"Kay, I on da way, tell me what happen."
I ran down to the garage and cranked the moped.

I barely heard from my sista ever since my father banish me. But I would keep up on her, you know, that's my sista. Brianna her name, but I always call her Gummybear cuz she look like one Gummy Bear. She was one real round sista my sista, but real girly, real soft, not fat, just her shape, like one Gummy Bear.

She get one mean singing voice. I heard she kill over at da karaoke bars. And back in school at the bus stop when girls would rag on her cuz her shape I would slap dem, pinch dem, for Gummybear. I know some guys would say you wrong for slap one chick but if you ever met Gummybear you would slap dem too for her. I would tell dem girls, "May be you just all skin and bones. You never think of that? You skinny bitch, no ass, no tits?" Gummybear watching from behind, with her hand on my back, all proud of me.

But then Shelly our older sista ratted out both of us to our mother when she heard about um and we both got scoldings.

I was there when Gummybear had her boy Bobby, and she let me come over play with him for little while even after I get kick out. She got a nice condo but she work three jobs and she had two room mates.

I try to show her son how for punch with da second knuckle. I figure I teach him cuz he no more father around for teach him that kine stuff. Then her getting all salty at me cuz how he too small for learn all that and I not his dad.

I told her, "I dunno what schoo you think he going to. But if he going to dat schoo up the road he better start training right now. I jus teaching him to throw, the odda boys know already how to grapple. Oh and yah, by da way, while we talking about Mista Right, da proud fadda, I like go slap dat fucka wit my left, see what he do afta, tell him pay money for his son or he gon see da close hand right."

I guess she thought my yelling was too loud, plus she said I was gon scare da boy talking about his father in front him li'dat.

I dunno, I guess I never got one invite back after that. I guess she never like me around da boy, be like da man figure to her boy with all my tats and swearing all da time and shit.

I heard da boy Bobby big for his age, like his gramps, but I never seen him grow.

Gummybear not the type to make drama. But she said she locked herself in the condo with one chair up against the door knob.

I found out every thing on the way, she was telling me while I was flying it.

Gummybear work this one house keeping job with this one butchie Cathy. Cathy was one tough chick, she used to bang cars before with her girl friend Cutchies. They was shack up together, Cutchies and Cathy, tweaking together. For life kine. True love kine. Bonny and Clyde or Bonny and whatever.

They was like married, more than married cuz they would do every thing together and never spend time apart. So when they got busted together, Cutchies wen eat da charges for Cathy, told da cops was only her that did um. She told Cathy make one statement, be one witness, rat her out.

Cuz, I hardly know any guy girl couples that been together for twelve years, plus she wen jail for her.

And when Cutchies got lock up, she make Cathy promise she gon wait for her, and Cutchies too she promise she not gon get one other girl friend in cell block. Plus, they was gon get clean, quit da shit already and work one regular kine job. That way they never get taken apart again.

All the time Cutchies was in there, in detox li'dat, fiending for clear every night, sweating, pulling out her hair, she never gave the business to any kine girls in side. As lonely as she was, Cutchies was true game li'dat for Cathy.

Cutchies was one prime dike tita too, real cut, from far away she look like one pretty cut guy, with one strut and wide man shoulders with one small waist.

But I guess Cathy, mopping floor every day with my sista Gummybear, telling her about how Cutchies lock up, my sista telling her about how her man wen dig out on her, left her with da baby, I guess Cathy got one little crush on Gummybear. They was all they had, pretty much, those two girls. Four in da morning they come work together, grab one Breakfast Jack or one breakfast bento from Seven's. Then they mop da floor, wipe down windows together while the sun rising outside, da clouds rising up da Koʻolaus.

And my sista one real nice girl too. She was da one always help out my mom and dad dem when they was beefing. When you go tell Gummybear your problems you feel better after.

But you know da messed up thing too? I never thought about till after. I dunno if my sista was innocent in all dis, like how she was saying, with her and Cathy. I know she wen bought Cathy all kine perfumes like that from da mall when they was working. And Gummybear was going out all da time trying for find one new guy for herself, I know cuz some of Dingo's boys told me they seen her out in town at Mai Tai's. But my sista, she one pretty large girl, not thick, but you know, round. And her with da kid already too, I no think too much guys was really trying for that. I think prolly she just like da attention or whatever from Cathy. It made her feel special cuz she never get attention like that from guys. Made her feel sexy even. I no can say, I no like really think about um.

I drove by my sista's condo and there was Cutchies with one bat. She prolly never even know that was the neighbor's old Cadillac she was smashing up either. I parked down da block, in case the cops came I could run for it. Cutchies's Silverado was park side ways in da front lawn with da engine still running. She had one bumper sticker, KEEP THE COUNTRY COUNTRY–YOU LEAVE THE COUNTRY.

"Cutchies," I tell her. She was smaller than I was expecting. I was kinda laughing on the in side. I wen tell her, "Put down da bat Cutchies, we go figure um out. Cruise, cruise–"

She dropped da bat and start strutting up to me, shifting her shoulders. Her nose was huge, all mis shape, you could tell she ate plenty man punches before. Her two man legs in her baggy jeans.

She was so amped I knew she jus blasted off, she prolly jus launched her first rips of da pipe since she got out from all those years in side, her face all frozen stiff like she wearing one mask.

Her getting cheated on, and the years she was lock up, and all in side one human being, then to put that in to one clear frenzy? That's like mixing trouble with trouble, nitrogen and glycerin and soaking in gasoline. Guarantee, you hear on da news some guy shot his wife and kids then himself, that's what happen.

"Cutchies," I tell her. I talk to her like she one small kid kine. "Nuff already Cutchies. We go figure um out."

And then bam, she false crack me so fucken fast like one mouse trap going off. My head spinning. I feel da waves coming up my throat. Then that quick buzz feeling, that high feeling when time get all fuzzy. One punch, she almost laid me out on top the drive way.

"What?" I was saying. Not like "What!" Like "What? What da fuck even happen?" I was astonish. Trying to figure out how she wen reach my mouth even. And before I could swing back she go shouting with dis super deep voice for one chick, "Get-da-fuck-outa-hea-brudda. Dis-none-of-your-fuck-in-bid-ness."

"Cutchies!" I shout back, holding my chin, pointing at the house with my other hand. "Dats my sista in side dere."

And her shouting back, "Your sista one slut."

Bra, any confusion li'dat I was feeling, gone already. Cutchies think she bad ass? Fine, ask about me. I ran up swinging but I never land nothing, how she duck and weave, bouncing, dancing around, shouting, "You fucka! You fucken fag!" Our arms got all tangled up, she know all kine ju jitsu moves. She jump back and sweep kick me in my knee and I heard some thing pop, then she whacked me in my rib cage, and I was slumped forward leaning on top of her just to stay up.

Then she push me off and caught me with two quick rights, then the one two combo and one left hand wind mill. Fuck, I was thinking, no way, no way. I gon get knocked out. My rib cage all swelling up, I had to lean side ways.

The neighbors all watching like, what da fuck? Cuz there was one good size man getting mopped up by one medium size butch. And now Gummybear coming out the house shouting, "Get her Jesse! Get Cutchies!"

Now I was da one fighting like one chick with my hand on her face, scratching, pulling hair. I never like chance um standing up any more so I used my weight and took her to the ground. I had her all pinned down and her arms and legs kicking around me like one up side down ca ca roach. Then she wen spit on my face, head butt me right on da lip. So I wen head butt her right back in to the drive way. She start biting, shouting, spit, blood shooting out her mouth, slurring her words, "Fffffuck yoush, yoush fffffucka!"

I thought I had her now. I wen push up with my upper half and start landing on her with my elbow over and over, shouting, "Tap out! Tap out!" Whack, right in her fore head. "Nuff! Nuff!" And finally I wen smash her with one solid right on her temple and I thought that would stop her but she just keep kicking and screaming, scratching and biting, amping off clear, feeling no pain.

And me, she wen crack my rib, and I could feel my eye swelling, covered in sweat and dirt and gravel and blood and spit, running on empty, sucking air, about to pass out.

"Cutchies," I tell her once I had her arms pinned down again. "Give up fore I dent your fucken head."

"Fuck you," she said, and she start breaking free again.

That's when the other neighbor comes running out da house, this old man.

"What happen to my cah?" The old fucka was salty, bra. This old pake. "What I did to you guys, huh? What I did?"

I was working my way up, trying to get my right knee up to her arm pit to get her mounted, pin her arms down under my knees.

But Cutchies, some how she reach from under neath my ass and bang me right in the nuts.

Then I could hear da cops coming, cop engines and they was gassing it up over da hill.

So I jump up and start trying to run. But Cutchies was grabbing on my leg until my shoe came off. And my rib and my balls hurt so much I running in one zig zag line, leaning for ward when I dove in to da bushes, crawling when I looked back and seen da cops.

They was walking up to her jus like how I was before, laughing on da in side, talking to her like one little kid, "Calm down, calm down, we'll get um figured out." So she jumped back to her feet and punch her own hand with this loud smack sound. She put her arms up.

"Dis-none-of-your-fuck-en-bid-ness! I-lick-all-you-fuckas!" Yelling to da four cops. "Come on! Come on!"

Bra, I was jus planted, watching her through the bush. The cops shouting for the neighbors go in side, after she threw my Air Jordan at the main cop. She started charging, the cop spraying her down with da Mace, in her eyes, in her mouth. Her shouting, "I eat dat fugga! I eat dat fugga!"

Still screaming and throwing cracks all blind. "I-lick-all-you-fuckas!"

They had to carry her ass in da car, blind, kicking, grabbing on da roof. The cop that got bit called for more back up. Next thing you know had seven cop cars up the road. All for one tweaked out love sick butchie. Clear is like that for some guys. No fear or pain, no tomorrow, just love and rage right now.

I walked in to the Urgent Care trying to tell them I fell down a flight of stairs. Jus cuz they gon call up the cops and then they might send me right back for more paper work.

They said my rib wasn't broke, I jus had in ternal contusions and if it start swelling more I might have hard time breathing. They said I better go hospital, stay over night. I told dem let me out cuz I no more medical.

They jus said to come back if bone chips start falling out of my nose that could get infected.

When I got out Pika was waiting for me. She never have to do that. I told her I wasn't going to her place.

"I not gon let your dad see me li'dis," I said.

"Jesse," she said. "You always think my dad's against you. He really, actually, hates to admit that he likes you."

She was super mad. But I had to go back to Robby's house any way.

"Well then, I'm coming too," she said.

Chapter Twenty

They was all sick at the house cuz I wouldn't tell them what happened.

Robby was calling up guys. "Who wen fight Jesse? Eh, no fucken lie you. Was Kody? Was Kody?"

"Wasn't Kody," I told him. "You jus spreading da news even more."

I jus lied there in bed, Kapika beside me, and Amber told Dingo bring the TV in for us. I was falling in and out of sleeping listening to Amber telling Kapika about my fish.

Then on da third hour I could tell Mikey found out. That guy find out every thing some how. Mikey hardly never laugh, but he get dis one real evil half smile.

I told him, "No fucken tell Dingo and Robby."

And Mikey smiling back like maybe I gon tell um, maybe I not. But he never. Unless it cost Mikey any thing, he kept a good secret.

It was the first time Kapika ever came near the house. She hated Robby but Mikey jus made her sick to look at. I told her you gotta get to know him. She said, "No you don't."

Pretty soon her and Amber they had the lap top out and they was checking out each other's MySpaces. Usually you get two girls that think they fine in one room, bra, that's one cold war going on. Especially if they know the same guys.

Even more, I pretty sure Kapika knew Amber was one free spirit. I knew in side Kapika's mind was going, gross, ew, gross. But there they was, laughing about me like I wasn't even there.

I must have fell asleep again cuz when I woke up Amber was gone and Pika had changed the channel from her Korean soap operas to CNN.

"Eh Pika," I said. "Why you still hea?"

"Just cuz," she said. "Nothing better to do, I guess."

My face hurt when I smile.

"Eh Pika," I said.

"Eh Jesse," she said, making fun of my voice, scratching her little neck that weigh so much.

I tell her, "You coulda got yourself one older guy, one stevedore. Or one college boy."

"Oo," she said. "Keep going, I like college boys."

I got up to piss and every thing hurt even more.

When I got back now she was brushing her hair in the mirror. Then tapping the fish tank, trying to get the fish to move. Then we just looked at each other for the longest time.

Then she said, "You know Jesse, you ever see those gangsta families, the ones with the momma gangsta, the poppa gangsta, and little kid gangsta with Fubu wear and little Lugz, cornrows and dreadlocks? That's never going to be us. Okay?"

Jus as I was falling asleep again I turned my head to the fish tank. Behind the fishes I had a white paper, the girl Charlene's mssing picture. I left the edge jus sticking out before but it was gone. I figure Robby found um or some thing.

Chapter Twenty-One

Rawlings and De Luca were sitting on the hood of the Lancer in the beach parking lot. They were in their swim shorts, sunburned. Something in the water had bitten Rawlings on the ankle, and it was stinging and throbbing. He stretched out his leg and poured Steinlager on the red criss-cross marks.

Two girls walked by, tanskinned, hips swinging, wrapped in towels, on their way to the shower.

"Hey, beautiful," said Rawlings, and he tilted his Oakleys up at them. The girls looked through him and walked on, faster.

Rawlings put his shades down on his nose again. "They'll be back."

"You think?" said De Luca "Pulling away, accelerating, not looking in the rear view–that's usually a sign they aren't coming back."

"They don't know what they're missing."

"Looked to me like they knew."

"Damn," said Rawlings. "All this time in beautiful Hawaii and I still haven't seen a coconut bra. All I got in-country is this damn bite on my leg."

He stared at the redness. It looked angry, even through the sun glasses. He poured more Steinlager on it.

De Luca's cell vibrated. He checked the caller.

"Hey, Rawlings, it's Janice. I'll put her on speaker."

Her voice was calm and controlled. "I got a call from someone who knows where Charlene is. He must have seen the flyer."

"He knows where she is?" said De Luca. "You're sure, Janice? He tells you he knows. Do you think he really knows, or is he playing you for the reward?"

"I've had other calls. I dread when I hear the phone. And then when it's bogus, I could scream at how cruel people are, and afterwards I cry. And then I dread when there's a day when there aren't any calls. But this one, he knows Charlene has a mood ring and a dolphin tattoo on her ankle, and–"

"What kind of voice?"

"What they call local."

"I mean, does he sound like you can trust him?"

"One thing, he says he won't deal with the police."

"What do you think that tells you?"

"Well–"

"I think it means be very careful."

Rawlings leaned in close and took the phone.

"Janice, this is Rawlings. Listen up. The guy won't deal with the police. You don't want to be dealing with him by yourself. This is hard core. So what are you going to do?"

She took a big breath and went silent. Then, "He said Jesse. He said the name Jesse. That was the name I heard, on Charlene's phone."

De Luca took the phone again. "Are you going to call him back? Or is he going to call you?"

"He's going to call. To be sure about the money."

"You're guaranteeing him money, right?"

"Yes."

"You can tell him that. But you don't need to tell him that me and Rawlings, we come with the money."

"You mean that? You will help? Oh my goodness. Sergeant De Luca, Corporal Rawlings–I am truly grateful. I thank God for you both."

Chapter Twenty-Two

Vili was right, Kody-Dos knew what they was doing. Cuz when the raid came, Vili was the one sleeping in his chair with the Heineken in the one hand, phone in the other. Vili was the one there with the red devil gas can, the Sudafed box, the hot plates. Vili was the one seen his kids still holding they water balloons, getting picked up in the air by the cop with the rifle. Vili was the one who seen his wife get thrown to the ground crying out for him. You know when Vili seen that he charged the guy and gave him one for real peace maker, put the cop to sleep, he never wake up till the next day. When the other cops shot Vili they shot each other too, no one killed but all kine blood. Now Vili three counts attempt murder and the guy never own one fire arm.

On the news you never seen my friend Vili. You just saw one Tongan in hand cuffs, no shirt, one look on his face all rage. And you know where Dos was? Maui, bra. Kody? Big Island. That's what one of his chicks told me when I tried for find them. Kody was gone for almost one week before. That never sounded right to me.

Every body came court for Vili for arraignment. His wife too, but they let her go. Before it was done they made Vili sound like one king pin, Tony Montana, Don Mega Godfadda, so no bail. Even in the court his own friends was laughing, shouting when the prosecution wen say all that, cuz every body know that's bull shit, but we all got escorted out. Vili jus look at the ground the whole time, unless when his kids would try shout for him.

And I never seen Kody or Dos. I know Vili never rat them out. I no can say why, whether cuz he was one stand up guy or he jus fear um that much. I know one thing but, between Kody and Dos they had couple million buried some where. And still yet they let Vili go down with one public defender.

How me and Vili came up, you make justice with your heart and your good name to one brother hood of men. But in court you gotta pay big money for justice ah? And on the news every body was all happy. They never even found drugs at Vili's house but they never mention that on the news. Was one big show for the camera saying stuff like meth lab seizure, we have the individual in custody, safer community. Sucken Vili.

Every body was so fucken cool with the raid. The real HPDs prolly know they had the wrong Tongan but they never care, long as they get one for put on TV. Some body got one promotion. And Dos jus bought one A-6, probably from Kapika's dad, so he was happy. And they cop friends on the in side too was gon buy one new Mustang or Chrysler 300 from the police auction. It was all bull shit and every body was cool with Vili in jail except for me and the god damn chronics.

Mikey said drug laws are like nature laws. Places that get cold get snow. After the flood comes the raids. After the raid comes the drought.

Now in the drought chronics get desperate, calling you, when when?

Strange things happen in droughts. Dealers cannot turn on their phones cuz a lot their chronic customers is more nuts. Guys go in to hiding. Chronics switch up habits. Chronics come geniuses, coming up with new ways to scam. All kinda bunk, bull shit drugs, fake drugs going around.

Dealers re freeze one ball of good dope and make three balls. Sell the pellets from the little bag in side mochi crunch packaging and call it clear. Guys cut coke two three times already by the time you getting it. Chopped up codeine. Pretty much any thing white. Tylenol has the coating around and you can see it in the coke if you look careful. In drought times guys might jus sell baking soda and novocaine or any thing that tingles. I even heard this one guy chopped up soap, covered it in bread crumbs for the taste, tried to sell it as rock. I heard he got beat down. Hard times.

Fuckas you don't even think they know each other team up on you. Hard enough already when you lower level like me, then in a drought it's every man for him self. All kinda guys trying to get to the new lines coming in and old lines that broke ties with before. Some fuckas get rich off the drought. Some ordinary working fuckas take they life savings, go up to Vegas or Reno, Cali, come back with pounds and quit they job and go back Vegas.

Yah, every body is cool to you cuz you the one make the bags. But the minute you need them, where every body went? Hard drugs, your customer is not really your friend. Your customer tell the girl he smoke with come polish you, he goes in the car, takes the stash and you never see him again. The girl no care, she smoke too, she like be your girl friend now. Until she take your whole car and goes on to the next guy.

No body feel sorry for you.

No body loves you.

Jesus no even like you.

Count on your self.

Game up. Game on. Run um hard.

Chapter Twenty-Three

I sitting on my moped blowing smoke at the stars. Out side the chicken fights in the old abandoned hotel. The sky had the kind of stars you can see far away from towns.

There was about twenty five cars and trucks parked on the grass.

Two ounces of white in my bag. White boy. White girl. White cocaine.

A small cloud of feathers blew over toward the banana patches.

There was Dos's new A-6 with dealer plates, the kind Kapika's dad sells.

The whole place look shady, or may be I was jus paranoid, sitting there with two ounces in my bag. The fights could get held up at gun point. Or some body forget to pay off the cops and the place could get raided. What was that bark, one dog cop?

Killas said he gotta meet over here, that was like hour ago. He keep texting me, 5 MIN, 5 MIN. That's Killas slang for twenty minutes. Ten minutes is an hour and two hours means tomorrow.

He had call me up asking, "Why? How much is for oranges?"

The O, that's the ounce.

I told him, "Times is hard, even though you my friend gotta go nine fifty."

"Yah," he said. "I know not gon be da pure like how was before, but what? Not gon be bunk either?"

"Better den da other shit going around, dats all I gon say."

"Tanks Jess."

He never even complain. He better not. Even in good times ounces can cost fourteen hundred. He was going to cook it, rock it up, chop it, get about twelve grams of rock per ounce. May be less.

When one big line goes down the other lines dry up fast. Even the other drugs. That's why he not complaining.

In side you could hear all the yelling from the chicken fights.

My phone text again, 5 MIN. This fucka. Five minutes I gon be gone.

I thought I know the guy Killas good, he was there the day with Charlene, but I no like this kine set up action. We doing him the favor.

A guy carried his cages in to the door by me. The birds chirpin, cluckin, going nuts flappin, rattlin the cage. This one bird had one little hood over his eyes.

In side was the chalk board under the over head light. New planks holding up the old hotel roof, new wood, sap dripping. Then the circle of guys, some of them holding they roll. Couple of them had ladders to see over every body else.

It was too hot in there. I wasn't going to try and squeeze in. From out side I jus heard the feathers in the air and guys cheering out, some guys waving their money around.

You wonder if the chickens knew they was chickens. Strutting around like the world should fear them. The rest of the world didn't even know they was there.

Let the bird have name. You know?

I not one activist. I mash one mochi chicken plate from Food Co. But if you gon raise the bird to be one man killer bird, grow him up in the sand pit until his leg is too strong for him to walk normal, he have to strut. Then you tie him to one stick, or cage him, train him to kill. Then you go put one hood over his eyes and throw him in the ring against one bird just like him, and even if he wins you might still broke his neck to protect your blood line. All I saying is, you do all that, at least give him one name. Let the bird have a name.

"Jesse Gomes," said this slick voice.

I saw the lights flash on the A-6. I seen Dos walking out the door. He must have made bank, he all fucken happy, hugging me, slapping my back. Kissing my eye brow. One guy come with him, standing back with a smirk.

"Eh Jesse," said Dos. "How you my brudda? You all right?" He look all concerned. He kept patting my back, my rib. "I heard about you my brudda. My friend was telling every body how you got mopped up. I was all sick when I heard. Fuck. I had your back Jesse. I wen tell dem guys for you, girls now, dey no fuck around, dey scrap bra. And you know who else?"

"Fags," said Dos's friend.

"Fags Jesse," said Dos, looking over his shoulders like they could pop out from the banana patches any minute. "Getting bad nowadays Jess, da mahus. Get some game ass scrappy fucken faggots running around." He put his arm on my shoulder, looking in my eyes all fake serious with concern. "Next time call me up. I lay dat bitch out for you. Dats why you get bruddas my brudda."

His friend laughing so hard he started coughing his smoker cough.

Then Dos again. "Eh Jesse, you can drop my name. Any body around here give you trouble, you let me know boy."

He walked back to his car and looked back, yelling, "Tell your friend Mikey call me up. I gon need da money after

Christmas. If not I gon charge you da eight grand for disposal fees."

Mikey owe him. That was news.

I watched the tail lights as they left. You could feel the hum from the exhaust. Brand new A-6. Sick ass fucken car.

Killas never come.

Driving back to the house I had to make one last stop. One small one, only two points. I passed the school and went down the road with the fountain park and all the apartments.

It was across from the apartment where Vili's wife just moved in, with the kids.

I pulled up through the building parking, under neath by the coin laundry. I could hear the machines going and the clean smell of detergent where I always park the moped.

I ran up the zig zag stairs in my slippers. The halls all smelled like the beef stew some body was cooking and I heard a bag of trash banging down the chute in to the dumpster.

When I was on the fourth floor landing I stopped dead, looking over the rail.

I couldn't believe it. The Expedition with black rims parked in visitor parking in the building with Vili's wife.

Kody. This fucka.

Business right now but. I knocked on the customer door, he let me in and I was leaning against the ice box in the kitchen, thinking Kody while the guy's little ass dog was clawing at my leg.

The guy was all smiles opening the bag. "Ho you came through Jesse. Clutch bra. One drought and everything."

I told him, "You know dat. You know I gon take care you."

He put the dope on his scale and it weighed out with the right weight plus the weight of the bag.

He handed me a twenty and four fives, he was already loading up his pipe on the dinner table.

"Like one beer Jesse?"

"Nah," I said. I sat down on the table. "Why, you ever seen dat black Expedition around hea before?"

He said that same car was there twice last week, maybe even one time before that. "What?" he said. "You know dat guy?"

"Yah," I said. "Nice cah he get. All night?"

"Every time, same day every time," said the guy, nodding all slow. He give me this slick look like I was gon rob the car.

I wasn't gon do shit.

He shook my hand and I ran back down the zig zag stairs.

Driving back, revving the motor, I passed the fountain that never work, up the road by the school, and turned right back to Robby's house.

Chapter Twenty-Four

It's bad enough Vili gon end up doing twenty four years for Kody, bad enough Kody got rich off him and never help him out after Vili wen keep his mouth shut, bad enough the guy was supposed to be his good friend he never wen up for visit him one time. But Kody had to go fuck Vili's wife too? What, he never had enough girls for him self he had to have Vili's too? What, he never had enough kids already that he never take care, he gotta go play daddy with Vili's boys? Fuck. And Vili's wife too, that whore.

I figure I was gon have to tell Vili. At first I was thinking jus let it be. But Kody, that was just out of hand already, too far, too fucken far, bra.

I would tell myself every week, dis week when I up on da west side for community service I gon check out Vili after. That was da only one thing for do with your good friend, tell him the truth right? But every week I would fag out. But still I tinking, we gon get dis fucka Kody. I was tinking, watch, Vili not gon stand for dis. At least Vili could send his bruddas and they friends out to get Kody. We could match that fucka, may be.

I know you prolly gon think I bull shitting, but some how I end up meeting with Vili out of the main visitation area in this supply room area.

The guard that brought Vili in was one brudda, you could tell he was all respect for Vili. Vili's cuffs was barely even on at all.

Vili groan when he sat, the little ass chair never was made for Vili's big ass. He kinda did smile when he seen me. He ask me how was Pika, Robby, my cousins, all that. For a while he jus talk story about how he trying for be on his good behavior so one day may be he could get in to Annex 1, where they let you go out, work detail, eat plate lunch. Vili kept bringing up the plate lunch, I knew he wasn't eating good in there. The guy wen drop some weight. He said he would train almost every day but it's hard cuz you no can shower after. He said he get all stink plus at night the bugs come after him.

The guy would sit all different too, more tense like. I couldn't imagine the guy falling asleep now in one chair. He look all different now, he wen shave his head for keep cool.

The guy is one cigarette smoker now too. He took out dis little roach looking cigarette and threw it to me. Was rolled in some kinda weird paper with words on it. Vili wen light his one up and slid me his book matches.

"You jus smoke up in here?" I said.

"Can. Da guard no care, he one cool guy."

I look over at the guard, he look like he was talking to his chick on the cell phone. "Sucken Vili, you running dis place already?"

He wen squint his eyes when he took one hard drag. "I da bitch over here."

He keep fanning him self with his shirt, some parts of his suit had big wet patches. He had some serious over growth of nose hairs, usually his wife would clean him up, before.

I ask him, "What about Lepa, J.J. Wong, every body else, you met up with dem?"

"Oh yah, like your high school reunion in here, Jesse."

The surprise thing for me is he never ask me about none of his old friends, or even his family. The only guys we wen talk about was the guys in there or my friends. Was kinda weird talking story with Vili now. I kept trying for joke with the guy but he jus nod. Where stay the girly ass laugh now Vili, huh.

For a while we jus stop talking out right. So I was reading the words on my cigarette, King Ahasuerus subsided, he remembered Vashti. What?

"Eh Vili, what kine paper is dis we smoking?"

"Bible pepas, you."

"Bible? You guys smoking da Bible in here? How come you never just smoke one regular cigarette?"

"You no can jus burn one whole one in here. Guys break um down in to chrees, fours even. If you get skills you roll um up in to little piners with da Bible paper."

He had one half page and showed me. I read and I had to laugh after. "He gave also their increase onto the catapiller and their labor onto the locusts."

Vili look down at me and smile jus a little. "I know, Jesse. We going to hell."

"I going any way, no matta, " I said. "I jus no like fuck around wit dem locusts."

Nothing from Vili. I give up already trying for make the guy laugh.

"Eh Vili," I said.

"What?"

"Vili, I got one thing I gon tell you, my brudda. Long time I thinking better if I never tell you, but if was me, would have to know."

Vili look all serious. I figure he already wen guess. Then I was thinking oh fuck, Vili gon rage bra, his friend the guard gon carry him outa here. But I keep going.

"Vili, I jus gon tell you what I seen myself first. Four times may be, I was making drops over by the apartment where da kine lives, your wife. When I was leaving, I seen your one friend from before, da one with da pukas in his face, I seen his car."

I stop and look back at the guard. I never like say the name, what if some body hear?

But Vili say right away, "Kody?"

"Yah. I got da word too, he over dere every week, his car dere real late some times."

Vili sat back in his chair and jus look at the ground.

"All night kine," I said.

Still yet Vili never seem that mad.

I lean in to him. "What you tink Vili, you like reach out from in here, give da guy couple love taps? All your friends still get plenty love for you back home. I gon call up your cousins every body, plus my friends."

Vili face never change.

I said, "Give me da word Vili."

He jus start playing with his sock then fanning him self with his shirt again.

Then he said, "No Jesse."

I don't know, he kinda said it like I was stupid too. Not no thanks. Jus no.

I figure the guy must be shame or maybe he jus never like get us in to one mess over him.

"No shame Vili," I said. "Or what, bra? You tink we no can handle dat guy? We handle dat guy for you Vili. I go call him right now from da phone, tell him we coming. For Vili. For you my brudda."

My chest starting for swell up.

"No Jesse," he said. "No call no body."

I never felt so denied, you know. I said I do it for him, and I wen mean um too. Then Vili jus shake me off like that.

"What? Why, Vili? One guy out dere f– . . . doing your wife."

Vili finally looked up from the ground. I could see all the white in his eye.

"What Jess, you never figure um out yet?"

"What Vili, what?"

"Jesse, I going be in here for ever. If any thing, if you gon see Kody, tell him do her right."

All this stuff in my mind. Kody control the thing. He think he gon get ratted out, me the rat, or I tell Robby. So Kody rat to his cop friends on the pay roll, tell them the big Tongan, that's the guy you looking for, he's the big boss man of us, then he give them the envelope.

The night after the raid I had this dream. Me and Vili was running. First we was running around this loop like those haoles with the white sun screen on they nose. I keep yelling to Vili, "Vili, come on you fucka," and he would just mutter to him self, pouring sweat. Then we ran to the dump and he was all happy. It was one good dream, like we was running away.

When I woke up after, for little while I thought it was true.

Chapter Twenty-Five

When I got back to the house there was like three cars pulled up I never seen before. At first I thought some tweakers was holding up the house.

Then I could hear Robby yelling at Mikey t0 tell his tweaker friends get out the house. They came out the door in their ratty ass clothes and pass me on the stairs coming up and never even look at me.

I came in the house. Dingo was sitting on his chair with pants around his ankles. His stomach hanging over his BVDs. Sweaty red skin. Mikey sitting away from him just being Mikey in his hood even in the house. And Amber sitting on the floor against the table next to Robby. Her bag and the ash tray was in between them. Their feet almost touching.

"Hi Jesse," she said, all sexy.

I ducked my head under the black light. "Hi you."

"You still my favorite Jesse," she said.

She was wearing this red spaghetti strap top, showing pretty much every thing, and tight blue jeans. She rolled in to that cat woman pose on her stomach, but school girl face, flapping her feet up and down, watching Robby watch the hockey game.

She put her fingers in her cheeks making fun of my dimples. I took off my shirt and she passed me the joint from the ash tray.

Robby was yelling again, "Dingo! Pull your fucken pants up."

Dingo pulled his pants up.

I said to Mikey, "By da way Mikey, I seen your friend Dos. He said give him call."

Mikey jus gave me the blank look. Just for fuck around I told him, "Like use my phone Mikey?"

Robby got quiet when the commercial ended. He had his gambling note book out that he use for track his bets. Holding the cold Heineken bottle against his head. I guess he had the migraine again.

Amber saw me looking at the flower arrangement she put in the beer bottles on the wall unit. "I had to pick my own flowers Jesse, cuz no body gets me flowers."

Dingo got up. "Like one Jess?"

"No," I said. "I not gon drink."

Kapika says I been drinking too much for one guy trying to get one job.

"Every body's doing it Jesse," said Amber.

Dingo came back from the ice box.

"Dat better be one beer in your hand Dingo," said Robby, without looking up.

Dingo sat down in his chair and open the can passion orange.

"Jesse," said Robby, looking now. "Look dis fucka. You seen dat? Dis fucka."

There was like four cans of passion orange juice by Dingo's chair.

Robby said, "I know I said go grab as much you like. But what da fuck, Dingo, drink one beer, we get plenty beer for drink."

"I got Robby some juices," said Amber to me. Her voice all cute.

It was getting harder to tell who was playing who any more.

All day Robby would get all nuts if any body took the juices. I think he jus like open the ice box and see the orange cans. It seem like one thing one girl would buy.

And Amber made it her business now to be by the front door. So when girls would show up looking for Robby, they would leave all shame with their tail between their legs.

And one day Robby asked Amber who was the guy in the white Jetta that drop her off and she ask him, "Why, you jealous?"

He jus looked over the sink, out the crack in the window. "Jus tell him turn off his sounds next time. I get sounds. I no need his sounds."

Each time Amber came over now she had a little bit less make up. The gel lotion was gone now.

She patted the floor next to her and I sat with her.

She started pouring me shots and pretty soon the room was spinning. Then she was doing little dances around Robby but it didn't work.

Then I felt a tap on my shoulder. When I looked back down my phone was gone. She always do this.

I was running through the kitchen. Me chasing her. Titties going all over the place.

Jus when I was about to catch her Dingo came flying over the table and tackled me, so she could read my messages to Kapika. "'I miss you too. 'I love you too sexy. You gon get it.' Jesse, wow Jesse, eh, I had no idea Jesse. It's always da quiet ones."

She jus kept going and after she read all of them she said, "Aw . . . Jesse-got-a-girl-friend, Jesse-got-a-girl-friend."

Even Mikey was laughing. Finally she gave me my phone back. Then she made this little huff noise. "You broke my heart Jesse."

"Fucken scrub," yelled Robby at the TV.

Mikey tilted his head and Amber nodded back. Then she tip toed around the table, over Robby's legs, with her finger over her mouth.

"Don't tell Robby," she said, right in front of Robby. "I'm going to smoke drugs with Mikey."

And when they was done smoking down stairs she came back and she was wearing Mikey's black jacket and Mikey jus had a white tee. She came by Robby and took her mouth wash and her lip gloss out of her bag and went back to the bath room.

Robby didn't look up but he was smiling. I knew she didn't give Mikey one head job. She jus wanted to make Robby think.

Even more when she was telling Dingo how she had to have reduction surgery. Dingo got all nuts telling her, "Dats like slapping God in da face."

Me hope less drunk by now, laughing so much my eyes tearing up, my face getting sore.

"You see?" said Amber. "Be happy."

And every thing was going pretty good until my phone rang.

I got up and went out to the porch and closed the door behind me. Lights came in around the edges, through cracks through the barred up windows.

"Eh," I said.

"You didn't text me back," said Kapika.

"Some fool took my phone."

"Oh," she said. Her voice was quiet.

"What's wrong?"

"Nothing. I had a long day. Can you come over?"

"I'm all drunk," I said.

"I don't care this time," she said. "As long as you're nice drunk not mean drunk. Nice drunk Jesse gives back rubs."

"Why Pika? What's wrong? You no can jus tell me what happen for once? You always hiding tings."

"I don't like getting you mad when you're drunk."

"So jus tell me stuff when I sober."

Now the snappy voice from her. "Bra, when was da last time you were frecken sober?"

I stumbled back wards, almost tripped on the punching bag lying on its side.

She sniffed, jus from her allergies. "I'll tell you, but you have to promise not to get mad or be jealous?"

"Kay. I try, I try."

"Jesse–I didn't tell you before, there's this guy. I don't like him. He keeps coming by my job."

"How come you never tell me before?"

"See, you? Can I talk? There's lots of guys, Jesse. I can't tell you every guy. But this guy, he's so gross."

"Ho, sorry, ah? Lots of guys?" I said. "And dis guy? You told him you get one boy friend?"

She waited, her mind thinking, "I told him your name."

"What?"

"He said he heard you were dead. It was terrible. I got sick. That's why I kept texting you."

I got red. "Who is dis fucka? Say I dead? I smash dis fucka. How come you neva call me first ting? I would have come down."

"Cuz I know you would come, stupid. You would have made a scene in front of my boss and everyone."

"Tell me his name, I go give him couple love taps."

"He told me. But I forgot, I was so angry. He has cat eyes."

"Dat no help how he look," I said. "What kine people he look like?"

"I don't know. He jus look gross. He has a limp."

I felt the air leave my lungs.

"You know him?" she said.

"Yah."

After a while she said, "You still there? Jesse, say something."

After a while I said, "I no can come ova. May be later."

"Why? Are you mad at me? I didn't do anything. Jesse?"

I turned the phone off, put it on the rail and looked out over the town.

All the lights of the houses to the beach.

The light where my Mom and Dad's house was. Third street, five lights to the left.

I went back in to Robby and Mikey and Amber.

"Dat fucka Kody," I said. "He gotta go."

Mikey look all serious at me and start making the clicking noise with his mouth, his thinking sound.

"Kody?" said Robby. His eyes going back and forth. "How come Jesse? What he did to you, he wen mess with you again?"

"Before I never know but now I know for sure. Da guy wen rat out Vili to save him self."

"What?" said Robby. "Kody wen rat out Vili?"

"Dat's how come da cops wen raid his house. Next time could be us."

"Vili wen tell you dat? You seen Vili?"

"Yah, I seen Vili today," I said. "Kody gon die tonight. I know where he stay right now."

Dingo speak up, shaking his head. "I tell you dis, Jess. You like fight dat guy, good luck."

"I no like scrap da guy," I said. "I gon kill dat faggot rat for what he did to my friend. Da guy fucken Vili's wife too."

Amber said, sitting up straight, "No, no, no, Jesse."

I shouted, "You guys all fear him. I no scared him."

Dingo shouting over me, "You know how fucken linked up all Dos's family? You like dat kine action on us right now Jesse?"

Robby too looking all skeptic, trying to grab me.

But I walked right past him in to my room. Got my shoes, long sleeve black t-shirt and baggy jeans with big pockets. And the mask cap.

I lifted up my dresser. I felt for it. But there was jus the empty box of cartridges and one empty casing.

I went back out and stood in front of Robby, him trying to make like he never cared any more.

"Where you put um, Robby? I had da ting right in my room two weeks ago."

"What?" said Robby, sipping his beer, munching his pop corn.

"You know what—my chree five seven."

He said, "Jesse, you go do dis, you know you're on your own."

I said, "I gon bury dat fucka Kody tonight, with or without you."

Robby wiped his nose, stood up, went to his room.

After about two minutes he came back. He had a can of WD-40 with the red straw part still sticking out. Wrapped in a towel his Glock-9 he kept in the safe and he never let any one see.

He opened the slide, checked the sight, and showed me how you had to push in the safety. Then he wiped it down and handed it to me, his hand around the linen cloth.

It was way heavier than I thought and still greasy.

"Kay Jesse," he said. "You on your own now boy, you pay your own way. Dis one five hundred dollar piece. Da guy dat sold it to me said he called it in stolen. I gon charge you two hundred for da gun and clip. Da money now. And all da dope you got fronted. Any thing you leave in my house I gon trash um. Forget my name. I don know you."

"He told my chick I was dead," I said.

"I no care," said Robby. He burped. "Get how many guys looking for Kody? Da feds couldn't get him. One O.G. couldn't get him. But you go get him Jesse. You so fucken hard core. Get da fuck outa my house."

"Kay," I said. "I leave my bag on top da bed, every ting. If you wouldn't mind jus holding da fish tank for couple days."

"Fuck your fish," said Robby. "I gon eat your fish. Den I gon call up Dos, I gon tell him I never knowed you. You never was."

I went back to my room. I took my money. I left six bills on the bed and the dope and the scale. Robby like hundreds he always said.

I put the gun in the bag and fed my fish.

Robby had the TV on as I was walking to the door.

Then I stop.

"You guys," I said. "You gotta go out. One public place, one party. Some thing. Every body see you around, dat way every body know wasn't you guys. Was only me."

Mikey scratched his head hard, then looked at his fingers like I said some thing stupid.

"Was only you?" said Robby. "One public place? I go to da fucken main precinct, I turn myself in for witness protection, not gon matter, dey gon find me. You know how fucken linked up dat family?"

He finished the last half gulp of his beer and let go the bottle. It hit the floor and bounced on the wood without breaking.

After a while Mikey stood up and punched my shoulder. "Might as well do um right."

I knew he would come through for me but I had to tell him, "No Mikey, you gotta sit dis one out."

"Sit down Mikey," said Robby. "One big time dealer go missing, you know you da first guy every body gon think of. Plus you owe Dos money and you ducking how much warrants on you already. Dis fucka Jesse get one death wish, let him go. You and me go back before him. Stay here Mikey."

Robby turn back to the TV and say to me over his shoulder, "What for you waiting? Go, hurry up fore I fucken palm you."

I wait for a second before I say back, "Robby, you never wonder why Kody never challenge you?"

Amber sitting there all this time, never saying nothing, never taking her eyes off Robby.

He didn't look when he talked. "Bid-ness, Jesse. Dis one bid-ness."

"Or maybe cuz Kody know you da only fucka dat would bring him down."

Robby feared Kody, always did, I know dat cuz how his eyes get when he hear the name. But Robby like fear. He get that rush, like he enjoying it. Him and Kody was same same li'dat. They love it, the rush. That's why they was both legendary status, and they was both gon die young.

All of a sudden Robby stood up and put his arm around my shoulder and hugged me. He smiled, kissed me over the eye brow like the old school gangsters.

"You really thought I would let you go alone?" he said. "Come, get your shit, we go."

"You guys are nuts," said Dingo looking all sick. "Dat fucka Kody is game."

"We gon find out how game he is," said Robby.

Next thing we were out side and he was flying buckets in to the bed of the El Camino. He threw me the ski mask and the duct tape. "Put um in side your bag."

I heard some thing move on the porch. I looked up. Jus creeping out from around the pillars I saw the long red nails coming from the long fingers, then came the frilly hair, the nose, the small mouth. I read her lips, be careful.

Robby looked back over his shoulder and she went back in to hiding behind the pillar.

Robby held the cold Heineken against his head for his migraine. "Get in da car."

Chapter Twenty-Six

By Vili's wife's apartment get this one three tiered fountain with three bowls that was supposed to trickle down. But the fucka was shut down or maybe it never work. That's what it seem like. The only good the thing did was give one place for the kids to cruise and drink beer at night, sitting on the bottom tier. Tag um with spray cans. Give the tweakers a place to meet up on foot or bikes.

I think how prolly the politicians say eh, dis fountain gon fix up dis area, every thing, make nice. Dats what we need over here, trickling down.

But the water never trickle down like how they said, jus one big puddle rain water in the top.

We parking by the fountain in the dark, behind the long wire fence with vines and weeds across from the apartment.

"Second floor," I said. "203."

We could see the Expedition, but no body could really see us from that side.

We were in the old Honda we stole from Bay Town Golf Course parking lot. We left the El Camino by the old boarded up theater with the dumpster where we put Charlene.

The gun was in the bag between us on the seat and most of the coke was already in my nose. The window was fogged,

I guess it was pretty cold. I had to use my right nose cuz my left nose was all clog.

Robby kept telling me take it easy on the rails.

"No worry," I said, "I'm on it." One or two is good.

I poured the last of the coke in between my thumb and pointer finger and held it under my nose.

"You're on it like a chronic," said Robby, throwing his empty bottle out the window. It landed on a huge pile of leaves. Then he open the door and got it back. Prints.

Was one long ass wait until the police shift change. About five thirty a.m. we would get ready.

Even though that was the best way I was hoping the fucka Kody would hop out earlier. This waiting was killing me.

Worst case, if Kody made it to the Expedition, I was suppose to drive out through the fence and block the truck in, den start shooting up the wind shield.

Robby kept shaking his leg trying to concentrate. His eyes never looking away from the 203 door for more than one look at any thing.

"Kay Jesse," he said. "Dis guy gon start talking fast once we get him. Fuck him. He dead already."

Another half hour then–

"Oh no, look," said Robby. "Side road special ova dere."

I looked at the lady standing under the street light in a jean skirt and sweater by the parking lot.

"Too early," I said. "She no look like da type."

"I dunno," said Robby. "Either way, dats your witness right dere."

Some places you see tweaker women walking on the side of the road, real certain places, certain times. Hoping some tweaker guy or some drunk ass driving by would see them and like party. Mikey said most time they would know each other already. Tweaker community.

Robby hopped out the door and took out his money in the rubber band. She came over by us.

Robby peeled off three twenties. "How's every thing tonight, Aunty? You safe? You feeling good, or you feeling sick in side?"

"Good, good," she said. "Could always be betta."

She had all the signs. All skin and bones. Teeth all fucked up. Clammy hands where the drug comes out your skin. Could be Amber in fifteen years.

Robby handed her the sixty bucks and told her, "Go eat. Go enjoy. Whateva. But no come back down dis side. No good dis road, kay, Aunty?"

She took the money like she didn't even need it, leaning for ward, looking at me. Poor lady, her mind not breathing too good any more.

"Jehova," she said.

"What?" I said.

"What?" she said.

She laughed at me and left, muttering to herself, walking by the fountain, shouting back so the block could hear, "Dat God's name boy."

Another hour went by and by now I was sweating through my shirt, drug sweat.

Robby gave a groan. "No way," he said, and he put the beer against his head.

The lady in the jean skirt had walked back up past the fountain.

"Cuz, what she doing?" I said.

She looked all high. She was prolly out already again. That was fast. In one drought too. Her jus walking up the road. Couldn't hold still. She would prolly soldier around like that the rest of the night.

Robby was gonna go say some thing. But then the door to 203 opened.

The yellow diamonds. The long black Ecko shirt. The pink skin. The white scar. The Guccis shades even, on one dark night.

He stretched his back, stretched his shoulders, he looked every where, at every car in the lot and the cars across the street. He even looked where we were, behind the fence under the tree. But he wouldn't recognize this Honda. Then his slippers going down the stairs, the sound slap slap back and forth off the two sides of the building, on to the side walk.

Robby looked over the steering wheel with his hand slowly opening the door handle.

The door to 203 opened again and Vili's wife came out and whistled. She threw his other pants down over the balcony and they landed in his arms.

"I don't gotta go, you know?" he said up to her. "I can play nice."

She gave him the meanest look. She went in side and it was so quiet you could hear the door lock.

He put his hands in his arm pits cuz the air was wet and cold, walking to the Expedition, watching the tweaker lady.

He called to the lady, "Ho! Sup?"

She walked over the street, up to the parking lot by him.

"How much for half hour, Aunty?" he said.

Robby pulled the mask down over his face, took off his slippers and swung out of the car. I saw him in the rear view mirror, running around the fence, up the side walk without making any sound.

"I get my car right hea," said Kody. He bumped the Expedition with his elbow. "I get my whistle too if you like dat kine."

Robby ducked in the shadow behind the first car in the parking lot.

Only I knew the lady saw him.

She saw me too some how, but she just looked like what she was, paranoid, crazy. She started backing up.

"Short time," Kody said. "Short time only."

I'd say it was about four and a half seconds.

Robby got his bare foot up as high as his chin and kicked once. The plastic on the Guccis sun glasses broke and flew spinning in air before Kody's head hit the door of the Expedition. He bounced off and landed right in to Robby's left fist. His fore arms went over his head trying to block. Then the knee, and after every thing landed and the face opened his arms just flopped to the side.

I jumped the fence with the duct tape.

I forgot to put the mask down until I crossed the road but the tweaker lady had already ran away.

Kody was lying on his back, Robby's knees on his arms, fingers and thumbs on his wind pipe, choking. The legs kicking, me trying to hold them down. And the tape going verp verp wrapping over and over around the ankles. The bleach blond head with the streak of blood that looked brown in the light. Eye brows spreading up and wide over the fore head. Eyes wide open, looking up so much you could just see the bottom of the pupil, looking in the holes of my mask. He knew it was me. Sup Kody?

The nose and cheeks getting huge trying to suck breaths when we got the tape over his mouth. Then the legs stopped. Then I got the hands with the tape, verp verp.

Robby opened the back door to the Expedition and we pitched him in. Robby pushed the legs half down the seat, took the keys, ran to the driver's door, going ding ding ding.

By now some of the doors up stairs started to open, but the Expedition was already down the road and I jumped the fence back to the Honda on the other side of the vines. I tried three times and finally got it going.

I flew it down the road trying to catch the Expedition, street lights on both sides flying past. Robby turned his blinker on, waiting for me before he turned off and took a back road and I followed him.

I heard the cop sirens going the other way.

I was still too amped up on nerves and coke to realize it really happened. Not until I wondered who was going to be the first one to tell Vili.

Robby knew one spot perfect for dis. Up in the valley, one off road up in to a trail area. The Civic hardly never even made it up behind um.

I wen turn off the car and check around. I never seen any body. Just Kody and Robby with the gun on him.

Robby threw him to the ground and I wen kick him right in the face. "Ho, wassup Kody?"

I just lost it, I kicked him in the head. I could feel all the vibrations of his skull all the way up my leg, he down there in the dirt with the broken glass and gravel.

He start for look up at me all hard from the ground so I threw one hand full of dirt in his eyes.

Robby was just watching it, loving it. I no tink he ever seen me get that nuts before.

Kody sat up and wiped the dirt out of his eyes and shook his head and spit blood out his mouth.

Robby gave me the gun. "Eh Jesse, if he try stand up, no hesitate, just go blass um."

And he went over to the Expedition and cut the gas line so could torch it.

Kody said to me through the blood in his mouth, "You know you dead too. You tink you just gon walk out of here like nothing. I get outa here I going kill you, kill your moms, kill all your friends."

Robby coming back. "Get outa here, you Kody? No worry already, you gon die."

He turn to me. "Kay Jess. Dis your beef. Put dis fucka out. One shot."

I lined up right with Kody's head.

Kody started for make a kiss mouth at me. "You not gon shoot shit, Jesse. You one fucken fairy."

I froze one second, two seconds, five.

Robby took the gun from me. "I got one better idea. No use da gun. Why leave rounds? We keep bot guns dis way."

He held the gun on Kody, tossed me his lighter to go torch the Expedition, and he push Kody in to the Civic.

I lit the pool of gas and ran to the car.

I drove, Robby in the back with Kody. He made Kody sit on his knees with his head on the seat, that way Robby could shoot him quicker if he try some thing, plus just in case we pass any body Kody no can signal for help.

I light up dis joint, smoking make me feel better. Robby took the joint and put um in Kody's mouth, him with his head down in the seat. "Here. Take two hits before you die." Kody spit at him.

The lookout on the mountain was where Robby said.

We wen drive by couple times in case of cops, then we wen park on the other side of the road where no body could see, and we made Kody walk all the way up the trail. It was cold, my hand holding the gun right to the back of his head was cold, the gun was cold, and I had a little shake in my arm.

We got to this one spot where was jus one straight fall all the way down the cliff.

Robby was fuckin around, telling Kody he should write one suicide note.

Then he ask me too, "What you tink Jesse? You tink da fall gon kill him or what?"

"I no can say," I said.

"Cuz I heard dis one guy wen jump off here and da fucka live. You heard dat before Jesse?"

"I heard dat, yeah."

Robby start slapping Kody's back.

"You gon live, you know Kody? Yah, I tink so bu, for a while any way. Probly couple hours, broke leg, broke neck, yelling out. No body gon hear you but. Jus wait, da red ants gon munch on your nuts bra."

Then he push Kody right to the edge. "Time for walk da plank."

Robby grabbed my arm and pulled me towards Kody. The wind was nuts up there.

"What, Kody," said Robby. "Any last words?"

Kody looked at me, face all bashed, eyes blood shot. "Yah. See you soon."

Just one little push.

And I couldn't do it.

"Jesse," said Robby.

But I couldn't.

Robby pulled me back and kicked Kody off the cliff.

Kody tried to grab Robby's leg, take him with him, but it just slipped off.

He never yell either. Sounded like he hit pretty hard on some thing, then the bushes.

I love you Vili.

Chapter Twenty-Seven

I thought Kapika's door would be locked. I even waited jus a second, but it opened. I took off my shirt and it felt good to take off my shoes.

I thought she might be asleep. But when she really sleep it's always mouth open, drooling, snoring like one chain saw.

When she felt the hands on her back I saw the little smile. She pulled my arm over her. Then she opened her eyes and saw the red letters on the clock, 4:18. She looked at my hand in the red light.

"Is there something you wanna tell me?" she said.

I remembered to keep breathing the same pace. "Sorry. I was drunk earlier."

"You smell like dope." I saw her nostrils moving.

She took my arm and turned back around. After a while she clicked the light on and rubbed her eyes, looking at me.

I held up my right hand and said, "I'm a changed man." And I meant it.

"Okay," she said finally. She turned back around with the neck on the arm. She smiled. "You are, yah? You're changing?"

She pulled my top hand down on her stomach.

I said it again. "I am change."

I couldn't smell her shampoo, my nose was still clogged with cocaine. I took my hand off her stomach and laid on my back watching the fan blades spin. Still thinking drug thoughts. Kody thoughts. Then Charlene thoughts. The weight of my shape going in to the mattress, and the mattress pressing back.

I'm a changed man.

Chapter Twenty-Eight

Over at the house Mikey was saying not to hide out, that gon make it more obvious, we gotta make like we don't know. He told Robby go out, ask around about Kody, that way word get back to Dos guys.

Robby looked over the rail, hazy sun set up the mountain, with the house phone on speaker phone and us sitting dead quiet, Robby calling up every one until this guy swore on his baby sista's life was Dos got Kody.

"No fuck around?" said Robby.

The guy said all serious, "I no shit you. Was Dos dem. Guarantee."

We was all rolling.

Robby even call up Dos and tell him he heard it was guys from this one other crew in town that got Kody.

After he hung up the phone we all laughed cuz Robby got all in to it.

"Dos don't know shit," he said. He slapped me in my head, smiling. "I think you got lucky dis time Jesse."

Next Friday me and Mikey and Dingo was going the fights with Killas guys. Robby already knocked two of the guys fighting that night so he was staying in with Amber, watch movie. Yah, really? No, not really.

Mikey and Dingo was in the car already arguing over some thing. Them two never get along. Total opposites.

Robby had his arm holding on the top of the door way, could see his coarse arm pit hairs, the beer in his other hand.

I told him, "Tell Amber move in already."

Robby sipped his beer and looked down. "I already tell her dat. She said we'll see."

"We'll see what?" I said.

"We'll see if can . . . you know . . . be one good boy friend to her."

"Boy friend?" I said.

"Yah you," he said. "I told her if she slow down on da dope, may be quit even. I told her I quit. I try and help her get her kids back. I dunno. She say da dick belong to her now."

I laughed my ass off. "Whateva happen to girls all scandalous? Fuck da system? You gon get one job too?"

"Why?" said Robby. "You gon end up with Kapika afta she pop out da kid. Your family gon take you back too, you give dem gran child. Your girl, she just testing you Jesse. And one girl li'dat? She not gon wait for ever. But you do good, she gon give you one kid whether you like him or not." He waited a while. "It would be different if never was for da ice. If your chick can hook you up one job bra, take da job. Take all da hours you can get. I get me one job and–you never know Jesse, one day we could be old men given lickens to da kids for da same fucked up shit we did. Think about every ting dat happen since you live here. You like your son doing dis kine shit?"

I tell him, "How come you always tink you know what I tinking?"

"Cuz dats why, you not dat smart." He slap my back. "Now get da fuck outa here."

But just as I was leaving Amber came up totally naked. I tried not to look but I couldn't help. She put her hands around Robby's waist and hugged him from behind with her face against his back smiling at me. She always messing with me.

"Jesse-got-a-girl-friend," she said in the sing song voice. "I couldn't wait for you for ever."

"You really think you can keep dis guy on lock down?" I said smiling.

"Eh," said Robby. "How come you guys tink I da one gon fuck around. What about her fucken ass?"

Amber squeezed Robby around his rib cage. "You talk like that in front our boy Jesse?"

"You not his mom," said Robby. "You just da girl he never wanted. Get outa here Jess, I take care your left overs."

Was one mean fight too, at Dole Cannery. MMA East Side verse West Side. East Side took plenty fights. Was so loud, all the crowds. They get some game fuckas from West Side.

There was only one thing Mikey notice. Dos wasn't there. Usually he never miss one fight, not one East Side West Side. I thought Mikey would be happy he never have to see da fucka, he still owe da eight grand.

Chapter Twenty-Nine

When we got home the Toyota was gone and no more Amber. We saw her bag. We finally found her, all smoked out, hiding under Robby's bed all paranoid.

She told us Robby went to go store. She found the dope he was hiding from her and she started smoking as soon as he left. Half hour later she called. His phone was off. She call again, phone still off, now she don't know how long.

"What store?" said Mikey.

"I dunno," she said. Her arms crossed over her stomach. She was so high. "He went for cigarettes."

We got in the El Camino and went to the liquor store down the block and ask the guy if he seen Robby, he knows who Robby is.

"Yah," said the guy. "He leave long time ago. Chree hour."

"He was good?" said Mikey.

"Good," said the guy. The guy look all sick too. I know him and Robby would always joke around.

Mikey's mouth made the clicking noise. His mind going in to over drive. Already I could tell from looking at him this wasn't good. Then finally he looked at me with the coldest look I ever saw him give, like it was my fault.

"Here," he said, and he wen work the surveillance video, winding back.

He turned the screen from the camera for us to see. Some body's hand reached up and put gum on the lens, but it didn't cover the whole thing. The picture was all fuzzy and the film only went in two second jumps. We jus saw some guy in a white shirt and a beanie walk out of the picture by the driver side of the Toyota that was hidden by the gum.

Then Robby came out the store heading toward the truck. For the longest time nothing happened. It almost looked like the truck moved from in side. Then an old grey car went past, could have been an Intrigue or even a Town Car. The Toyota flashed its lights and followed the grey car out.

There was the gum on the lens, the lights flashing. You couldn't really say anything happened, it jus never look good.

The store guy's face was jus like Mikey's. "Call police?"

Mikey nodded. "Yah. I give you one direct line numbah I know."

I watched Mikey write on the receipt, he drop the pen twice. You knew it was bad if Mikey said call police.

Two days later Killas called up Dingo's phone that Mikey was using now cuz Dingo was too drunk.

Mikey jus nodded and hung up. Then he looked at me and started clicking his lips, then he took a deep breath.

"What?" I said.

It was about six in the afternoon when we all got down the road to the dump. We passed the field with the kids flying kites and the remote control planes buzzing around.

We parked past the telephone pole marked 43 by a rusted up side down shopping cart.

I ran. I ran over the kiawe branches and dead wood. My slipper fell off and I let the other one go when I ran up the embankment through the tire marks in the clearing, through the bushes. I ran down the slope past the monkey pod trees following the tire marks, the dirt bike marks.

It was in the field by all the scrapped cars. The blue Toyota truck. Torched, right next to the burned out black Expedition.

Mikey and Dingo came up.

"Jesse, they got him," said Dingo. All the fat in his face sagging.

"He could jus be fucken wit us," I said, hearing myself, not believing.

Mikey jus eyeing me out.

"What, Mikey?" I said.

Mikey just eyeing me out under his hood.

Chapter Thirty

I cannot remember what really happened the week after. I remember this or that, but not all together. I know I told Kapika Robby went missing. For good. She said, oh my gosh. She jus said come home. I said I had to stay with the guys for a while. She said okay, call when you're ready.

Then she said, "Please call me. Please don't do anything stupid, Jesse. Please. Please. Please."

After that I jus got texts for couple days. I didn't pick up her calls.

Soon enough all these random fuckas started showing up at the house. Guys from Dingo's distant family. Some of Robby's old friends, but mostly fake friends, saying fake things like he was like one big bro to me.

That's why I came down here with Mikey, in the garage. I figure I been up for two days already smoking rock I might as well.

Only me and Dingo knew the combo to the safe, but Robby never kept his savings in there, if he had any the bookies didn't get. I know Mikey was hoping dat, cuz Dos called for Mikey the day before.

Saying he was sorry when he heard about Robby. Heard. He said he lost a good friend too, even if Robby must have had it coming to him. He said we all lost enough friends already. But he still gon need the eight grand from Mikey, jus on principle. He cannot have his own guys knowing that some one never paid.

"You gon get paid," Mikey told him. Then they hung up.

Up stairs I could hear every body moving, the feet on the wood floor moving around like old drunks. Every once in while the voices coming through the floor in to the garage like low murmurs. By the porch I could hear the birds chirpin around, prolly waiting for their hamburger bun like Robby always gave um around this time. They never figure out yet Robby wasn't coming back.

The flame on Mikey's face. Both of us sweating. The garage door was down with jus a little day light coming through. No windows. Sitting on buckets. Mikey's shoes crunching around on the pipe I broke. His face all red.

I told him, "How much times I gotta say I sorry about da pipe, Mikey?"

There was broken glass all over the floor from the second time he tried to melt it for me and I dropped it. Glass every where, hundred dollars worth of ice still in side. He almost killed me but I went and got him the last of all the dope we had, only about two grams, and I told him we smoke it all until it's gone.

Mikey blasted the flame on the blow torch and it made the hissing gas flame sound. Making the new pipe. He smacked the end of it. Made the hole in the top. He held it over the fan jus for a second. If the glass cools too fast it cracks. When it was still orange it collapsed from in side and sagged.

Mikey shook his head. He was off his game too. I never seen him shook li'dis.

Worse, he blamed me for every thing, he just didn't show it.

He put the pipe down on the towel and got the sheet of tin foil. He folded it. Unfolded it. Folded again until there was a small crease down the middle of the diamond shape. He put a small pinch of the crystals in to the middle. Up stairs I heard some body fall down. I was looking up but Mikey just sat there looking at me, not saying any thing. Holding the foil.

"Wait," I told him. "Tell me again."

I still never took my first real hit of ice my whole life.

"Follow da smoke down da foil," said Mikey. He handed me this hard thick empty plastic pen. "Slow."

He heated the crystals from under the foil with the lighter. When you look from out side the pipe it looks like the dope is black grey when it melts. But when it's in the foil you can see it turns white, then to bubbling liquid, then smoke.

"Breat soff, soff," said Mikey, sweat drips down his fore head from his short buzz hair. "Follow da smoke."

I breathed too much and I was out of breath. I blew out. I breathed again from the beginning, slow, more slow then I would have thought. Letting the smoke build. Small holes starting to burn in the foil.

"Slower," said Mikey, all piss off. Then, "Kay, go."

I sucked deep in to my chest like was weed, even though you not sposed to. The draw was clean. It felt pure. The sour sweet taste. I watched the small white stream leave.

"I never caught um again?" I said.

He jus sat there watching me like I was stupid for wasting dope. But it was my dope and he knew it.

I got up and got the dust pan. I swept up all the glass. The sound of it, more shattering when it landed in the trash.

Then I got the Windex and sprayed the head lights of the El Camino. So much shit around here needed cleaning. Then I started putting tools away. I started getting the table all organized while he smoked his turn, me wondering why I couldn't feel any thing yet. Did I feel any thing?

Mikey just shook his head. "Jesse," he said. "Watch and learn."

I sat down on the bucket. He ran the flame up and down the foil.

For him the smoke seemed to jus cloud, shrink and disappear in to the tube. None of it got away.

I held the pen again. I tried what he did.

Small breaths, not too much, little by little. This time when I let it out I saw my first cloud. It drifted up and spread out along the roof.

"Dere," said Mikey. "Now." Jus watching my eyes. Watching my mouth open. "Mean ah, da dope?"

I remember thinking, all this time I was lied to. I get it now.

Here's what they don't want you to know and I don't want to tell you.

If God made one more pure thing than that first peak of clear he kept it for him self.

Forget your first time. Forget what's her name, she made the sun shine. Forget that guy was supposed to be for ever, who? Forget when your kid said dad for the first time.

That was da old world, your old life, the old you.

You just cracked out your shell.

Taste air for the first time.

You just got born again.

You just put on your cape.

Before you never like the smell. Now your mouth water. One more rip. One more bing. One more blast. That white stream. That hard knock. That speed burst. That turbo charge. And the little prickles.

You can hear every thing. Every thing zoomed in, tweaker vision. This is the real world, that other world was the lie. This is the more real world.

Put your mouth on that glass. That fire hose. That devil's dick. That crisp rip. The hard knock. No fear. No pain. Jus clear. Until each breath is clear, clear. And each heart pump is clear, clear.

I don't remember every thing. I remember when I was getting to the end of it. Mid night by the H-3 over pass. Parked off the road in the high grass. The cars flying by on free way over us.

Bottles all over the ground. Mikey was taking a piss. Four weeds different heights in the breeze, like a family on a mid night stroll.

I was on my knees, hunched in to the car, looking through the sand on the floor under the pedals for one last crumb of sea crest, that little crystal.

I loaded it, I took the pipe, burning it. Sucking for any thing left.

"Gone, Jesse," said Mikey. "You smoking glass."

I breathed out. I thought I could see a faint trail of smoke. But by now I seeing stuff. Things moved around. I would get up and not know why. Sit down. Get up again.

"Jess," said Mikey. "Hold my hand."

I sat down in the seat. I tried to close my eyes. I could hear my heart beat in my ears. Wondering if I was still made of flesh and blood, cuz it no feel that way any more. The drug playing tug of war in side. It didn't want to go away.

Then I remembered. I had money at the house. I could buy.

When we got back every body there was about the same thing as us. Getting smoked outa their mind. Make the pain go away again.

Chapter Thirty-One

I heard some thing and stopped what I was doing and looked up. The clock by Robby's bed said 4:47. The naked blonde girl was under the sheets.

"Jesse?" she said. "Why do you keep calling me Charlene? Who is Charlene?"

I heard some thing under the bed. It was moving too. I put my hand over Charlene's mouth.

"Sh," I said. "I gon get dis fucka."

The girl pulled my hand away. "Jesse, you're scaring me. Let me go, please."

I put my hand over her mouth again.

"Shut up," I said under my breath. "You can leave afta. Not safe right now."

I put my feet over the edge one by one and tip toed to the safe. I spun the dial. I tried four times before I finally remember the code. I took the Glock out and it was lighter than I remembered. I knew Dos was under the bed. Before he was in the closet and the day before that he was on the roof. Jus waiting for the right moment.

I dropped down on my stomach holding the gun with both hands under the bed.

"Ah!" A girl's voice shouting.

Two huge eyes looking out from under all the frilly hair. Amber. She looked small wearing Robby's huge white sweat shirt. She smelled like piss.

"Jesse," she said, all panicking. "Thank god."

She took my arm and pulled me under the bed. "Your legs too. Quick. Hurry."

I got under the bed and I saw the blonde girl's feet on the floor. Her hands picked up her clothes and she ran out and slammed the door.

"Jesse," said Amber, holding on to me. "They're coming for me." Breathing fast. "Do you have a bolt cutter? Kay, kay, thank god. Go climb up da pole out side. We have to cut da power to da house before dey get here."

"Who?" I said.

"Dem," she said. "Dey want my babies, Jesse." Her eyes so wide open, looking out from under the bed. "What day is it?"

I didn't know. But I know she'd been under there since Robby, felt like for ever ago.

I told her, "Amber, no body's coming. You jus tweaking out like me."

"No Jesse," she said. "Dey always wanted my babies. Dey took my babies, Jesse, dey took my babies."

She cried and reached around me, slow panting, my head against the top half of Robby's sweat shirt. Stroking my buzz hair. Scratching my head.

I felt shame for the first time. I was still in my dirty drawers. At least she get clothes even if she piss her self.

"Dere on top da bed, Jesse," said Amber. "I heard them. One guy and one girl."

When one person gets paranoid it makes the other person normal again. And only one way to deal with some body sketching out this bad, you have to take them seriously until they figure it out on their own.

I told her, "I get um for you, kay?"

I got out from under the bed and pointed the gun at the pillows. I picked up the sheets and threw them, they hit the door and slid down.

"No body here," I said. "We safe."

She back away under the bed, wide eyes. "You're lying."

"I never lie to you. Come out, see for your self."

I lifted her out from under the bed and she looked all around the room. Jus all Robby's shirts hanging in the closet. I threw them on the ground. I knocked over all his jewelry on the computer desk. His watch. All ten thousand of his porns, hitting the floor one by one.

"See?"

After a while her eye lids came back down. "Sorry."

"Nah," I said, "I was losing it too for a while."

She touched my neck, all over my neck. All the hickeys.

"She marked you pretty good, Jesse," she said.

"It jus happened," I said.

For the longest time we sat on the floor against the wall, not saying nothing.

"Can I ask you a question?" she said. "You remember your birthday? Dat first time I came. How come you didn't want me, Jesse? Was it because I'm old?"

"I did want you." After a while I told her, "Maybe I jus wanted to be da one guy dat didn't try and fuck you."

She leaned in on my shoulder and reached under my arm until our arms were like an old couple. And Charlene wasn't there.

"Jesse, you gotta go back to your girl now," she said. "Don't ever come back here. Don't answer your phone, not even if it's me. Jus go. And tell her every thing. Every thing from da day you was born and tell her you done with it now."

"I can't tell her every thing,"

"Every thing," said Amber. "It's da only way. But she'll forgive you. Dat girl loves you, Jesse, you get one big forgive as long as she hear it from you, and den never again. Go now, hurry before you start coming down again and we end up smoking together."

Smoking with Amber, jus the thought, and I knew what she meant, it made that good bad shiver all over.

She went in to her bag, took out some pills for me and I swallowed them right away. Whatever pills she had they were always the best. Better than Mikey's.

"Go back to your girl," she said. "Remember–every thing. Promise me."

She took a bunch of Robby's shirts and sweaters under the bed with her. She made a pillow and blanket out of them.

Jus as I got to the door she yelled for me.

"Don't remember me like dis," she said. "I used to be–"

"Pff," I said. "Nuff. Quiet."

What I really was trying for say was, you still are, girl.

"Why didn't you ever want to know my real name, Jesse?" she said.

I smiled. "I already know your real name."

She put her fingers in her cheeks, making fun of my dimples again.

I reversed down the drive way. I had to drive over the side walk and knock over the mail box jus to go around the cars.

I couldn't figure out why this guy in a Nissan was driving on the wrong side of the road. After he honked I figured it out. Was me.

I pulled over on a side street and parked until the pills started to kick in.

I realized it was going to be Christmas in a few weeks.

Chapter Thirty-Two

It was seven in the morning when I got to Kapika's. I sat out side the gate on the side walk, hiding behind a parked car so the neighbors out jogging wouldn't see the chronic in their neighbor hood. The red flowers hanging over the gate. But I was jus staring in to the ground. Zoning.

I remember after the first time she made me go beach with her. The red flowers behind her. Hosing the last of the sand off her feet, in her bathing suit. Then looking back. "What?" she said. She knew. She smiled.

I started to see all these black bugs flying around. I would close my eyes and when I opened them they'd go away for a while then come back. I couldn't stop scratching. I smelled my own smell.

I felt a hand come around my shoulder. A cold bottle of water rested on my arm.

"I thought you left for good," said Kapika.

I looked down. Her eyes looked at the hickeys. She smiled, but different.

"I'm so sorry about Robby," she said, still looking at the hickeys. She took her hand off my back. "I have to ask. Jesse, did you break up with me? I had the strangest feeling all this time that you were breaking up with me."

I shook my head. Then said right out, "I smoked ice with Mikey. I cheated on you. Da only time. I didn't know what I was doing. I never wanna get high again."

"With Amber?" she said, all still.

"No," I said. "Just some stupid girl was at da house."

She let out a deep breath like she was relieved.

"So," she said. "We're together?"

"I don't know," I said. "If you still want."

I leaned down and she held me around the neck. She kissed the back of my neck. I could feel her nose smelling the other girl on me. "Let's get you inside before dad comes back. He runs now in the morning."

She took me in her room and laid me down and told me to sleep, not to worry any more, that's why we have each other. She said she had some thing to tell me too.

"You gon dump me den," I said.

"No," she said. She smiled. Then she looked sad. "I can't have babies, Jesse. I knew when I met you."

"But you told me—"

"I told you what you wanted to hear. I lied to you because I thought you wouldn't want me. I always knew what you wanted. I can't give it to you, baby. You can't have one with me. That's why I waited to tell. Maybe not right away, but you would have left me."

The worst part is I don't know if she was wrong. I wouldn't have thought of her the same. But now it all seems so small.

"Do you still—" she said, letting the hair fall around her face, hiding.

I pulled her up by the arm. "It's not even a big deal to me."

I kissed her. After a while we both laughed a little. Amber's pills coming on, I felt almost normal for a couple more hours.

The next two days was me getting ice feelings, and the yelling came from Kapika.

She said I gotta throw away the phone. Get a new number. She said if I ever cheat again it's over. If I ever smoke any kine dope it's over. She said I couldn't drink until she tells me I can.

"I can't ever see you like that again," she said.

She told me never go back to that house. Keep the car, leave every thing else. She said for Christmas I would get all new clothes. She would take me out shopping for them of course. As mad as she was, that part she sounded happy.

Then mad again, she told me I can't ever call my friends, they can't come by her house.

"Know what, Jesse?" she said. "No worry. I'll tell them for you," And she did. I heard her on the phone telling Mikey off, "I no give a shat, kay?"

I felt like when I was little boy and my mom was giving scoldings to the bullies for me.

When ever I had done some thing wrong I knew Kapika blamed Robby, she never blame me. Like I was her own kid. I was kind of her kid I guess. May be I finally figure that out, figure her and me out.

"Never again?" she said.

"Never," I said.

Chapter Thirty-Three

Up the mountain, the volcanic sun set over the park. A long weaving road through pine forest, De Luca driving, Rawlings shotgun, Janice in the back seat, no one talking. Past a Board of Water Supply station, to a gate in a wire fence, with a broken lock hanging to the side. The road ended there.

They got out, Janice holding Charlene's teddy bear. Rawlings opened the trunk and took out a long canvas sack.

There was a small path that split in two, a higher and a lower. They took the lower. Janice said the voice on the phone said that was the one.

Janice was walking ahead, shakily. She recited to herself–go about half a mile through the pine trees, then look for a white coral block.

She saw it and stopped. Rawlings took her arm; she shrugged him loose. "Let her go first," said De Luca, and he and Rawlings hung back.

The dirt around the coral block looked like it might have been patted down, pine needles and cones scattered on it.

Janice knelt, put her hand out, then pulled back. She stood, swayed, and caught herself. She closed her eyes. "I've got to see. God knows I don't want to. But I've got to."

De Luca said, "It's going to take a while. Why don't you go rest?"

Janice nodded. "I'll be praying. I have to believe–"

De Luca put his hand on her shoulder. "We'll be praying for you."

She walked away, hugging the teddy bear.

Rawlings said, "Let's do it."

He stooped and opened the canvas sack and took out the two shovels.

They did not speak while they were digging. The wind was making slow sighs in the pines, every so often a hushed whistle. The dirt was loose. They eased their shovels into it carefully. The deeper they went the slower they worked, spading up only a few clods at a time, squatting to brush with their hands, until Rawlings uncovered the hand with the mood ring, green, on the index finger.

In the car on the way back De Luca said nothing, Rawlings either.

Janice sat stonefaced. Then, "He's going to have to give me Jesse. He wanted four separate checks made to cash, and he gave me an address, one of those mail drop places. I told him I would be sending them one at a time, and when he cashed the first one I stopped the others. He's going to have to give me Jesse."

Chapter Thirty-Four

One word guys say some times is "clean."

You know when you were born you didn't crave poisons. So you think one day, may be, you not gon crave any more. You wrong. Like Robby said, the cravings never really goes away.

Jus when you think you past it you start getting angry for no reason. You see other people out drinking. You tell your self it's not that great, drinking with friends, with strangers, getting high. But you know you lying. You know it was the best part of your life and if it's over now then what the fuck you got left to live for?

My phone would be buzzing, Kapika texting, HANG IN THERE! pikabu. I WISH I WAS HOME! pikabu. MUH! MUH! MUH! I LOVE YOU! I LOVE YOU! I LOVE YOU! pikabu.

But you can't quit for any body else. If you do you jus gon fuck up and bring them down with you.

I couldn't sleep good but I never really felt awake.

Being sober is like being high. Nothing looks the way it's supposed to. Nothing ever feels right.

Most of all you have to face this stranger. This boring sorry cowardly fucka wearing your clothes.

Even your girl think you boring, she jus don't tell you that. You try and fake your self back to your old self but then the old cravings come too.

The more sober you get the more you remember. I really did that? No way, what the fuck was I thinking? I'm never drinking again. And an hour later you jus stop your self walking in to the liquor store.

You used to lean on drugs to make the hurt go away, and it worked. Now you just fall on your face. I remembered what Robby said. Be a man. Handle your pain.

I mow the lawn for Kapika's dad. I take care the cars. Change oil. I go to inter views. I watch basket ball with the dad. I even go back to the courts I went to as a kid with my basket ball. I get in the water. Feeling the salt, coming up from deep water, breathing air after. But still yet in the deep water with me is hammer head thoughts. Kody. Charlene. I never tell Kapika about Charlene and Kody.

Ater two weeks I was getting up when it was still dark. The dad told me I was one bus ass worker the way I take care the yard and the cars. And I don't owe rent. If any thing he owe me.

He said I should come run with him in the morning. I wanted to tell him to go get fucked, but I figure he letting me crash, so I came with him couple times, feeling like a queer, watching the sun come up. I had to make myself so tired at night I fell right to sleep.

May be, may be, day by day running, playing ball, breathing good again, I was starting to believe there was some thing else. Some things I forgot long time ago. The dad was still a prick, but jus because that fucka don't know as much as he think he does, doesn't mean he don't know some shit too.

Chapter Thirty-Five

The day before Christmas Eve, in the El Camino, driving through town. All the stores with their green and red decorations.

I spent the morning at Macy's looking for one gift for my sista Shelly even though I wasn't invited to the wedding or the pre Christmas party. Fuck it. I was gon crash the party, see what they doing for the after party. And bring gift, cuz if I jus give money I look like one drug dealer.

Dwayne, my cousin the ex-chronic, called me up the day before. He told me I should come by, show face, even if they never like see my face. Even that fucka Dwayne was gon be at the wedding and my own sista neva invite me.

I guess Dwayne jus got out re hab. He trying to be dad with his baby now li'dat, so my family like help him out. Me, they jus remember I got arrested over that fucken moped. They think I'm the chronic.

Kapika wanted to help me cuz she like her shopping. But I know she gon want come to my house after, meet my family. She never really believe that my family jus cut the line on me, my sista Shelly neva even tell me she getting married. I tell her my dad is one strick fucka.

At da party I jus like see the guy going be Shelly's husband, dats all. Make sure he see me, jus one time, so he know dat I there for my sista.

In Macy's I was about to say nuff already cuz I couldn't find any good gifts.

Then I seen.

I couldn't believe they still sold um even, same place, every thing. Then I knew I had to go to the party. I had to give Shelly this gift, if even jus for that.

The Macy's lady wen gift wrap um for me too, free. She could tell I was all charged. It couldn't have been more perfect, I was jus wondering if my sista would remember. That was long time ago.

The house was different from how I remember. But our house was the nicest on the street cuz my dad would always work on it. I could tell now he jus put one fresh coat of paint on the fence. Probably for the wedding. We had one decent size yard behind the fence and I could smell the barbecue already. Kapena playing on the radio. The sound of ice poured in to a cooler.

It's not like I could jus roll up with shades or nothing. I was trying for think of one fake job for tell my dad just in case he ask. Termite, I was thinking, I could bull shit about termite pest control.

Every thing look so small in the front of my dad's house. My dad land scaped the whole front lawn, put gravel, plumerias, and the red flowers had at Pika's house. But I guess he never bother to take down the can on the string hanging from the tree. The one I used to shoot with my pellet gun. All rusted now.

Walking up the path with the gravel all the sleeping grass closed around me. That's how I figure my family was gonna be too.

The party was loud. Then every thing came quiet, the gate creaking when I came through and every body just look and stare at me in the over size aloha shirt I borrowed from Kapika's dad.

Was about twenty five, thirty people there. They looked at me, then down and away. They was all sitting at these six round tables, had to be rented. It got so quiet all you could hear was He Aloha Mele playing on the radio. There was color paper and napkins and balloons. They going all out for my sista.

There I was walking past all my family, thinking I never back down in one fight before, but I might run from these old folks.

But then I seen Gummybear and her boy Bobby. She let him go and he came running up and grab my leg. I surprise he even remember me he came so big now.

"Uncle Jesse! Uncle Jesse!" It took one little kid dat never knew better for any body talk to me. He start throwing little combos like how I taught him before, yelling boom bam boom.

"Who taught you for do dat?" I said.

Gummybear came over and kiss me in front every body, jus to show them she no care if they hate me. She look so pretty with her dress and the flower in her left ear now, oh!

"Introduce," I said.

She wave the boy friend over. He look like one scrub, but hey, he like my sista, good enough. He get one cock eye, small kine, but more better for catch your own back.

Gummybear was never the type to make statements, took some thing for her come up, kiss me in front every body. She jus stand there with me, giggling.

All this time too I could feel my dad. I never look right at him yet but I knew him and my sista Shelly and my mom was all by the grill making plate for every body. No body knew exactly what to do about me crashing the party.

I heard my dad mumble and my mom telling him real soft, "Dats your son."

I was feeling a lot of heat coming from that grill, and I never like be where I not wanted. So I figure I give Shelly the gift and leave, be one gentle man. I walked the gift up to her.

"Here you go sis," I said.

"Thanks," she said, real business like. No kiss, no nothing. She look so old I swear I never would recognize her. Her face and the way her voice sound now, from Punahou and the main land college. Even her hair, all flat with high light. It seem like I never knew her my whole life.

I could smell the steaks and sausages starting to burn, but no body was gonna tell my dad dat. I still couldn't look up but I could just see him and his arms over the grill with the tongs.

No sense waiting for them to make me one plate, tell me Jesse, grab you one chair, go grine. They wouldn't even let me pretend I was home again. I turned to leave and waved without looking at them.

But then I turned back around and asked Shelly, "What, you never like open your gift? Then I go. Promise." She crossed her arms just in case I thought I was getting a hug. "I just like see if you like um."

"Okay," she said. She made this one polite smile, the kind girls make when they like tell some guy to get lost.

She started fumbling with the ribbon. The Macy's lady wrapped um up good, Shelly had hard time. I jus wanted to see her face when she saw. The paper fell on the cooking table.

She was holding the box open by her stomach, turning it around.

She bit her lip and covered her mouth with her fingers. Her eyes came small. When I seen her looking up at me I knew she remembered.

When we jus little my mom never had any where to leave us when she go work. She take me and my sistas to come work with her back when Macy's was still Liberty House. We was having the time of our life jus running wild, playing hide and seek in the clothes racks. My mom chasing behind trying to fix every thing, fold the shirts back up. And you know my mom, she get hard time really raise her voice li'dat.

But the supervisor keep snapping at her telling her go put us in the employee room so no body see us. Gummybear was scared, but me and Shelly snuck back out, crawling up the escalator.

Up there we was playing spies and we never got busted. Shelly jumping around on this fake bed, her bangs all bouncing.

We hide in the clothes rack when the grown ups came by. Shelly peeking her head out, she seen this bamboo wind chime. For some reason she love that thing, jus the sound it made I guess, when some one walking by flick it.

She knew better than to ask our mother for any thing. My family never had that much money back then. And there was all these other moms with their daughters, buying all kine girl stuffs and perfumes.

I figure Shelly should get some thing, she was always the good kid, book smart even.

So I told her, "I try grab um for you sis."

"Okay Jesse," she said, smiling her little mean smile. "Don't get me in any trouble."

I was gonna take um out, stash um by the rubbish can, and come get it when we going home. But jus as I getting to the door I felt the supervisor tugging at my shirt.

The manager gave my mom scoldings like she was jus one kid, to bring us here and her son stealing. Was shame for the whole family. Then my dad telling me I must be no f–ing good to steal one thing I never even need. He never raise his hand to me one time my whole life, but that night he came close.

I don't know if my dad ever thought of me the same after.

I never ratted out my sista but. Never tell them was for her.

"Jesse," Shelly said, all grown now.

She put out her arm like she wanted one hug and tilted her head for one kiss. And jus for that one hug I was little brother Jesse again. She put her hands on my fore arms, right on my tattoo.

She look at our last name there, then she whisper all soft, "You have a good heart, Jesse Gomes."

"I told you I get um for you one day Shelly girl," I said.

"I want you to meet Steve," she said, with a guilty smile too. "I always wanted you to meet him."

She wanted for me and him to have our moment. But the guy was gone.

Funny, I guess he took one look at me and dug out.

Was so much fun, drinking my can juice like the little kids. It was good to see so many healthy kids running around. No meth babies in my family, just Dwayne and me.

I met all dis new family I never knew I had, from new marriages, every body introduce.

My one hot aunty, Aunty Kimmy, I tell her, "Ho, where you been all my life, Aunty Sexy?" Making like I never met her before.

My Aunty Gracey call me over. Her and my Uncle Ron was some serious talkers. Uncle Ron was the rich guy in the family too. He started his own company and now he just kick back, count his money. Him and Uncle Frank was sitting on one side the table, all kine alcohol sweat dripping already, Uncle Ron telling his joke about how come all the black guys died in Vietnam. "The sergeant said, 'Get down in your foxhole.' And they all started dancing." He used to tell the same joke when I was ten.

Aunty Gracey and Aunty Kimmy on the other side. They was all decked out for the occasion, heavy make up, their perfume so chronic I like gag.

"Come here," said Aunty Gracey, bouncing in her seat. "Kiss aunty."

I kissed her and she jus go off with the stories about how I used to run around the house naked, no matter what she would say I wouldn't keep the pants on.

"Ho, finally you come see your aunty. I told your uncle I know Jesse gon come today, I told every body. Then when I seen you, you make one old lady cry," she said, wiping her face with the napkin.

"You da most handsomest guy in da family," said Aunty Kimmy.

"I hope so." I point my juice can at Uncle Ron and Uncle Frank with the Elvis hair. "Look at dese ugly fuckas."

Uncle Ron opened a beer and put it on the chair next to him. "Drink one beer already Jesse, I not gon tell your P.O." His face had heavy creases now and his little bald spot wen take over his whole head. "All dese years I wen tell your aunty you our retirement plan. I no more one 401k, no more da kine IRAs. Me, I jus waiting for see you on da crime stoppers, I gon turn your ass in for da reward, go catch mahi."

"So what den?" I ask him. "You never finish your throw net or what?"

"Chree years I work on dat fucka," he said. "One half million knots, I tie um all my self. Da next time time I go launch, dis fucken barracuda more big den you wen eat right through um."

Uncle Frank shaking his head, like was one different version of the story.

Uncle Ron had one thirty footer and one twenty two footer. He went plan um out when he was in the army, how he wasn't gon take no orders ever again. When he got back from Vietnam he decided he gon have his own boat. Now he get two. Funny thing, he was one shitty fisher man, but that never stop him.

"Ho Jesse," he said. "I was gon call you up for holoholo, you know. I never have your number."

I gave him my new cell number.

He kept trying to make me drink and I kept telling him no.

"You join Jehova witness or some thing? Morons? Mormons?" he said.

"I'm a changed man," I said. "I found Moses."

"Good for you," he said. Then he whistled super loud for my little nephew. "Eh Bobby, get one shot for dis change man ova hea. Get one beer for God's chosen."

Bobby came running up with the Heineken Light, but I let it sit there.

We talked mostly about fishing until Dwayne came walking by with his sideway Ecko hat, saggy board shorts, big smile. At least he stop wearing that fanny pack.

Dwayne get real long girly eye lashes. Every body was saying how he wen pack on some size now that he clean his shit out. Me and him too was looking nice and wide. I think the family like that, cuz they know when you tweaking most guys come skinny.

The guy Dwayne look happy too. He jus came one dad three months ago. Uncle Ron was telling me how he gave him a couple thousand for take care the kid. Some other guys in the family gave some thing.

Dwayne kept going table to table telling every body how he turn his life around and he gon find work, be one good dad. I never seen him like that, so happy.

When you see guys that just came dads, it's a look that they don't get from any thing else. I wouldn't know for myself but.

I heard Dwayne tell Gummybear, "My son, he not gon end up like me, fuck up every thing in my life." He pounded his heart with his fist. "I get one reason for live now."

"Oh no," said Uncle Ron when Dwayne came over. "Now we get both da criminals. Eh, Dwayne, you no can rob Uncle Ron, you already rob me, you monkey," he said, cuz how he gave Dwayne money for his baby boy. "My wallet stay in da car, you not gon rob Uncle Ron."

Dwayne told me to check him out before I dig, on da side kine. And he went back making his rounds, telling every body, giving the same speech, "If never was for my son, my life would be about hard drugs right now. He saving me more den I saving him."

Uncle Ron start rubbing his nose and looking away, like he heard enough of it already. If you a man you don't gotta go around make your struggles public to every body. I would never do that.

Our family, all our family, was always real legit. Our grand parents was real strict Christian before.

I still like talk to my sista Shelly more before she go back to Cali. I was telling my Uncle Ron, good for see you again li'dat.

The guy tell me, "Sit down, Jesse."

He said um real tough too.

"Jesse," he said. "When you gon stop fucken around, come work for me finally?"

"Me?" I said.

"You. How much more years you think you got left? Listen. I know you one smart boy and dats how you got dis far. What, I gotta twist your arm for give you good work?"

I start laughing. "Dats da beer talking, Uncle. I tell you da truth, yah. I need one job bah. I would jus let you down Uncle Ron but. I dunno how to hang dry wall, pour slabs."

"Fuck," he said, "no matta, neither do we. More good for my boys dat way, we get paid by da hour."

I had to laugh. "What, you guys jus milk um?"

"Fuck yah, Jesse. We in da milk business and I'm da milk man. Da Better Business Bureau call me up every day, I tell um what for do with my nuts. But me, I work in my office now. Dats what I thinking for you one day. First we get you one company truck, company cell phone, you work front lines for couple years, den I get you in management. You Mistah Gomes afta dat."

"Mister Gomes?" I said. "Nah, I never heard dat since court."

Some people was already walking past us, saying they good byes li'dat. Shit Uncle Ron, I trying for leave already.

"Yah," said Uncle Ron. "Guys all would respect you, you one born leader. Dese young boys, dese punk guys, dey no listen to me. But one young punk li'you, dey gon listen. If not you gon broke dey ass. Couple years, I let you buy one piece, ten per cent, fifteen per cent, some thing, I front you the money too. Not management, owner ship. Dass when you gon make real money, Jesse. Plus, you never know, I no more one heir to da throne right now, may be one day I put um in your name, I go catch mahi." He waved his beer all around. "I know you grew up dis house, I know you one hard worker. You gon have to learn how for do accounting too. Me I do every thing, pay roll, GET taxes, banking statements. I get one girl for help me but I can do um myself."

"How you learn all dat? You went back school?" I ask him.

"School?" he said. "Fuck school. I never wen school my whole life. I teach myself. Cuz when it's your money you learn fass. You would trust one other guy with your money? Me, I only trust family. Family firss. And you most of all Jesse."

"Me?"

"You. Long time I was hoping for run in to you."

The guy was serious. Seriously nuts. I could tell he was thinking long time before today. He had all the mischief in his voice. He plan out dis whole speech when he was fishing, guarantee.

"Uncle Ron," I said, "you always was da coolest to me of every body. Dats why I gotta be honest. I jus would let you down. I never work one regular kine job my whole life."

"Shit," said Uncle Ron, "you work hard at da gym, right? You work hard on your house I bet. Same same. Not as different as you think."

He never stop but. He keep going on and on about being one boss, and having legit money, real money.

But can you see me some body boss, telling them get up early, no show up all cut, no give lip? Me? Shit.

I not gon lie, I think I would do pretty good.

He gave me his card and said call him up the day after Christmas for work. Then after he said call him up for go fish.

I had to stand up for get the guy stop talking. I told him I had to go piss and I would call him. I said thank you. I wen shake his hand and tell him, "Eh, Uncle, I dunno. If guys no like pay or some guy hassle you, try mafia you li'dat, dat part I know I can help. We family. Family firss."

My uncle went rage laughing.

"You wannabe syndicate fucka." He laugh even harder. "Kay, I gon call up my little nephew Jesse for strong arm next time, yah? No. I know guys too. I let dem live dat life, I leave dat life alone."

He threw some trail mix in his mouth and start crunching. Jus looking at me. "Eh Jesse," he said. "Why you throw your life away for dat shit, drugs?"

"One kid wen ask me da same thing."

"What you told him?"

"I know dere was one reason before, I guess so. I just cannot remember now."

"Huh," he said. He sat up in his chair. "Tell me you wen hear dis joke before. One pake ask one Portagee, 'What you think is more far, da moon or Flo-ri-da?' Da Portagee say, 'Stupid, you no can even see Flo-ri-da.'"

He slap my shoulder, tell me, "No be one fucken Portagee, Jesse. You call me up for work."

After I came out the bath room I stopped to look at the old pictures. It was nice to be in one house that no smell like smoke. I was looking at all the baby pictures of my sistas, then as they got older, and after I was gone from the house. Last time I came here was with Mikey. Was hard to believe I only lived couples miles away. Might as well be on the moon.

This one picture of me was from the day my dad took me to the harbor. The one of my dad smiling, me in my life jacket. I never even seen one picture of him for how long now. I know you think my dad was one shitty dad. I know you think family first and a father gon for give his son for any thing, never turn his back on him. But fuck you, you never knew my dad. Most guys, they no take responsibility for what they do in life. But if any thing, my dad he take more than his share. He take it all on him. Every body blames the dealer, the user, the government. Any thing that happens around him, my dad takes it on him self.

When I wen turn around my dad was right there, making like he was putting the pillows on the couch.

"Get angel cake out side," he said. I never know if he was trying to tell me go back out side or he just like me try the cake.

"Kay," I said, "I go check um out den."

My dad get dis gorilla shape to him. His hair too was like one gorilla, and he start scratching, looking at the ground, and it seem like the ground bend under him.

"You working?" he ask me.

Yups, you know I one Gomes, dad, one hard worker. I work termite. I wen rack up mean over time last week, boss man getting angry, had one inspection right down the road from here.

But still all these years I cannot lie to my dad.

"No," I said. "You was right to kick me out Dad. But I trying Dad."

"Dwayne said you stay with your girl friend's family?" he ask me.

"Yah," I said. "I left da drug house after my friend died."

He start nodding.

"Kay," he said. Then he jus walk away, out the front door around the house back to the grill. I went out the gate by the red flowers.

Well, that was it I figure. Shoulda been one termite guy. Still piss me off, lying get you farther in life than the truth. But may be I was wrong.

Jus as I was gon leave my dad came out the house with one tray food containers and he put um down in the truck bed.

"For you guys," he said. He wiped his fore head. "Dwayne said you dating one nice girl."

I smiled. "Yeah."

He start looking around at the El Camino, the blacked out windows, the chrome rims. He was looking at the safety sticker.

"You gon need one new sticker pretty soon? You illegal," he said.

"Pff," I said. "Not gon matter, Dad. Dis cah get how many warrants already for being illegal, we still never pay money."

He laughed. My dad actually laughed.

Then for the first time in years my dad looked me in the eye. He rub his mouth shut from smiling. He sniffed. He jus there staring in to the car for a while, with his arms cross and his chin to his chest. He was thinking real hard about some thing.

"Pig," he said.

"Pig?" I said.

"Pig, for dinner Christmas." He look away and made like he was scratching his chin.

"Yah?" I said.

"Your modda probably gon ask for you bring your girl friend. Da mom and dad too if dey like, get both sides together if dey not too busy. Make more family."

Before I could say any thing he already start walking back to the house.

"Kay," he said, not looking back.

"Kay den Dad," I said.

That's my dad you know.

I was thinking, what was the number again? Shit. Now I remember. I took out my phone and dialed and just kept pressing zero through all the menu.

"Longs Drug Store," said the lady.

"Yah," I said. "I like talk to da big boss man over dere. I like make one complaint."

"Is this Jesse?" said the lady.

"Dis not one joke. Dis serious business. I like talk to da shift manager over dere."

The lady transferred the call.

"Hi, this is Kapika."

I make my voice all different.

"Yah, eh. You guys get job opening?"

"What were you looking for? We have cashier or stocking."

"Shoot. I take one stock room job. Eh, you guys get drug test ova dere or what?"

"Yes, we do."

"Kay, kay, no problem. Eh, I one hard worker you know. Most guys is one handed, me I both handed. Am-bu-dex-tress. Eh, you not one prick boss, ah?"

"Jesse! You!" she said. "You know what? I wish you would get a job instead of bother me when I working."

"I know, I know, I know. You always doing some thing important. Big tings going on. I know I not important. You right, I jus wanted for bother you, be one bother to you. Eh, merry Christmas any ways. Are you by da chimney?"

"You drunk?"

"Never been more sober. I jus wanted for ask, what you was doing for Christmas?"

"You know what we doing for Christmas."

"You guys like meet my mom dem?"

"What?"

"Yah you," I said. "My dad said come down if any thing."

"Oh my gosh," she said. She even did this little excited laugh she makes. "I'll have to make something for your mom."

"Oh nah," I said. "No need."

"I gotta bring something. What you trying to say, I can't cook?"

"Eh Pika"–

"Eh Jesse," she said. Making fun of my voice.

I waited for a while.

"Tanks."

"For what?" she said.

"For I dunno."

"Eh Jesse," she said, making fun of my voice again. But then serious. "You know the thing I always always tell you, right? What I been telling you every day for two weeks?"

"Yah."

"Do I have to tell you again or–"

"No," I said. "I get um. Straighten up, fly right. I get um. I tell you what else, I coming straight over dere and wait for you for when you pau work."

"Okay, Jesse." Then her voice start break up. "Hey, Jesse, Jesse, you're cutting out, your phone's cutting out."

And it died.

Dwayne came out the gate jus as I was closing the phone. By now it was getting night and I wanted to head over and wait for my girl. Dwayne, he smiling so big.

"Wassup play boy," I said.

"Like one stoge?" he said, reaching in side his pack.

"Nah," I said. "Eh, I tink you was crazy da other day when you said come by here."

He light his cigarette and start puffing out his nose, getting all in to it like was weed or some thing.

"Wen work out all right?" he said.

I nodded.

Now he start talking about the old days when we both grew up play fighting in this house. Real fighting some times.

How we would shoot centers, go out and walk around, we always had each other's back. No matter, even the time I was gon get mobbed by five guys, we got mobbed together.

He seemed all charged. I know he setting me up. Shit, I never really like talk to him.

Then he told me about how his chick and him been beefing. Right now they not even together.

"Look," he said. "I no like even come at you with dis, but I don't know any body else dat could help me."

"I no more dat much money right now," I said. "I no more incomes coming in. But if you need it dat bad bra, I prolly could give some thing small."

"Nah," he said. He took off his hat and put it on the cab. His face look all sick. "My son. He stay with my chick's family. He stay in one ice house right now Jesse, you believe dat? I dunno if he eating good or what. Dey smoke cigarette all day around him. Cuz when me and my chick started beefing, mostly cuz how she still tweaking, she took my son and went back to her family. We was staying with my aunty up dere and every thing was fine. But now Jesse, she even worse den before, I heard. Now I no can even go see how my son doing cuz I know I show up alone the family gon rob me, take my money dat I bring for da baby, buy dope."

His eyes came all sad. I know what he like now.

"Jesse, you da only guy I know right now could get my son back for me."

I took one deep breath and start leaning against my truck bed.

"You never think may be could call da cops or Child Service for get your son outa dere?" I said.

"Yah, but I da one jus get out re hab, I no more job, no more house, I got da felony charge on my record. CPS get my son, fuck, I dunno how I gon get him back afta," he said. "When I get my son back, my girl will come too, I know it. Dat fucken housing, bra. Dey call um Tweakerville. Dats where dey get my boy. I no need dis kine action right now, but if I gotta draw blood for my son I gon do it Jesse. He cannot end up like me." He look down and kick at the ground. "I jus thought I ask my cousin if he still my back up or what? I know it seem like every thing going good for you right now, but I got no body else Jesse. No body else gon get my son outta dere."

I watched the mountain and I laughed for some reason. Through all the clouds the sun was going to set over by the other side where Dwayne's boy stay. Then I thought, Kapika. She would tell me come home. Let the police handle family matters.

If I know her she prolly already had all kine plans, what she was gon bring for my mom them. She prolly made a list too, she like making her lists, her names.

I could say to Dwayne I had to call Kapika, go pick her up, but my phone was dead.

I sucked in until I could feel my lungs was full with air and let it come out slow.

"Kay Dwayne," I said. "We go get your boy."

Chapter Thirty-Six

We pick up Dingo and Mikey and go.

Mikey told me, Tweakerville? He say I must like die for come all the way up there on this kine domestics action. But he came. He jus said I had to come with him after, he had his own scam for later and he needed me for it.

Tweakerville was at the end of one of those back roads in the country that go on for ever to the end of every thing. Past one lard plant that reek for miles, past couple small farms. The kine road you could bury the needle, shoot past go ninety if you like, no more any body around.

Dwayne was saying that Uncle Kurtis house was the last one in the housing and when we get there go in slow, in-fill-trate, park by the house, but jus cruise um.

We was coming to the end of the road, no more street lights, you couldn't see more than fifty yards in front the car even with the yellow moon, and that road jus getting more and more dark on us.

"Try slow down," said Dwayne.

I cut the lights, then I seen the fence to Tweakerville.

It was small for one housing, ten small houses, five on each side of the road, one small parking lot in the back, with couple old trucks, one sand pit for fighting chickens. The houses was all the same color, light green, nice paint, no peeling, porch light above the door. The front yards was all pretty clean too, some dog shit but other than that top shape. I was surprise, I was expecting one rubbish dump.

We stopped right by the gate. The place quiet, no body strolling around. Was jus the sound of crickets and the long shadows from the orange porch lights. Far away we start hearing some body on one uke from behind us. Me and Mikey start looking around cuz the music getting more loud.

Whoever jamming was unreal, like on the radio kine. Then we seen him walk out from the shadow, this kid, fourteen about there, jus staring me down, blank face no expression. He get all mis match clothes, like one turtle neck shirt and bright red board shorts, one kango skull cap. He jus jamming the fuck out of that uke, the rest of him all chill but his hand like one blur on that thing.

"He missing one string too," said Dwayne, getting out the car, pulling the back of his shirt. He never shake the kid's hand, he never say wassup, jus, "Sale you fucka, you know where my son stay?"

The kid look jus look blank face.

"Sale!"

The kid's eyes was like the fish you see on ice at Safeway. But his ice had him jus full on tweaked out, tuned out.

"No give me dat look Sale," said Dwayne. "You know if my son stay up Uncle Kurtis house?"

Still no answer, was coma tose the boy. He more stiff than one rock too. Was jus his hand jamming away, never getting tired. That's the clear power in him, charging him all night, no food no sleep.

"Dat kid is nuts," said Dingo, talking in to my ear. "Get him one recording contract, I like be his agent."

Dingo's breath was straight fumes. He was the only guy still sucking the warm beers. Since Robby was dead Dingo was on one liquid diet, dats why his stomach look like beer and he smell like one brewery.

The kid never turn his back to us. He jus walk back wards back in to the shadow so you couldn't see. You could tell he getting farther away cuz the music start getting quiet. He never said one thing the whole time, never blink, never lick his lip.

"Fuck you den Sale," said Dwayne, getting back in the car. "We jus go cruise up."

Mikey was looking skeptic.

Dwayne told him, "No worry Mikey. We gon be all right, jus cruise."

Back in our town guys would say that even without Robby, then me, Mikey, Dingo all together pretty much can handle whateva. This not our town but.

Still for some reason I never felt sketch. Had good air up there, nice breeze. It seem peaceful. Like one grave yard. Even the dogs and chickens was quiet. Hardly any TVs, or boxes, no house parties, no Christmas parties, no beer drinkers, no card games, no nothing, just clear. Clear and leaves blowing off the trees, whirl winds of leaves, caught up in the wind they fell in to.

We was creeping down the road now real slow. Was dark behind the house windows, how they get all boarded up. But I know they all looking even if we no can see them. Every body seen us, guarantee. In one dope dealer car too. They probably figure we out collecting from some body else that live there. Not they problem. No more such thing as Tweakerville loyalty.

And there it was, end of the road, Uncle Kurtis house, where Dwayne's son stay supposedly. We pulled up right in front and let Dwayne hop out the car.

"Kay," he said. "I no think my chick is home. But I going any way boys. I dunno how long gon be, I got business with this house, so. Please, no get out the car for little while, and no look too long in side. Jus listen. If any thing happen you gon hear it."

He wen shake our hand, looking up at us through his long eye lash.

"I love you guys bra," he said. "I love you guys, I die with you guys, if any thing happen to you."

He took one breath and start walking to the house. The door wen open before he got there but no body look out side. I think I could see Kurtis, barely, through all the window panes there was one dark out line figure. He was watching us, guarantee, wondering how Dwayne know us. Probably thinking Dwayne owe us money and we took him there to collect from them.

After a while me and Mikey get out the car, standing with the car between us and the house, looking over the top. We told Dingo no get out, cuz Dingo gon make big noise guarantee. That's why some times I never like take him out places. He get too nuts when he kill cases, twenty five plus beers li'dat, and this not the place for one guy like Dingo.

"Jesse," said Mikey to me. "What, you never like take your hat off?"

"Oh shoot," I said.

Mikey was right. Wearing one low hat li'dat I look like I there for make trouble. Even him, he had his hood down.

For the longest time me and Mikey was jus standing there, leaning with our fore arms on top the car, trying for look like we know what we doing there. We couldn't hear nothing in side. I thinking, come on Dwayne, get your son, we go.

The house next door it sound like some guy pounding one chick in there. But when you listen hard it sound more like one porno movie, had that kine music. Then this baby started for cry and this girl voice telling the baby shut up.

Me and Mikey almost jump back when the door wen open and out come this young girl, bubble gum, short skirt, white t-shirt, pony tail, big hoop ear ring. She had choke make up on, covering up her butt face she get. Her head look like one skull, with barely one nose at all. Her body not that bad, flat, but real, real skinny, short too. Couldn't be more than ninety pounds. Couldn't be older than seventeen.

She go sit down on the stairs to her front porch, knocking her knees together, showing bean, smiling at us with her butter face.

"Eh," she said, "you guys get one no menthol cigarette?"

Right when I taking the stoge out the box, Dingo went hop out the car and thief um right out my hand.

"You gotta come over here get it," said Dingo to the girl, sticking out his chest. She start smiling all sexy, or trying for be sexy. That's all she like, was one invitation. Guarantee she thought we was out dealing. One dealer with one car li'dat, that's one dream husband for one ugly ice slut.

She wen reach for the cigarette. Dingo reversed couple steps, make her work for it.

"Hey," she said.

"Hey you, what's da deal sex appeal?" said Dingo, waving da cigarette by his chin. "Come, you could get it." He start smiling all sly. "You definitely would get it. Front ways, back ways, up side down ways. Ways you never imagine."

She giggle. "You guys not from around here? Where you guys from?"

"No where," said Mikey.

"You know, around," said Dingo, bobbing his head, giving her the cigarette to light. She put her butt down against the car and run her hand down the side.

"Ho, you guys get one smooth cah too," she said.

"Dis right here?" said Dingo. "Dis cah is out. You should see my odda cah."

She smile more big, she think Dingo one dummy in one good way. She kinda smell like one cross baby powder and mosquito spray.

"Nice chains you guys get. You guys slang dope? I like dat kine, I know you guys already," she said, blowing smoke slow out her nose.

"You don't know me," Dingo snap back. "Your modda warn you about guys li'me. I break your heart, play girl."

"Break my heart?" she said, putting her fingers on her chest.

"You know dat," said Dingo. "I hang for hours."

"Shit," she said. "Dass what all guys say, before. You probably da kine one minute marcher."

Dingo starts laughing real loud, too loud. "I one rocket launcher, watch out, you one super soaker."

Them two was in love already. Me and Mikey start walking away a little, still watching the house. Could hear the uke playing again, the kid making his rounds wandering around Tweakerville like he security. The girl start inching more close to Dingo.

Now she telling him she used to give lap dance at this one pretty decent strip bar in town. She said she got busted for no more age. Dingo start telling her, "Why you drive all the way down dere just for do dat? I get dollars bills right here." She tell him get in side the car, she go give him one VIP lap dance, jus for him.

We let Dingo go already, he gon get more loud if we try tell him no do one dumb ting over here. The uke was getting so loud again I know the kid Sale was coming over by us. He stroll right up to me strumming his uke with that blank stare, right up in my grill. Was off.

"Ho," I said, trying for be cool to him. "You jam dat thing?"

He wen play deaf to me too, just stand there.

Mikey spit, looking back over his shoulder at dark space between all the houses.

"Eh Mikey," I said. "If Robby was here he would just go in dere. We would already have da kid, be half way home already."

Mikey looking back at me like, yah, where's Robby?

Dingo popped opened the door to get some air in da car and we could hear them two again. She ask him how was her lap dancing. He tell her, "Not dat good, I seen your pussy but I never seen your ass hole."

"Dingo," I said. "Her fucken family lives right hea, you like dem smash you, you like us scrap all dem?"

He hopped out the car.

"She said only get her kid in side. Her kid only small, he no care. We going in side. Relax Jesse, dis one cruise place bra."

Right after he take the girl in side her house we hear this old truck pulling up the road, lights off. One of the wheels was loose and the truck sound all sick, creaking, screeching. The truck pull up two houses down and out come this sixty year old fucka with one bat.

He start limping up to us, but he walk right past us like we nothing. I seen his face up close when he step through the light. He was wearing one in side out grey t-shirt, jeans and tape slippers. Both his front teeth was missing. It take plenty years hard work ice smoking for your teeth start falling out.

Me and Mikey jus back up couple steps out of the light, get out his way. He wen stop right in front Kurtis house.

"Kurtisth!" he shout at the house, his voice all slurry cuz his teeth. "You wen taxsh me for the lash time you fucka. Get my power drill or I gon bat your housh."

You could hear the window open where I seen Kurtis before. We seen the nose from the twenty two coming out the window. Mikey grab me by my shirt and pull me down, both of us peeking around the car. Pah, pah, pah, the shots all echoing through the mountains. All these roosters started running from the back yard across the street, them squawking and feathers flapping. But the guy, that old ass guy was game, he never flinch. Even the kid Sale he never stop playing his uke, never blink even, he still looking at me with fish eyes.

The old guy shout, "Kurtish, I go get my gun, I coming back," and start limping back to his truck.

Me and Mikey was both leaning down against the car now like we in one fox hole, both thinking the same thing, we no like be there for the shoot out.

"I told you, Jesse," said Mikey. "I told you, but you like get involve with dis kine domestics."

"Yah Mikey," I said, "dis not our town, not our beef. But we wait little while for Dwayne pull through, get his baby."

The old guy never had one gun in his truck, he wen reverse down the road and pull out.

As much as I like dig out, take my friends outa there, I couldn't flake on my cousin. Now I know what it is to crave clear, it feel like your soul like jump out your body. And most my whole life my arm was four foot long, clear was four and one half foot in front my face. You start thinking about it and you think if this life, life without clear, then give me clear or give me whatever behind that other door. Then you start pouring sweat, your throat start itching.

That's why Dwayne need his son more than his son need him. His son was one twelve pound anchor. We was gon get them out if I had to bust out Robby's Glock 9, show Kurtis who he fucken with. And Mikey and Dingo was gon stand right by me cuz that's what our life was about. I know you think my friends is bad guys too. So fuck you for that. Unless you gon stand next to your friend in one gun fight with no gun over some shit no concern you, no say my friend's name out your mouth.

One whole half hour more go by knowing that if I heard any kine ruckus in there I would go in, pull trigger.

Finally when Dwayne came out he was carrying his son in one car seat. I tell you, was one big relief.

Then he ask me if I could hold his son for him, he jus had to go back in the house one minute. He was all, "You cannot smoke in front him, Jess. Not even cigarette." I told him I wasn't gon smoke in front the kid any way but since he giving me orders, fuck it, bus is leaving right now, get your shit, we leaving. Dwayne was like, "Fuck whateva, go den." He start strutting back to the house. I standing there holding his fucken son in his car seat, every thing. What is this?

"Dis fucken guy," I told Mikey.

Then the kid start crying. I put his rattle in his hand, he start cruising again. His rattle was jus one plastic Pepsi bottle with some dog food in side. I put the baby down on the trunk. He was a little ugly fucka. His skin was way lighter than Dwayne, guarantee the mom was more pale.

Mikey keep looking at me like time to go.

"You get Dingo outa there, den we go," I said.

I look at the baby on the car seat. The kid's feet was so small. I guess that's all babies but I dunno, I never seen that much babies before. His fingers too, I never know babies' fingers was so small. I put my pinky in his palm and he start gripping um.

"I'm Uncle Jesse," I said. Just so he know who I am. I mean, I dunno how introduce to one baby. He look like he trying for burp or some thing, he keep opening his mouth, all kine snots and bubbles on his chin.

Mikey call Dingo on his phone, tell the guy come out the house or we coming in there. Then we start flashing lights.

Finally Dwayne come running out Kurtis house with the baby bag, all the diapers li'dat.

Kurtis yelling to him from right at the door step, "I no fucken care." He had one real high pitch voice. "Take da puppies too you like, cept for da baby pit. Just give me da money."

I could tell the guy was all gon already, three brain cell left at most.

Dingo come out the girl's house scratching his crotch. He was all dragging too, burping. He look like she wen wear him down and all the beer catching up.

She come flying out the door with just her t-shirt, talking about, I never even meet your friends? you guys leaving? you no like stay little while? But I knew this gon happen too. She was expecting to catch whacks off us.

"Fuck dat," said Dingo. He go jump in the back seat, almost wen crush the kid, looking like he about to throw up already.

Da girl wen yell at us, fuck you, then go back in the house.

I put the car in drive and start pulling out, thinking she might be one problem. I never even notice Sale standing in the road, I almost wen whack him too with the car.

"Oh my bad," I told him, braking. He came up to the driver side window and stop playing for once.

"I like come wit you guys," he said. His voice was real soft.

"Oh, he talks," I said. "Sorry but, you gotta get your own self outa here."

He nod and start playing the uke again, wandering around his housing. Out in the middle of the night.

Dingo and Dwayne was arguing in the back over leg space. In the rear view I could see the baby, all the bubble drool still on his chin.

We went past the fence, I told myself whatever happen that's the last time I ever going to Tweakerville. Let them rest in peace. Let the ghosts have the night over there.

Dingo said we should stop at the drive thru for piss and get some thing for grind, but then he crashed out. It was like four already. Dwayne never like eat, but he said he catch our breakfast for us cuz we wen help him out.

Me and Mikey was pissing on the side of the Jack in the Box. Only lights was working in the parking lot. There was leaves all over, fat leaves. You couldn't walk without them crushing under your feet. They was just blowing around, more blowing off the trees too. The whole place need one good raking.

"Eh Mikey," I said. "You tink Dwayne high right now or what?"

Mikey look at me like I stupid. Then he told me Dwayne was high the whole time. He was prolly high at my sista's wedding party, high the day he got out re hab.

Mikey waited till I got it. And this was it. We never came out for get Dwayne's son back. We came for Dwayne pay off his credit with his father in law and pick up clear from them. The clear was all in the baby bag, guarantee. Dwayne jus needed us to make the deal go smooth. Maybe even he jus needed a ride.

Dingo was snoring pretty bad, him and the baby sitting next to each other look like twins. The only other guy around was one older guy standing against the door to the Jack in the Box. He was standing by one rake in an aloha shirt, but there was all kine leaves every where. One haole guy.

Dwayne came back with the bags of food. "Ho!" he yelled. "Where's my son?"

He wen pick up da kid in the whole car seat and start giving the speech again holding him, "If never was for my son my life would be about hard drugs right now."

He go pound his chest with his left hand, real hard too. In his right hand the car seat was swinging around. His eyes was like fish eyes, he yelling super loud about his new life, how he one changed man.

The worst part too, he believe him self. "He saving me more den I saving him." He's there swinging his son in the car seat around like one loaf bread. He start telling us how he would scrap every night before, to get his dope li'dat for the night. But not any more, now it's about the kid. He go telling all these fight stories swinging at the air while we all eating.

Sure enough he go drop the car seat, pick um up again, start swinging um again. The kid start crying.

"Eh you fucka," I said eating my break fast sandwich. "Put your son in da car you like fly him around li'dat."

"Fuck dat," said Dwayne, all charged. "I never putting him down again. You staying wit me now. You staying wit your daddy." He start hugging the whole car seat super hard, flexing all his back, da ting start creaking. He came all red, with rage and love. The baby cry even louder.

"No cry," Dwayne said. "Be a man. You no fucken cry. Soljas no cry, even little soljas."

He start rocking his kid back and forth, whispering to him about some thing. Then all at once he go nuts yelling at the guy by the wall. Big guy but real soft, not the kind you would expect trouble. But there he was staring down Dwayne with this really weird kine eyes.

"Who da fuck is you?" said Dwayne.

"What?" said the guy. He start panicking. But his eyes, it still look like he staring Dwayne down.

Dwayne is all, "Who da fuck is you?" I jus wish he put his son down before he go rush up in the guy's face li'dat.

The guy jus look, his eyes not changing.

"Why you looking at me?" said Dwayne. "You never look at me, never, never, never look at me, not in your whole fucken life you do one thing li'dat. How come you looking now? How come? How come?"

"I'm sorry," said the guy. "But I'm blind."

Yah, the guy's eyes was off. They didn't move, dat's why he look li'dat to us.

I figure even Dwayne would jus let the guy go for dat, he no can help be blind. But Dwayne still like fuck with the guy, alk the guy out.

"For real?" said Dwayne, right up to the guy's face, his son by the guy's knee. "What you see when you looking at me, you see all black out?"

"No," said the guy, "you're just a big blur."

Dwayne start screeching. "I one blur?"

I guess he never like being one blur. Den he came all teary eye.

"Dis my son right here," he said, holding da next generation ice tweaker up for da blind guy to see.

Dwayne with his shirt around his neck, his side way cap, holding his baby in one car seat, all fucken high, ice addict, ice father. Talking so fast you could barely understand, like he one crazy person, and the blind guy couldn't even see him.

"Eh eh eh," said Dwayne. "I like ask you one question, is you blind right now or is you scared?"

"What?" said the guy.

"You could only be one thing at one time," said Dwayne. "Is you blind right now or is you scared? Cuz you gon always be one or da odda." All the veins in his neck was popping out.

"Scared," said the guy.

"You scared?" said Dwayne, and he laugh little bit. "Since you scared, go back to being blind."

More leaves was falling off the trees. The whole place was just wall to wall leaves, caught up with the wind they fell in to. The rake still sitting against the wall.

Chapter Thirty-Seven

Dwayne said he like stop off real quick at some body else's house, check um out real quick. Mikey start shouting about no have da time.

But I just told Dwayne, "Yah, no problem. Leave da kid in da car, I watch him for you."

He start walking toward the house with the baby bag, the dope in side. He looked at the bag for a while. Then he looked back at me, like he knew what I was gon do. And I think some part of him knew it was for the best.

My phone was dead for hours. But after we left I get Dingo's phone and texted Dwayne, YOUR SON IS WITH FAMILY.

Dingo wanted to stay up with some of his family for a couple days so I dropped him off.

I had to wake him up when we got there. He rubbed his eyes, burped, scratched his crotch.

There was all these bees buzzing in the trees in front of the house. Mikey rolled up his window. Mikey don't like bugs, spiders.

I said to Dingo, "Wen work out all right? Just another day for you. Da life and times of Dingo. Maybe I write one book one day, Dingo, Da Younger Years."

Even Mikey smiled.

Dingo tells me, "Guess we not gon be seeing you around for a while again. Kapika, she gon like you be da stay at home dad now. Like one house mom kine."

I nodded. Then I said, "You know I never did like you Dingo."

"I never like you either Jesse," he said, smiling, bobbing his head.

And I had to shake my head again as I watched him walking toward the house, opening another warm beer.

When I started the engine the baby started flapping his hands around with the t-shirt.

I gave him my under shirt to use, like one blanket, an older one I had. Jus cuz babies need blankets, I guess. I pulled it back under his chin.

When I was pinching his toes I said to Mikey, "Eh, you did some thing good tonight. May be Robby was wrong. May be your heart get one soul after all."

Mikey jus said, "We go Jesse. Now I gon need your help. I gotta get da money for Dos."

"No problem Mikey," I said. "Jus let me drop off da boy. What you gon do, sell da car? Sell all Robby's shit?"

He still look all pissed off, "Not even four grand all dat."

"Come on Mikey," I said. "It's Christmas."

But when I looked up he had the hood back on.

Driving to Kapika's I was thinking of her house as home.

On the way the kid dropped his rattle, the Pepsi bottle. It rolled around and almost got under the brake pedal.

"You know what boy?" I said. "We gon have to get you one real one."

I threw the rattle out the window and watched it bouncing off the road onto the side walk. I smiled.

When you around kids, you get to be a kid again. Start over with them.

Chapter Thirty-Eight

When I got to Kapika's was like six fifteen already so I figure they was all getting ready for the holidays, like all the neighbors. It was Christmas and I got my chick the only thing she ever wanted and could never have.

I was gon walk through the front door holding the baby, still in his little car seat, not even scared, not crying, just cruising.

But the door was locked.

On the bench I saw a box that had all my hats stacked up in side.

Under neath was the shirt with the stain from the day I met her. The one she would never give back.

I could hear the mom yelling, then I saw Kapika's hand coming around the out side of the door.

Her hair was half tied up over her head, the rest of it jus fell around her ears. Her eyes was all baggy and she had little wrinkles on her face, no make up, no ear rings. U.H. Colt Brennan foot ball jersey. Little white shorts. Look like she was up all night.

I said, "My phone died." But I couldn't talk, jus cuz the way her face look. Not even mad. Way past that.

"Dis Dwayne's boy," I said.

"Give him to me," she said.

The baby started crying super loud.

As I handed the kid over I felt her grip tighten around the handle of the car seat, and she held it propped up against her stomach, jus looking down at the kid crying.

I put my palms up facing her and tried to talk soft.

"I can tell you mad," I said. "But I got da baby. Dwayne, da dope get him for good. I not dis boy's dad, you not his mom and I know dis sound crazy, but we sposed to raise dis boy together, Pika. Me and you Pika, dis boy like our own, dis boy. I ready. I not ready before, but I ready now for be one man for dis kid"–

"You not gonna be part of his life," she said. She still wouldn't look at me.

It felt like one dagger. I was trying to think up any thing to say to her.

"I shoulda told you yesterday, I gon work for my Uncle Ron, work–"

Now she look at me. "I went to the house, Jesse," she said. "I thought you were high. Stupid me. I was gonna give you one last chance cuz I just couldn't help myself. I talked to Amber. She's not doing so good, Jesse." She waited for the longest time, she looked behind her, she looked down the drive way. She whispered super quiet, "Jesse–that guy, that I told you about. Amber said–she said you and Robby killed him."

Her mouth was so wide open and her lip was jus shaking, like she was shivering.

I looked down at her feet.

"Look at me," she whisper yelled.

She leaned for ward like she was going to be sick. The kid crying away now.

"For you," I said. "For you and my friend and my town and every body else."

"Jesse," she said. "I asked you not to do anything stupid. I begged you. Stupid me. I just wanted you to come over, that's all I wanted."

"Come on," I said. "Guys die in war, some fucka blow up a school dey give um a medal. Dis fucka sposed to be dead Pika. He no bleed blood, his heart pump Kool Aid. You seen him."

"Jus go," she said, sick face looking away. "Don't ever come back."

"Pika," I said. I took a step closer but she took a step back wards, holding the baby seat up with both arms.

The kid looking dazed, looking back at me, trying to figure out what happened.

I put my arms out to hold them both, but she stepped back and twisted away from me. And her cold flesh was gone from my hands.

"Never touch me again," she said, walking back wards. "I know what you're going to say. You're going to tell me I'm a spoiled brat and in your world you think you're some kind of hero. I don't care. I don't even care if those are all things I thought you were the day I met you. I don't care if you would be a great dad. That doesn't matter. None of it matters. You chose. Now go. Get away from me."

Slowly I started walking down the drive way. Looking back at her, hoping she would look up, one last time she would look me in the eye.

But she was still looking at the ground. Then she looked up and to the side of me.

"You can't be around this child. He'd spend his life trying to be like you."

"So what den?" I said, pointing up at the window where I knew they were spying on us. "You gon raise him to be like your dad?"

"I'll tell you another thing, Jesse, my dad's not out to get you. You don't need anybody to bring you down. You do that on your own."

I saw the panes close on the up stairs window.

When I was almost to the car, I looked back one last time.

She was taking the kid out of the car seat. "I know, I know," she said in that same soft singing voice she used to me, "I got you now. It's okay. It's okay."

Walking around the corner to the car, I saw the black hood was in the driver seat now, texting in to his phone.

"We go, Mikey," I said. "We go do your thing."

Mikey looked up, then back in to the phone.

Liquor stores can't sell until seven. Some times you might see chronics that's been up all night waiting out side. They need hard liquor to make the cravings go away, to make them come down more numb. Christmas day, and there was about six of um lined up by that same liquor store where they got Robby.

The Korean pulled up in his car and opened up the store, and I seen one of my long time customers, Will, coming from around the corner.

I remember the guy Will. Before he always used to bitch because his dad would make him clean house, clean yard, clean his mom's car and do the family shopping. He seen me when he came out of the store with his bottle in the bag. He swallowed up the gin like it was nothing. That's how it is but. He prolly barely felt it under the power of clear.

"Hard night?" I said.

He wiped his mouth and twisted the top back on. "Hard life."

He started walking around the corner of the store to the high grass.

Behind the building was all the plastic bags, the mattress of news paper and card board and I knew he lived there now.

I went in side and got a tall bottle of Smirnoff. In the car Mikey's phone beeped and he started the engine and drove.

I sat drinking until every thing came all blurry again. Mikey under his hood. I still never sleep, my ears was starting to pop again. I saw all these wavy lines just from not sleeping.

Mikey said this was the easy part, what he was going to do, why he had me with him. The second part was the hard part.

I told him I didn't even care what part this was.

We pulled in to the under ground parking lot by the strip mall, empty cuz it was Christmas. Day light just coming through from up stairs. Christmas music playing from the mall, O Holy Night. The only other car there was this blue Plymouth Lancer with no body in side.

"Gotta wait," Mikey said, looking in to his phone, making his clicking thinking noise. Then, "Fuck, I gotta take one mean piss."

"You went like hour ago," I said.

"Prostate," he said.

I smiled all tipsy, leaning against the in side door. "I gon crash pretty soon Mikey."

He nodded, still looking in to the phone. "Take chree of dese." He gave me the pills from his prescription bottle. They looked funny.

"Dass Amber's pills," he said. "Amber get da mean ones."

Amber. She did get the mean ones. Who needs Kapika and her little ones.

"I take one too," said Mikey. He put one in his mouth and tossed his head back. I took mine, the three. Then he looked up the ramp to street level.

"I gon piss," he said. "You know what, I going store. I gotta grine some thing. You like some thing Jess? Jerky?"

I shook my head, all wobbly. Then, "No, wait. Hell yah, I take some jerky."

"What kine?" said Mikey, getting out. "Teriyaki or regular?"

"Fuck yah, teriyaki," I said. "Tanks. I get money."

"I get um for you," he said. "If da two guys show up, jus tell dem I coming right back."

I nodded.

He reached in from the window and shook my hand. "Eh tanks Jesse. You save my life bra. Put your seat back if you like."

"What if I crash?"

"Nah," he said, "go crash. Not gon matta. Either way. Dem guys, dey not gon hassle you. Dey not like us."

We laughed.

I put my seat back. My head sinking. The car spinning. Mikey walking away, spitting some thing out of his mouth.

Ten minutes and Mikey wasn't back yet.

I think Mikey gave me the wrong pills. I was getting more tired.

Little Drummer Boy from the mall.

Fighting my own eye lids.

My stomach.

And the song, bum bum bum parumpa pum pum.

I took another drink, wobbling.

I thought about Kapika and the kid. I felt my mouth stretch.

My eye lids.

I woke up when the car hit a bump. All I could see was black. Then the small out line of light coming in and I knew I was in the car trunk, my mouth taped shut. I pulled with my arms but they were wrapped up behind my back. A cord around my ankles. I was breathing hard through my nose, rocking back and forth, thinking about Kody when he couldn't breathe. I yelled but there was no sound, only in side my head from the vibrations.

The car hit a dip and I hit the roof. The car going too fast. It was off roading some place. Then the next bump.

I was breathing so hard the in side of my nose was touching my nostrils flat, then wide. Flat. Wide.

My mouth filled with the taste of vodka, pills and stomach acid and the Breakfast Jack that Dwayne got me. I started choking. I knew I had to stop trying to breathe through my mouth and I did. Then I only breathed through my nose.

I swallowed as much of the vomit as I could.

By the time the trunk opened I didn't even care who the two guys was. My nose just sucking up that air. Cold air. Wet air.

"Aw Christ," said the big one. "Look at him." He looked huge. Barrel chest.

The short one took the tape off my mouth and I spit vomit at him but he was ready for that, he leaned to the side and just a little got on his shirt.

"You dead you fuckas!" I shouted. "I bury you fuckas."

"That's him all right," the big one said.

"Who?" I said. "Who am I?"

The short one took the driver license out my wallet and read it to me.

"Jesse Gomes, right? Jesse Gomes."

Then, all calm, "You like to rape and kill little white girls?"

"What you mean?" I said back at him.

He lean in to me. "Charlene."

My chest swelled up. For the first time I noticed all the pine trees. The bright sun almost over head.

"That's him all right," said the big one. "He's not even trying to argue."

The short one said, "Janice said you'd remember her. Charlene's mother."

I said nothing. I just couldn't believe this was happening. No matter how many times I told my mind what this was about it felt like a dream. But then I saw the white brick of coral, and I jus knew Mikey must have put it there. That was the signal.

The big one said, "You remember her, don't you, on the phone, Charlene's mom."

I couldn't talk.

"She said she forgives you. She'd like you to forgive her. She said it would mean a lot to her if you did."

"Fuck her and fuck you too," I said.

"All right then," said the short one. "Let us know if you change your mind, and we'll help you dig the hole. If not, it's going to be a long day for you."

He un tied my ankles. I tried to run but I was too drunk, too high, too tired. I didn't get too far, I fell over. They didn't even need the gun. I couldn't hardly stand any more.

They un tied my hands and I spent the next hour with the shovel. The dirt going in fatter piles, some times falling back in the hole.

I heard the blades of the helicopter. All three of us looking up, watching it coming toward us. I looked at them. They looked at each other. Then all three of us looked up. But it took a right turn and went up over the mountain that split the island in half. Tourist helicopter.

It felt like hours and hours. More and more piles. Hot sun. Every thing spinning. Sweating. The shitty taste in my mouth. My ears popping. My own puke stink.

I remember what Mikey told me the first time I dug the hole here. He told me to square the edges, shape it.

Mikey.

I almost laughed.

I was supposed to be with family. With Kapika. Pig, my dad said. Pig for dinner Christmas.

My eyes getting blurry. I yelled super loud, jus to stop from crying and get mad again. They put tape over my mouth again.

Then right away I felt the butt of the gun hit the back of my head and I fell side ways in the hole, deeper now, and landed right on the shovel. From both sides the dry dirt caving in on me until I was covered in dirt, dirt in my nose, my hair, my eyes.

I just wanted it to be over.

I stood up and picked up the shovel.

I pretended I was digging the hole for Charlene, pretending it was for me again. Like last time. Trick the mind, but back wards now. I threw the piles of dirt faster.

I was gonna be the one with the warm dirt covering me up like one blanket, little by little. I was gon get to sleep, finally, with no noise any where, no loud music, no fighting, and no drugs, just warm dirt.

The short one was holding the .45.

They took the tape off my mouth one last time.

I coughed. I tried to get angry, just to stop from choking up, but it didn't work that good.

"Tell da mom . . ." I cleared my throat and spit. "Tell da mom I never seen her daughter get raped, not by me or any body." I coughed. "Tell da mom da real guy is da one she pay da money to. When you tell her dat, she know it's true." I waited for a while. I swallowed. "But tell da mom was me too, may be. And yah . . . kay . . yah . . . I forgive da mom or whateva. I would do da same ting as her if was my kid."

I pumped my legs, like for foot ball practice from Pop Warner.

"Shit," said the short one, looking down, shaking his head. He gritted his teeth. He pointed the gun down then lifted it up again. "Shit. You couldn't just be an evil fucken bastard for us, could you?"

"Sorry bra. Dat never was me."

I looked up at the sun. The tree tops, all the pine cones creaking in the wind.

I took a deep breath and stretched out my neck. I bounced on my feet, like how Robby trained me. I made sure I was looking up, always up, never down. Always, Robby said.

"Jus go fucken do it already, pussy," I said stretching my back, looking over them. "Come on. I forgive you too, you ugly fuckas. Fucken grammas, hurry up. I got places to go–"

And the sky went away. My ears ringing. I went numb. I took one breath. I fell back wards in the hole.

Like how my mom used to put the laundry pile in the living room, I would go dive in, smell warm and clean and no one could find me.

Questions & Answers

1. How did you come to write the book?

At first I wanted to give a human face to a very dehumanizing phenomenon. Most people don't realize that the characters in this book are, in many ways, similar to us. They have talents, skills, compassion, and passions. They think. Some are born leaders. For whatever reason, they have ended up using their talents and energy to help drive Hawai'i's crystal meth subculture to epidemic proportions. The real question is why. I knew three young people who died using drugs, so the lethality, the power of drug abuse was always real to me.

2. What does the title "*Tweakerville*" mean? Is it a physical place?

The word doesn't have geography. It has no physical boundaries. It refers to and encompasses the mental and physical space of the crystal meth world. As Jesse says about Mikey, "Even when he's with us, his mind is there." We are all cohabitants and contributors to the ice subculture this book portrays, we just rarely see our role in it.

3. How do you know so much about the ice world?

It's hard not to be familiar with drugs growing up in today's Hawai'i. Drugs are everywhere, private schools as well as public schools, downtown offices as well as bars. Read the newspapers and you'll see any number of stories about drugs or about people on drugs and the consequences.

4. Are there any real life incidents in your plot?

None of the events are based on specific incidents. Some of the dynamics of the plot are so commonplace that they are after the fact, for example, the stolen scale from Jesse's science class. I later found out that a scale went missing years ago at my high school. Years after I had written the Charlene segment, I saw on the news that the body of a woman rolled up in a carpet had been found on the side of the road.

5. Where on O'ahu does this story take place?

The drug problem in Hawai'i is not limited to particular areas or ethnic groups. Some communities may conceal it better. The book isn't set in a specific neighborhood or area. Drugs are used, abused everywhere. No community, rich or poor, nor school is immune to it. Meth use and users are probably a lot closer than people think. Statistically speaking, you already know a user, whether you realize it or not.

6. Why is a character like Charlene the first victim of the drug in the story?

In the media, you can get the feeling that the life of one missing white child is worth more than the lives of many non-white children. So for that reader, there's Charlene, your dead white girl. But a crime has taken place and it's attributed to drugs, not to her depression or her reasons for taking drugs, her self-medicating, perhaps her crappy upbringing. There is a need to attribute blame which is exactly what Charlene's mother does.

7. Is there a connection between Jesse and Charlene? They are buried in the same grave even though they didn't meet in life.

Jesse's mind flashes forward as he's burying Charlene. Even this early on in the story, Jesse senses he's headed into that same grave, that death may be the only way out. The feeling that Jesse and Charlene have a causative role in each other's death is really an illusion. They're just two teenagers who found their way into a very dangerous world.

8. You like to use a lot of metaphors.

I try to write in a style without too much emotion. The first versions of the manuscript had a loud author voice that might have been distracting. I challenged myself to find other ways to allow those same feelings to play out. Metaphors can become a substitute for an author's personal emotions. Some examples: The blind man who can't see what's going on all around him; Jesse's description of the unnamed fighting birds, which spend their short life killing each other–right before Jesse's name is mentioned by Dos, and Jesse and Robby kill

Kody. There are also smaller metaphors: the stain on Jesse's shirt; Jesse and Kapika counting up thirteen pennies right at the start of their relationship; the red, white and blue stolen moped.

9. What were your reasons for not having a happy ending?

Crystal meth turns brother against brother, friend against friend. For the reader who thinks (like me) that Jesse is a hero, Jesse dies so that the child can live. For the reader who doesn't think it can be that easy, Kapika rejects Jesse. The ending needed to say something about the drug itself: tragic, complex and non-conclusive.

10. When did the ice problem begin in Hawai'i?

Meth may have been brought to Hawai'i by recent immigrants. One of the names for the drug seems to retain that heritage–batu. But it really matters little which country it came from. It belongs to Hawai'i now. Having three generations of abuse in the family, like Mikey does, isn't farfetched at all. Mikey was made by meth, born into meth.

11. The two marines—where did you get the idea for them?

I have friends and family who are former military. I have visited bars which often played out the saga of Military vs. Locals. What one person calls racism, the next person might call resistance. I've seen guys who are part-caucasian or even full caucasian participate in this so-called racial violence.

Most military are respectful. Many really surprised me with their openmindedness. I tried to make it clear that the two marines are exceptional cases of insensitivity.

12. Is there an appeal to life in the ice world?

The allure wears off once you are habitual. Then it all makes sense, and what is not normal to us is perfectly understandable behavior to those in the ice world. There is an alternate yet powerful code of morality in this world that doesn't judge with the familiar labels of mainstream society. People are conditioned very quickly by their environment. An entrant quickly learns new values, new rules, things that might horrify outsiders but can be totally natural and comfortable in this subculture. Jesse seems lured in from a good home by teenage angst at "the system" and the excitement of the outlaw lifestyle Robby lives. But by thirty pages into the story, all the costumes are removed and Jesse realizes that it's not a game. For most of the characters, the partying and camaraderie covers up deep-seated anger and revenge with nowhere to go, for example, Amber, who uses drugs and alcohol to hide from reality. It has been said that under the surface, there is some deep pain in Hawai'i, so great that meth addiction becomes the answer.

13. What other character types did you consider but not use?

Working single mothers who budget their addiction, and work very hard to minimize the effects of their drug use on their children; white collar users, office workers; older, former addicts who now in their lives offer hope and inspiration. For the novel to work, though, there was a need to focus. It's meant to be a fast-paced story, not inclusive of all possible character types.

14. In *Tweakerville*, is there gender equality?

The people running the business side of the meth world are male. Maybe in other tweakervilles there are women in leadership roles. It's entirely possible that a woman would have a position of power.

In my story there are no sexual biases. Amber is the only character who outhustles Mikey. Amber is miserable, but she's also comparatively in control of her situation. Here's a possible gender difference - in desperate need, the men in this book often revert to violence, the women are more likely to use their sexuality, but not always. Cutchies is nobody's victim, she doesn't hesitate to throw down with Jesse or the police. But readers, myself included, have a queasy reaction when the young mother offers herself to Dingo for drugs we know he doesn't have. The language about sex in this scene was so explicit that I considered taking it out because it embarrassed me. But the casual and routine way the young mother negotiated the sexual acts, which took place in view of her baby, shows the reality that many young girls are reduced to in order to feed their addiction. Males have more alternatives to get drugs, they don't have to sell their bodies, although with crystal meth now sweeping gay communities, it may be happening.

15. Whom do you blame for there being so much drug use and abuse in Hawai'i? Bad parenting, lack of law enforcement, flaws in society?

Drugs are used for lots of different reasons. The divide between public and private schools really gets to me personally. Iolani, Kamehameha and Punahou kids use drugs too, although public school kids discover the harder drugs at a younger age. Private school kids may be better insulated because they have an expectation of an easier future and they have been made to feel entitled by their parents and schools. Crystal meth is easy to get and not that expensive. Many say we were better off before the harsh regulation against marijuana which may have contributed to ice's rise as a substitute in the nineties.

16. Do people leave the crystal meth world and rehabilitate? What does it take? Why didn't you have one of the characters kick it and leave the world?

Robby quits ice in order to sell it which is a statement about his willpower. Jesse frequently points out to the reader the compassion that Robby feels for his customers. He tries to cut them off if they want to quit. It's false to say that drug dealers don't necessarily care about their community. I think Robby feels that in this tidal wave of an epidemic, what does it matter addicts are going to get high. Someone's going to make money. But in Robby's last statement he advises Jesse to get a job as Robby himself says he intends to. Jesse also quits drugs and alcohol for two weeks. It's implied that Jesse's father quit ice, presumably for his family. How one quits and why is not fully understood by the experts. Some say nobody ever really quits, that the urge always remains. Sometimes people go on two-week binges or reckless crime sprees because they just want it to be over with, either by going to jail or dying.

17. How realistic is it for a drug-free girl or guy to enter into a relationship with a user? Why would they do it, given the hardships that lie ahead? Or is love blind?

I don't really know, but it's a very common and tragic scenario. Opposites attract. A clinical psychologist told me that it's almost impossible for a non-user to understand the logic of an addict. Meth especially is a drug that prevents users from experiencing emotions the way they used to. Your agency, your free will, your decisionmaking is gradually eroded until at some point a lot of users are just going along for the ride. The drug is in control of their life. But love can be one of the best weapons there is against drug addiction. They say, change your playmates, change your playground. Recovering addicts need to be around non-users to remind them there is something else again.

18. What are you going to write about next?

I have text sketches and years of material for a prequel and a sequel. I'll probably call the prequel Clear, which was the original working title for Tweakerville. Clear will follow Kody and Dos's early life from childhood up to their rise to power. The prequel combs the early meth epidemic looking for clues and answers to many of the underlying issues that Tweakerville didn't touch.

The sequel to Tweakerville may be called White, which is slang for cocaine, the rich man's drug. One of the characters would be Steve, Jesse's would-be brother-in-law who disappears at the barbeque in Tweakerville. But now that Kapika's single, Steve might just leave Jesse's sister for Jesse's girl and end up raising Dwayne's son, as Jesse had hoped. We find out Steve was the "punk" who threw the M&Ms at Jesse's dad on the tug boat.

White will address issues that many haoles in Hawai'i think about but don't always like to discuss publicly. I hope White will help bring up some taboo conversations that too rarely take place openly but are at the center of Hawai'i's self understanding and direction. For White, I've also been documenting firsthand accounts of "Kill Haole Day," one of the many customs in Hawai'i that directly challenges white American influence and reveals the heated core of longstanding racial distrust and resentment. It will include the effects on those who were beaten and how it changed them.

19. Almost all of the story is told in different modes of pidgin rather than Standard English. You also sparingly use third-person narrative. How and why did you choose these story telling techniques?

I couldn't have developed Jesse's character using Standard English as he wouldn't be Jesse anymore. Jesse's narrative used to be even more conversational in the first drafts of the work. However, in later drafts, I had Jesse split loosely into different voices for two types of storytelling. One is closer to how a story would be told in conversation, i.e., it focuses on what Jesse thinks. In other places the reader isn't listening to Jesse, they're experiencing what he sees, hears, feels, smells with direct sensory access. Action and setting tell their own story in these cases and too many of Jesse's thoughts via a narrator would have prevented the reader from being drawn in and having their own thoughts. I decided both voices could be useful and that third-person narrative wouldn't work for Jesse.

20. Are there any observations you've made personally when writing this story about the greater ice problem?

My hope is that with the help of dedicated community members and loved ones, more addicts can quit ice. Also, our taxes are better spent on treatment and prevention than on imprisonment. Funding to treat meth addiction is cheaper than jailing users down the line, even if it only slows them down. For a long time, users have been getting waitlisted for treatment or finding that rehab programs are limited, unaffordable or have insurance requirements. At the same time because our jails are overcrowded, we're paying to export our convicts including meth users whom we didn't help when they openly asked for it.

It's important to say that help is out there for free and that there are no shortages of capable, dedicated, underpaid or unpaid heroes fighting the drug war on a case-by-case basis, or trying to prevent the next wave.

Glossary

Action—Dangerous or violent situation

Alk out—To back down

Amping—To be fired up or energized

Bang—To take property, usually a car

Banging rails—To take lines of cocaine

Banking —To make a lot of money

Batu—Crystal methamphetamine (see Clear)

Bing—A sizeable draw of crack cocaine or meth

Blast—A potent draw of crack cocaine or meth

Blasting tats—To get tattoos

Blazed—High on marijuana

Blind—Under the influence of drugs and/or alcohol

Bloodline—Many meanings, often referring to a family trait, as in fighting birds

Bump—To take a small amount of cocaine, often off a key or fingers, not a line

Bumping—To play loud music

Bull—Dominant male in a given area

Bunk—Fake or very poor-quality drugs

Bunked—To be cheated in a drug transaction, sometimes involving impure drugs, often with the dealer cheating the user

Burn—1. To smoke marijuana; 2. To cheat someone in a drug deal, often the user cheating the dealer by not paying for drugs

Burnt—High on marijuana

Bus—1. Drunk; 2. Damaged, beaten up, not functioning, destroyed

Butchie—Woman who possesses manlike traits, often lesbian

Burp—To punch or be punched

Cabbage—1. Not right; 2. Weird; 3. Drunk

Choke—Many

Cherry—Good, in excellent condition, brand new

Chronic—Chronic drug addict

Classic—Funny

Clear—Crystal methamphetamine (also ice, batu, sea crest, the stuff, dope)

Comatose—Unconscious or near unconscious from alcohol or drugs

Crack—1. Crystallized baking soda and cocaine; 2. To strike physically

Crash—Go to sleep

Crip—1. Strong-smelling; 2. Marijuana

Cruise—1. A pleasant, relaxed temperament; 2. To travel; 3. Statement of non-violent intentions

Cut— 1. Drunk and/or high; 2. Short for cut out, to leave

Cuz—1. Because; 2. Cousin; 3. Friend

Deadly—1. Good; 2. Attractive

Dig—Short for dig out, to leave

Dope—1. Meth, sometimes other drugs; 2. Attractive; 3. Good

Drought—1. When drugs are hard or impossible to find, opposite of flooding; 2. Demand is greater than supply

Dry—1. When a dealer is out of drugs; 2. Sober

Eating charges—Confessing to a legal charge, sometimes for someone else

Eighty-six—To be kicked out, banned, or cut off, as in a bar

Falsed—As in to false crack, to strike someone unexpectedly or wrongfully

Floater—Middleman drug user/seller

Flooding—When a drug is highly available, supply is greater than demand

For show—Disingenuous, duplicitous, showing off

Fuming—Angry

G—1. Everything is good, alright, or forgiven—all g; 2. Gram; 3. Thousand

Game—Brave or honorable for a man. Promiscuous for a woman, but often with a positive and/or respectful connotation

Gassing—1. To insult; 2. To travel quickly

Gone—1. Permanently addicted to a drug

Grab—Purchase or acquire

Grind—To eat

Grill—Face

Hammer—1. Figure of leadership, influence; 2. Large penis

Heavy—When a dealer has a great amount of drugs, often looking to sell for quick returns; opposite of light

Ice—Crystal methamphetamine (see Clear)

Inside—Incarcerated

Jam—1. To play music; 2. To do something with speed, jam um out real fast

Katsu—Mixed up, disorganized

Kills—High-quality drugs, usually marijuana

Light—When a dealer is short of drugs; opposite of heavy

Line—1. Connection; 2. Supply; 3. Drug supply; 4. Line of cocaine

Losing it—1. Losing one's temper; 2. Dangerously near chronic drug addiction

Load—Large quantity of drugs

Mean—1. Positive, complimentary, good, favorable, but

often less than nuts, or unreal; 2. Statement of being impressed, surprised, or in disbelief; mean ah.

Moke—1. Man who speaks deep pidgin or otherwise exhibits traits inconsistent with mainstream culture; 2. Term of endearment; 3. Unattractive man

Mobbed—A group assault upon a single person or smaller group

Nails—Unattractive for a man

Nab—To steal, usually shoplifting

Nuts—1. Brave; 2. Crazy or animated; 3. Favorable; 4. Exceptional

O—Ounce

O-Trips—Oahu County Correctional Center, or O Triple C

Off—1. Brave; 2. Uncool or unusually undesirable

Palm—To strike with palm or open hand; less hurtful

Pound—1. To drink alcohol or other liquids; 2. To beat physically; 3. To have sex

Poke—1. To get a tattoo; 2. To have sex; 3. To use a needle

Polish—Oral sex

Piece—Drug pipe

Pilau—Dirty; can be used to mean corrupt

Pinch—To take from someone else's bag of marijuana

Pures—Good-quality drugs

Pull—1. Influence; 2. To take out a weapon; pull knife

Pump—To sell drugs

Push—To sell drugs, sometimes implies an aggressive sales strategy

Put ink—To get a tattoo

Rail—1. To chop up pills or cocaine and inhale; 2. Line of cocaine

Rank—Reputation

Red—Angry

Roll—Cash

Rolling—1. Laughing; 2. Under the influence of ecstasy

Rolls—Ecstasy

Scooping—Making a lot of money

Scrips—Money

Scrub—Weak or unpopular person

Sevens—7-Eleven convenience store

Shack up—When a couple moves in together

Shake—Dry, faint marijuana, usually the remnants of a larger amount

Shoot, shoots—1. Statement of agreement and togetherness; 2. Friendly goodbye; 3. Short for shoot out, to leave or go somewhere

Shut D—Short for shut down; 1. Denied; 2. Rejected; 3. Closed

Shwag—Poor-quality marijuana

Sick— 1. Worried or concerned; 2. Having a desirable talent or quality; dat guy get one sick ass truck

Side whack—Secondary relationship

Skank—To dance

Sketch—1. Paranoia; 2. Reason for caution: the whole place look sketch

Slang—To sell drugs, also sling

Swift—Quick or clever mentally

Tag—1. To graffiti; 2. To have sex with

Tap—1. Good; 2. Muscular build; 3. Empty

Tap out—To concede, as in a fight

Tax—To take from someone weaker

Thick—1. Robust for man; 2. Attractive for woman; 3. Good

Trip—1. To be surprised; I trip out when I seen that; 2. Acting paranoid or abnormally; that guy's tripping out ; 3. To look for a fight or confrontation; don't trip at school

True game—Genuine or faithful

Tweaker—Heavy user of crystal meth

Tweaking—Under the influence of meth

Tweak out—When the drug has caused seriously abnormal behavior or permanent damage

Wax—To soften or dull a drug craving, often by using another drug

Whack—1. To strike physically; 2. To eat; 3. To take a hit of something; 4. Substitute for many verbs

Whistle—Crack pipe

White—Cocaine (also white girl, soft white, sniff sniff, haole, maʻa)

Wired—Well designed, planned or set up

Zap—Small sip of beer

Acknowledgments

I am deeply indebted to the writers who have inspired, taught, mentored, and encouraged me. They include the late Ian MacMillan, Rodney Morales, Witi Ihimaera, Morgan Blair, Susan Schultz, Gary Pak, Joe Balaz, Kenneth Quilantang Jr. and Daniel Hugo. I'd also like to thank Darrell Lum and Eric Chock, who were particularly supportive of *Tweakerville* over many years.

Also, special thanks to my family and friends, particularly my mom and brother, who shared their knowledge and passion for literature; to Sao, Sonny Boy, Kamren, Uncle Bu and all the family; also Darin, Uncle Danny, Uncle Dutch, Aunty Carrie, and Clinton.

Finally, my thanks to the people at Mutual for all their work on behalf of my first novel.

About the Author

Alexei "Lex" Melnick was born and raised on Oʻahu. He is currently in the M.A. program at University of Hawaiʻi-Mānoa, where he won the Hemingway Award for best undergraduate fiction and second place in the Seiki Award for local fiction. His writing has appeared in *Hawaiʻi Review, The Honolulu Advertiser* (winner of the 2008 Christmas fiction contest), and *Bamboo Ridge* (2006 Editors' Choice Award for best new fiction writer), and on the KIPO program "Aloha Shorts." He values most the life lessons that he has learned outside of books, from co-workers, elders, friends, and family. *Tweakerville* is his first novel.

Please email your thoughts on *Tweakerville* to melnick@ hawaii.edu.

used Arsonist Admitted Using Crysta

Father Pleads Guilty to Meth T

3 lbs. of Meth Seized in Bus

Teacher Charged
with Meth Trafficking

Death Toll Will Keep

Meth Linked to Abnorma

School Neighbors Spur Ice B

Man sought trea

$1.

Security Chief, Liquor Inspector Adm

Guilty Plea in
Meth, Rifle Case

Dr
Diap

Federal officials agree
lower percentage of imm

BY KEN KOBAYASHI